A Little More Sin

A Novel By
Parish Sherman

STREET KNOWLEDGE
PUBLISHING
Website: www.streetknowledgepublishing.com

A LITTLE MORE SIN®

A LITTLE MORE SIN

Is a work of fiction. Any resemblances to real people, living or dead, actual events, establishments, organizations, or locales are intended to give the fiction a sense of reality and authenticity. Other names, characters, places and incidents are either products of the author's imagination or are used fictitiously. Those fictionalized events & incidents that involve real persons did not occur and/or may be set in the future.

Published by: Street Knowledge Publishing
Written by: Parish Sherman
Edited by: Dolly Lopez
Cover design by: Marion Designs/ www.mariondesigns.com
Photos by: Marion Designs

P.O. Box Box 345 For information contact:
Street Knowledge Publishing

Wilmington, DE 19801
Email: jj@streetknowledgepublishing.com
Website: www.streetknowledgepublishing.com

ISBN 10: 0-9822515-4-8
ISBN 13: 978-0-9822515-4-6

Dedication

This book is dedicated to my Angels above. Thank you for watching over me. My maternal Grand Parents, Lula and Eddie Nash Sr. My paternal Grand Parents, Sylvia and Eugene Sherman Sr. My uncles Elmore (Sonny) Nash, Eugene (Sonny) Sherman Jr., and Ray Coleman. My auntie, Lois Maxine Addison. My father Michael Wayne Sherman Sr. A day doesn't go by that I don't think about you. I love you all always and forever.

This book is also dedicated to my younger cousin, Timothy L. Nash. Man, you in there with Life all because some bitch ass muthafuckas turned bitch on you (snitched). You and a couple other people are the reason I hate rats. Man the code of the streets ain't what it used to be. I remember when cats saw something and knew if they spoke on it, they would get their wigs put on flat, and they would be putting their fam in jeopardy. Hot (snitching) muthafuckas ain't got passes with me. They're right up there with child molesters. Well maybe not right up there, but very, very close. Cuzzo, keep your head up, blood, and I promise that I will make sure you never ever have another want.

R.I.P. Al Chatman, Seagram Miller, Dion, Dave, Mack Dre', Ray Mac, H.B., Floyd Finks, Pac, and anyone else I forgot.

I would also like to thank B.E.T's American Gangster for doing that Segment on Felix Mitchell. I've had to bust a lot of cat's heads for thinking Oakland was soft or something. The Tizown may not be a big as L.A., but we're just as deadly. Oakland is Los Angeles' little brother. Don't get it fucked up. If you ain't from the Tizown, stay the fuck out of the Tizown, because you'll get dropped in the Tizown and that ass will come up missing in the Tizown. Yadadamean?

Acknowledgment

First, and foremost I have to thank God for sparing my life on many occasions, and allowing me the many experiences that I have, which I put a very small spin on to write these books.

To my wifey I love you, and thank you for stepping up like you did. It's all about us. There's no me or you only us.

To my son, Damon Juwan; I know that I'm not there with you, and I haven't seen you since you were three, but you're always on my mind. I hate that your mother let me and her differences come between us, but it is what it is. You can believe that whenever I hit the streets, I will be in your life, by any means necessary. I love you.

My big Bro, Shaheed. Man we taking shit to another level. My oldest Brother Pastor Demorie Sherman; I love you man.

My Aunts Vivian, Janet, Evelyn, and Reneé. My cousins Donna, Sharon, Monica, Eddie, Darryl, Edie, Kelli, Nikki, Timothy, Alexis, Petria, Rico, Gino, Quan, Ray Jr., Andre and Janeé. All my little cousins, family and close friends. I love you all!!!

My Sister's Felicia and Kim. Thanks for holding me down. I love you both.

I'm not going to list all my potnas, but I will mention a few. Sherm, Thomas and Angela Ross, Big Mike, Shan-D, Bud, Lil' Potna, Vito, Black, A.F., A.L., Walter (Junior) Orr, M.A.K, Boss Mann, Hollyrock, Will Scott, Steve-Bo, L, Big Dave, Duck, Y.G., Tone, Tory (T.B.) Bell, Ray, Rick (Freeway Rick) Ross and Andy Au. Ali, thank you for helping me on the editing on this, and the synopsis for **Sin 4**

Life. To Mike MacDonnell; Thank you for reading the first book and giving me an outlook from a person that doesn't live that life. Also, thank you for teaching me about business.

My Editor, Ms. Dolly Lopez; I would like to apologize for the tantrum. I would also like to tell you that everything you said was right (as if you didn't know). You are very good at what you do, and I hope to work with you again.

To my other mother, Linda Williams; You keep me on my toes and always lace me up with game for this book stuff. I owe you the world for seeing that I got my foot in the door. Thank you for looking out for me like you do, and I hope we can take this book sh#t to another level.

Anyone I didn't mention because I don't fuck with you, fuck you. Anybody I didn't mention that I do fuck with, blame it on the kush not my heart, because it wasn't intentional.

Oh yeah, big ups to my man Souleo, the bookman on 149th Street and 3rd Avenue in the Bronx. Man you don't know it, but you were very instrumental in me meeting Lovely, and thank you for pushing my books.

If anyone wants to holla at ya' boy you can find me on the inmate locator on www.bop.gov inmate locator:

Parish Sherman #13080-097

Table Of Contents

Chapter One

It's About To Get Funky

Malika was sitting in her new house that Sin had gotten for her. She had just gotten off the phone with Sin. Him stopping at Everett & Jones and getting her something to eat would give her at least an extra fifteen minutes to do what she had to do.

She went upstairs and ran her bath water and added some strawberry bath beads that she bought from the mall earlier. She stripped naked and looked at herself in the full length mirror in the bedroom. *I look the same as I did when I was dancing at that club on Bourbon Street,* she thought. She opened the drawer that contained her lingerie and pulled out a pink silk teddy. She went in her panty drawer and pulled out a new pair of pink panties that were two sizes too small. She knew the panties would be all up in her heavenly-endowed butt and she knew Sin would love that.

"Nigga talking about he ain't staying the night. I'm getting fucked tonight, and I'm sure of that!" she said to herself.

Malika slid her tired body in the water that was as hot as she could stand it. She grabbed the strawberry shower gel and began to bathe. She pulled the stopper out after thirty minutes and stood and washed her natural curly hair with the strawberry shampoo.

As Malika stepped out the shower she heard the phone ringing. "Muthafuckas always pick the most inopportune times to call!" she complained as she ran into her bedroom. "Hello?" she answered without looking at the caller I.D.

"Malika, go to Alta Bates hospital, something happened!" Simone cried. The first thing that Malika thought was that something happened to Shamika or June Bug.

"Simone, what happened, sis?" she asked.

"Sin got shot, baby. You need to get up there right away. I'm leaving right now," Simone said.

Malika dropped the phone and started panicking. She hurried and put on her panties, her Baby Phat jeans, and a white T-shirt. She ran to the closet and put on her black and white Jordan's and a black hoodie. She ran downstairs and snatched her purse and ran out of the house. She got in her Tahoe and tore out of the driveway leaving rubber.

Malika had the Tahoe doing 100 on the 580 Freeway when a Highway Patrol car got on her. She pulled over and waited for the cop to get to the truck. She rolled her window down as the white cop approached. Out of the corner of her eye she saw his partner at the passenger side.

"Officer, I'm sorry I'm speeding. My husband was shot and he's at Alta Bates Hospital!" she cried.

"What's your husbands name, ma'am?" he asked.

"Simian Michaels," Malika said. The cop went back to his car and a made a call, then came running back to Malika.

"Follow us, ma'am. When we get to the 13 we'll take that to Berkeley. Please be careful. Although were escorting you we don't want you to lose control of this SUV," he said as he looked at Malika's pretty face.

The cops took off fast with Malika following closely behind. They made it to Alta Bates within fifteen minutes. Malika jumped out of her truck in front of the hospital and ran in.

"My husband was shot! Can you tell me how to find him?" she asked the receptionist.

The petite white girl rolled her eyes at Malika and covered the mouthpiece of the phone. "Ma'am, I'll be with you in a moment. Can't you see I'm on the phone?" she asked and resumed her conversation.

Malika looked at the girl standing behind her like she couldn't believe her ears. "Ahhh *hell* nah, bitch! I will beat your muthafuckin' ass!" she yelled as she reached across the counter and snatched the white girl by the shirt. "Now, what you say, bitch?" she asked.

The white girl's face turned lobster-red. She knew she was in for an ass whipping. "Wh... Wh... What' s your husband's name?" she stuttered.

"Simian Michaels," Malika answered and shoved her.

The white girl's hands moved across the keyboard at lightning speed. "Fifth floor," she said. Malika took off running. She got on the elevator and pressed five. When the doors closed she caught a reflection of herself.

Her hair was all over the place. She pulled the black hair tie out of her purse and put her hair in a ponytail on top of her head. As she was exiting the elevator she ran into a man. She looked at him closely.

"Shaqui?" she asked, surprised at how good Sin's younger cousin looked.

"What's up, Juicy?" he asked and hugged her.

When Malika and Sin started going together they were both fourteen and Sha was only twelve. The first time he saw Malika he said she had a big juicy booty, and had started calling her "Juicy" ever since. Looking at him now she didn't see little Shaqui; she saw a fine-ass man. Sha and Sin looked alike, except Sha didn't have the small gap between his teeth.

"How bad is it?" Malika asked.

"I don't know. The worst hit was in his back. The rest of the bullets made clean exits and the neck wound was just a graze," Sha said. Malika started crying again.

Sha put his arms around her and hugged her. "Juicy, you gotta pull it together. Auntie's taking it hard and you gotta be strong for her," he said.

Just as he was letting her go the elevator chimed. Tariq, Hasahn, Tayshaun, and Amir got off. Malika knew something was about to happen. They were all wearing black. They all greeted her. Everyone went to the waiting room except Malika, who went in the bathroom and straightened herself out.

Malika walked into the waiting room and Sin's sisters, Kim and Jas, as well as Sha's mother, Barbara all went silent. Sin's mama, Jackie stood and hugged her. "Oh, baby I am so sorry!" she said, feeling guilty for having a part in keeping her and Sin apart when Malika got pregnant fourteen years ago, and not mentioning to Sin that he had a daughter.

"It's okay, Mama Jackie. I understand why you did it," Malika lied. She would never forgive her or her own mother for what they did. "Thank you for paying for my schooling and sending Simina the money you were sending," Malika said.

Everyone else greeted Malika with a hug. The doctor came out looking tired. He let them know that the bullet in Sin's back would be hard to get. He also let them know that there would be a chance that Sin would never walk again, leaving him not wanting to do the surgery until he talked to Sin.

Tracy came running into the waiting room and Jackie explained what was going on. Hasahn got June Bug's attention and nodded towards the door. He, Sha, Tayshaun, and Amir all stood up and walked out. As they were about to start talking, Rod came.

"Look, we know who did this shit. Ya'll say he had some words with that nigga, Max. What we waiting for?" Hasahn asked.

"He's right. Ya'll mama shouldn't be the only mother crying," Amir said.

"Man, let's do this shit! Tayshaun, you in the car with me. Let's meet up at the Jack in the Box on my turf," Sha said as he turned to leave.

When the elevator came, Hashi was on it. Hashi was the only one out of all of them that wasn't in The Mad Circle. He was a close friend though. "I'm in!" he said as he stepped back and let them on. They all went to the parking area and got in their cars and left.

●●●●●●

Shaunté and Déja were at Lisa's house smoking weed when Lisa's phone rang. She saw Terell's number and answered.

"What up, Tee?" she asked.

"Lisa, niggas shot Sin up!" he cried.

"What?"

"I heard he's in Berkeley," Terell said.

Lisa looked at Shaunté with tears in her eyes.

"What?" Shaunté asked.

Lisa hung the phone up and Shaunté felt in her gut that it was Sin. "Sin got shot. He's at Alta Bates," she said.

Shaunté was briefly in shock. After a minute she ran out of the house and got in the Yukon and pulled off. *Please, God, don't let him die!* she thought.

●●●●●●

Sha, Tayshaun, and Hashi pulled up down the block from J.B. and his brother, Max's spot on 61st Street between Dover and Shattuck. They all cocked their guns and got out of the car. They saw J.B.'s Benz out front. They walked down the street and Sha shot the four dudes in front of the apartments with the silenced Mac-

10. They went to apartment D and stood outside listening to the conversation which took place inside.

"We ain't about to have no more problems up outta that nigga, Sin. I personally let that nigga have it," a voice said.

"You niggas outta pocket! I didn't tell you niggas to do nothing!" J.B. yelled.

"Max told us to shoot on sight," the voice pleaded.

"You muthafuckas don't work for him! I run this shit! Did you niggas even think about what kinda shit we about to be in? The Circle ain't gonna sit by and go for one of their boys getting hit!" J.B. yelled. J.B. knew that retaliation was going to come. A serious war had been started and as far as he could see it was over a bitch... again. *Damn!* he thought.

Sha had heard enough. He nodded at Tayshaun who stepped back and kicked the door in. He and Hash both went right and started shooting the silenced machine guns to the left. J.B. ran right through the sliding glass door. The other dude inside caught the wrath of Hashi's MP-5 bullets.

Sha ran to the balcony and started getting off at J.B.

"Fuck!" he yelled as he ran out the front door. He saw J.B. getting in his Benz and sprayed it. J.B. still ended up getting away.

• • • • • •

June and Hasahn turned on 68th and Arthur and saw a gang of dudes sitting in front of Max's spot. June looked in the rear view of the Benz and saw that Amir and Tariq had just made the corner. Hasahn leaned out the window and started busting the AK. June got out and started letting off with the M-16.

"Mad Circle, bitch!" he yelled. The shooting went on for a good two minutes leaving the dudes outside leaking. He then punched the gas. He had to get back to the hospital. He again wished for the hundredth time that he had never pulled Sin into the game.

"I know where that fool's people live," June said.

"Nah, June you know the rules. No kids and no innocent people," Hasahn said.

"Man, fuck the rules! Ain't nobody else going by them," June said.

Chapter Two

Getting Back to Business

Sin made it through surgery and had been recovering for the last three weeks. As he sat in his bed he thought about all the bloodshed. The other side's body count was at at least twenty. The Circle's was at three. The cats from The Circle that fell victim were only foot soldiers, but nevertheless they were down for the cause.

Yvette came at 9:00 with Sin's daughter, Simara. The little girl looked just like Sin, just as his other kids did. She was a four-year-old cutie.

"I'm fixing to leave. I got things I need to do. Drop Little Mama off at my mother's house and come back," he said.

"Sin, the doctor said one more week," Yvette said.

"I don't care what the doctor said. I'm getting up outta here today. Now please do what I asked you."

"Honey, give your daddy a kiss. We're leaving," Yvette said to Simara.

"I wanna stay with Daddy," said Simara.

"I'll see you later tonight, 'Mara," Sin said and kissed her.

After they left Sin grabbed his hygiene stuff and went down the hall to the shower. When he was done he put on the new blue Rocawear Jeans, the white and brown Rocawear T-shirt, and the brown Tims.

The morning nurse came in. She was a top-notch Asian chick with a black girl's attitude. Her name was Lei Woo. "Man, what you think you're doing?" she asked.

"I'm about to shake the spot," Sin said as he brushed his hair.

"Who said you was leaving? You a doctor now?" she asked.

"I would be if I could work on you!" he said.

"That shit was original! You gots way too many baby mamas for me, baby," she said with her hands on her hips and her neck weaving from side to side.

"You sure you ain't black? Because your body, the way you talk, and the way you carry yourself screams out 'black woman'," Sin said.

Lei looked like the actress Kelly Hu, but with a body and lips like the video girl, Karrin Steffans, AKA Super Head. Every time she came in Sin was at her.

"I'm trying to wife you and make *you* my baby mama," he said.

"That ain't gon' happen," she said as she switched out the room.

Lei and the doctor came back ten minutes later. The doctor tried to talk Sin out of checking himself out, but Sin wasn't having it.

When Yvette came back, she and Sin left. Once in Yvette's Camaro Sin pulled his phone out and called Shaunté.

"Hello?" she answered.

"Where you at?"

"At home."

"Meet me at my house at 3," he said and hung up. "Go by 4-6 so I can get some bomb," he told Yvette.

When Yvette pulled up at Teesa's, Sin called her and told her to bring an ounce of kush down. Teesa and Sha came out of her apartment and up to the car.

"Sin, I tried to get this dog-ass nigga to bring me to see you. Are you okay?" Teesa asked.

"Yeah, I'm good. Cuzzo, what's up with that loot?" Sin asked.

"Everything is straight. Where you want me to bring it to?" Sha asked.

"I'll call and tell you later," he said. He gave Teesa 400 for the ounce and then they left. After getting Sin's prescription filled they went to his house.

Yvette left at 12 to go back home to Reno. Sha and Shaunté both came at three.

"Cuzzo, I need you to keep handling this shit for me. I'm sending 'Tay back to Reno to stay with her sister," Sin said.

"I don't want to go back out there. It ain't nothing to do in boring ass Reno," she said.

"I ain't about to argue with you. You going and that's that."

After Sha and Shaunté left, Sin pulled his phone out and called Malika.

"Hello?" she answered.

"Malika, come get me. I'm at home."

"I thought you were going to be in the hospital another week."

"I got tired of sitting there. I feel fine."

Malika went off on him. She said he was stupid for not taking his health serious.

"Don't come. I'll drive over there. I don't want to sit up in the car and listen to you talk that shit all the way to Dublin anyway," he said and hung up. Sin snatched up his medicine and the weed, went to the garage, got in the SS Impala and went to Dublin.

As he was driving on the freeway he thought about how close he came to being killed. He pulled out his phone and called Anita.

"Hello?" she answered.

"What up?" he asked.

"Hey you! I was just thinking about you," she said.

"Can I see you later? We got some business to take care of."

"Oh, so you ain't scared no more?" she asked and laughed.

"First of all, I ain't scared of the loving. Second, I just didn't want to dick-whip you," Sin said and laughed.

"Well I'll be home tonight at about 10. So make sure the dick-whipper got energizer batteries in it!" she said. They talked for a little while longer and then got off of the phone.

Sin pulled into Malika's driveway and parked next to her Tahoe. He got out of the car and his leg started hurting. Malika opened the door as he limped up the walkway. He walked in and Malika started in on him.

"Sin, you need to stop this shit! The next time you might not be so lucky," she said.

"Malika, I ain't in the mood right now. Will you make me something to eat?" he asked.

Malika sucked her teeth and went to the kitchen. She didn't speak to Sin for almost the rest of the day.

At 9:00 Sin was dressed in a gray Phat Farm jean outfit and black Timberland boots.

"You coming back?" Malika asked

"Yeah, I'll be back," he said and left.

Sin put the Blackstreet CD in the car and went to the cut, *Before I Let You Go*. Once he got out of Malika's neighborhood he turned the music up and hit the freeway to Berkeley. He decided to pass Déja's house on the way to Anita's since he had thirty minutes to burn. The whole time he was enroute to Berkeley he was in his mirrors. Sin wasn't going to be caught slipping again. He gripped the MP5 with his right hand and felt a little better.

As Sin was passing by Déja's he saw Shaunté's Lexus. *What the fuck? When I talked to this bitch at eight she said she was already headed to Reno,* Sin thought. He busted a U-turn and saw Lisa's Acura and a motorcycle parked out front. He pulled his phone out and called 'Tay's phone as he pulled up to Lisa's car.

"Hello?" Shaunté answered with the sounds of 112 in the background.

"Where you at, baby?" Sin asked.

"I'm almost there."

"You should have been there!" he snapped.

"I got hungry, damn! Why the fuck you giving me the third degree?" she asked.

"Man, fuck you!" he said and hung up.

"Damn!" Shaunté yelled and threw her phone on the couch.

"Who was that, Sin?" Déja asked.

"Yeah, and he tripping," she said.

Lisa looked at Shaunté and shook her head. *This bitch is stupid,* she thought. Lisa was in her feelings about something else. She and the guy there with Shaunté, Chris, used to be a couple. She left him alone because he was too soft on her. Shaunté was out of line for messing with him though. They had a rule. None of them would fuck each other's boyfriends, husbands, or exes, and Shaunté was violating the rule. Lisa really didn't give a fuck, but it was wrong.

"Lisa, I ain't trying to go there with you," Shaunté said.

"You just don't care, do you? This bitch-ass nigga ain't worth what you going to fuck off!" Lisa said.

"Lisa, why you always popping slick when you see me?" Chris asked.

"Nigga, because you a bitch! Shaunté outta pocket for fucking behind me anyway!" Lisa yelled.

"Now I see. This is about me messing with your ex! Lisa, I know you ain't still carrying feelings for Chris," Shaunté said.

"Bitch, *please*. I dumped this punk because he was too soft for me. I want a man that's going to check me when I'm outta pocket. This nigga sees me at the club talking to another nigga, and don't say shit. It ain't about this bum-ass nigga. It's about a pact we made in 5th grade. We swore to each other that we would never go behind each other. Me, you, and Déja," Lisa said angrily.

"She's right, 'Tay. You foul for that," Déja said.

"Man, that shit was in elementary school," Shaunté said.

"You remember you said that," Lisa said.

"What's that suppose to mean?" Shaunté asked. Lisa didn't answer her.

"Anyway, I told Chris to come over here so I could tell him that me and him can't see each other no more. He says he accepts that and that's it," Shaunté said as they heard a car alarm going off.

Déja looked out the window and saw Shaunté's lights flashing. "That's your car!" she said.

Shaunté got up and grabbed her keys and went to the door. When she walked out she saw Sin sitting on the rail to the right. Shaunté got scared.

"Why you lie?" he asked.

She pushed the button on her key ring and looked back in the house. Sin had already heard the conversation through an open window. He got up and started walking to the door and Shaunté grabbed his arm.

"Wait!" she said.

He snatched his arm away and went in. The first person to see him was Déja. *Oh shit!* she thought. Chris was sitting in the chair like he was the coolest thing next to freeze pops. Chris was 6-1 and weighed 235. He had long black braids, gray eyes, and light skin.

"Sin!" Lisa said in surprise as she was coming out of the kitchen.

"Potna, you fucking with my bitch?" Sin asked.

"Why she gotta be a bitch?" Chris asked as he stood up.

Sin looked at Shaunté and asked while pointing toward Chris, "This what you creeping for?"

"Sin, prior to three weeks ago we weren't together. I started seeing him when you brought that bitch to my block. The only reason he's here is because I told him I could not see him any more."

"So *this* sucka is the reason that you said you would *think* about marrying me?" he asked.

Shaunté started crying genuine tears. She knew she fucked up. "Baby, please don't do this. I swear I love you and would never trade you for anything!" she pleaded.

"Shaunté, first of all you lied! Second, I don't know if that's my baby or this sucka's," he said.

Shaunté stopped crying and looked at Sin. "Muthafucka, you about to piss me off! Don't question my baby's legitimacy. I didn't fuck this nigga without a rubber! I ain't fucked nobody bare back in the last two years," she said.

"Shaunté, fuck *you!* Fuck *this* hoe-ass nigga, and fuck *you*, Déja for letting these muthafuckas kick it in your joint!" Sin said.

Chris started toward Sin. Lisa stood and pointed her gun at him. "Nigga, sit your fake ass down!" she said.

"Sin, get the fuck outta my house. You ain't going to come at me like that in *my* shit!" Déja yelled.

"Aww, bitch, you just mad because you ain't fucking her," he said.

"Nigga, who said I haven't fucked her?" she asked.

"Déja, don't be playing with him like that. You know God damn well that me and you ain't did shit," Shaunté said.

"I'm gone. You silly muthafuckas deserve each other. Lisa, call me tomorrow," Sin said.

"Baby, wait!" Shaunté pleaded and grabbed his arm. Sin looked down at her hand then back at her face and she didn't budge. "You going to hear me out, or you gonna have to kick my ass, but you going to listen to me one way or another," she said. He walked out and she followed.

"Sin, I swear on our baby that I didn't come over here to fuck with him. I invited him over here to tell him that I was getting married, and that he had to stop calling me. I only fucked with him a few times, Daddy. I love you and I want to marry you!" she said.

"I'll think about it," he said as he walked away and went and got in the SS.

As Sin was pulling off his phone rang. He looked at the number and saw it was Anita's.

"What up?" he answered as he drove off.

"Where are you?" she asked.

"I'll be there in a minute," he said and hung up.

Sin came back around the corner where Déja lived and saw Shaunté and Chris arguing. "Take your ass on where I told you to go," Sin said as he got out the car pointing his 9mm at Chris. Shaunté got in her Lexus and left.

"Nigga, you stood up in the house for what reason?" Sin asked.

"Sin, fuck that hoe-ass nigga. He ain't worth it," Lisa said as she was getting in her car.

"Get this shit away from my house!" Déja yelled.

Sin let one round off just over her head causing her to duck.

"Nigga, it's the muthafuckin' Mad Circle!" Sin said and got in his car and left.

Chapter Three

Unfinished Business

Sin pulled up at Anita's house and saw her in the window. He hid the MP5 under the seat of the car and got out. When he got to the stairs, Anita opened the door. He smiled. "Yeah, God is good to me," he said as he walked up into her personal space.

"Yes he is," she said as she untied the sash to her gray satin robe and shrugged it off. She then reached around him and locked the door and set the alarm.

"So, tell me, Sin. Are you worth me giving my body to?" she asked as she stood before him naked.

"Baby, I can show you better than I can tell you."

"Ain't no second chances. If you mess up your shot and don't live up to all this shit you talking, that's on you," she said.

"Let me get in the shower then I'll show you it ain't talk at all," he said.

"Follow me."

Sin was kinda disappointed that the house was dark and that he couldn't see all that ass. Anita led him to her candle-lit bedroom and took his shirt off. She then went to the bathroom and set the temperature on the shower and came back in and unbuttoned his pants and pulled them down. She pushed him back onto the bed and took off his shoes, socks, pants and boxers and laid them neatly on the chair. "I don't know what it is about you that has me wanting you so bad," she said as her gaze traveled down his body and lingered on his dick.

"You know," he said as he pulled her to him and tongued her.

"I think it's part looks and part personality. I also think you're a sweet person, but you're also dangerous. You're basically the type of man a girl could fall in love with," she said sincerely.

Sin had to cease those fantasies. He was really going to marry Shaunté, and when that happened, he was going to be faithful. "Unh unh, boo! I'm the wrong nigga to fall in love with. You need to fall in love with a cat that can bring a stable lifestyle to the table. I've been in way too much trouble. You need a black yuppie. That type of cat would compliment your life perfectly."

"Fuck all that, Sin. I like bad boys. I hate high-sadity, spoiled, sheltered muthafuckas. I want a man that has been around."

Anita walked him into the bathroom. "You ain't getting in with me?" he asked. "I'll be waiting for you in the bed," she said and turned and walked away, ass jiggling.

Damn!, Sin thought as he got in the shower.

Anita's phone rang. She reached over and answered without looking at the caller ID. "Hello?"

"Man, what's up with you? I been trying to see you so we could talk," the guy said.

Anita was really not trying to talk to her "friend with benefits", Nick. He was trying to see her that night, but she and Sin had already made plans to see each other. She told him when they talked earlier she was busy. Nick threw a tantrum. Anita reminded him that they were just fuck buddies and he didn't have the right to trip like that. She then reminded him that he was married.

"Look, I told you that I was busy. You making me not want to ever speak to you again. Nigga, you got a wife and three kids. Why don't you get on their nerves and get off mine!" she said.

Anita didn't hear Sin walk up behind her.

"Fuck you, bitch!" Nick yelled. Just then Sin kissed Anita's neck.

"Fuck *me*? Yeah, nigga I'll be getting *fucked*, but it won't be by your short-dick-having-ass!" she said and hung up.

"Man trouble?" Sin asked.

"This shit is over. That nigga got a wife. Harass her, not me," she said.

They went back to Anita's bedroom and Sin took the robe off of her. She took his towel off and laid back on her bed. Sin kissed her foot, ankle, calf, behind her knee, and licked between her thighs. He wasn't about to give her head because this wasn't that type of party, this time. He went to her stomach and then to her titties. The whole time that Sin had his mouth on her she was letting out little cries and light moans.

Anita gave it like she got it. She kissed Sin from the top of his bald head to his feet and back. She kissed the tip of his dick. "I'm really tempted, but it's too soon," she said.

She straddled him and reached under her pillow and grabbed a Trojan. She looked down at his dick. "This may not fit," she said. She rolled it on him all the way to the serial numbers and lowered herself down. "Oooh, baby!" she moaned.

If Sin thought he was going to put in all the work, he was wrong. Anita rode him hard. She had complete control until he flipped her over and started hitting it from the back.

Anita was screaming so hard Sin thought the neighbors would come knocking. When he put her on her back she threw the pussy. Sin thought he heard something. He stopped in mid-stroke. Sure enough, someone was banging on the front door.

"Don't stop!" Anita screamed as she was near a major orgasm.

Sin looked at her and frowned. He got up and went in the bathroom and took the rubber off and threw it in the toilet. He washed himself off and walked back in the bedroom, dick rock-hard.

"Sin, you don't have to go," she said.

"Anita, I know you in there!" someone yelled.

Sin shook his head and got dressed. He was mad as hell. He could have been out banging the back out of anyone, but he was there fucking a chick that had some bomb pussy and a jealous lover at the front door.

Anita got up and put her robe on. "Maybe you should go out the back door. Nick can be crazy sometimes," she said. Sin looked at her as if she had lost her mind.

Sin went to the front door and opened it. The dude saw him, and just as Sin hoped he would, he tried to throw a haymaker. The average dude would have run if they didn't have a pistol or nice hands. Nick was 6-2 and weighed in at 264, and was an ugly muthafucka.

Sin ducked and the punch missed him. He came back with a kidney punch that made Nick go to his knees. "Nigga, your problem's with this woman, not me. You ain't got no win with me," Sin said and looked at Anita crazy and left.

Sin decided to go back to Malika's so he could go buy some more stuff for his daughter in the morning. He lit his blunt as he got on 80. His phone rang. "What up?" he asked.

"When are you coming?" Malika asked.

"I'm on my way."

"I'll run a bath for you," she said.

"Nah, I just took a shower."

"I'll be in the living room waiting for you and the door will be unlocked."

"Okay," he said and hung up. Sin had a flashback of when they were together when they were younger.

When they had their apartment, Malika used to stay up waiting for Sin to come home so they could go to bed together. Most times she'd fall asleep on the couch.

As Sin was going over the interchange where he veered off 880 to 238, which connected to 580, his phone rang again. He looked at the number and saw Anita's. He let it go to voice mail. His phone rang again. It was Shaunté's sister, Destiny's number. "What up?" he asked.

"I'm here, daddy," Shaunté said.

"Why you putting me through all this shit?" he asked.

"Baby, I'm not putting you through anything. I told you what happened and that's the truth. Now you see how it feels, huh?" she said.

"Is that my baby?"

"Nigga, I don't believe you asked me no shit like that! Sin, I'll get back on the highway and come fuck you up!" she said.

Sin laughed out loud. He really did love Shaunté and felt that she was the one. She was about hers and would go to any lengths for him.

"You find something funny? You don't think I'll be there in the next three hours?" she asked.

"Nah, I believe you. Look, we ain't getting married. I can't trust you, baby. You got too much bullshit with you."

"Yeah right. Nigga, you gon' marry me. You gon' buy me a big ass ring, you gon' marry me out here tomorrow, and when this bullshit with the police passes over, we gon' marry again in the Bahamas."

"I guess."

"So what you gonna do bout Max and J.B.?"

"Sha said he heard the nigga, J.B. nut up on the cat that did it. I might just let it ride. Them suckas feel me."

"Watch out for them snake-ass niggas," she said.

"Fuck them and everything they love. You know as soon as you have that baby I'm putting another one in you," he said.

"No you ain't. When this one comes I'm retiring out the game. I'm going to use this AA that I earned and open up our legitimate business," she said.

"I'm going to see you tomorrow. I'm fixing to crash," he said.

"I love you, daddy."

"I love you too," he said and hung up.

Sin pulled up in front of Malika's house and parked. He got out of the car and walked to the front door, and just as she said it would be, it was unlocked. He walked in and locked up.

He looked in the living room and didn't see Malika. He went to the back of the house where the family room was and there she was, asleep on the leather high-back sofa. Malika was wearing a pink baby doll, matching pink panties, and white socks. Her long hair was all over the place. Malika was the most beautiful woman Sin had ever seen.

Sin lightly shook her. Malika opened her eyes and sat up. "You hungry?" she asked.

"Nah, I'm straight," he said as he picked up the remote and turned the TV off. Sin scooped her up in his arms and carried her upstairs.

"This is like going back in time," she whispered in his neck. "Yeah, it is," he said. When they got in the bedroom he laid her on the bed.

"I gotta go pee," she said and got up and hurried into the bathroom. Sin took his shoes off and laid down on the bed.

Malika came out the bathroom and wagged her finger at Sin. "Those are Egyptian cotton sheets. You can't lay on them in your clothes," she said. Sin stood and stripped to his boxers and laid down. Malika laid down in front of him and scooted back against him.

"Thank you for paying for all this," she said and kissed his forearm.

"Baby, you know ain't nothing free. I really need you to help me clean up my dirty money. I also want you to invest some money for me," he said.

"I talked to Miss Lucy earlier, and she said it's cool. I also Fed Exed my divorce papers," she said as she kissed his arm again.

"Malika, I don't want to mislead you, baby. I'm getting married," he said.

Malika sat up and turned the light on and moved a strand of hair out of her face. She looked so innocent and fragile right then that Sin almost reached for her. "What do you mean?" she asked.

"I mean what I said. I'm getting married. I'm in love with someone and she's pregnant," he said in a low tone.

"Damn, Sin! I don't know what to say. I had this thought of you and me being together. Sin, you're the only man I've ever loved. I've loved you for fifteen years, nonstop. When I decided to come back, I wasn't thinking of hooking back up with you until I saw you. Do you have any feelings for me?" she asked.

Sin knew that women had fragile feelings so he had to be careful answering. "Boo, you know I do. You're my first everything," he said.

Malika turned the light off and laid back down. Tears pooled in her eyes then ran down her cheeks. Sin put his arms around her and hugged her. "Baby, don't cry," he said. "No, fuck that, Sin! This is all my mom's fault! I hate that bitch!" she screamed.

Sin hated to see Malika cry. He kissed her forehead and each eye. "Malika, I love you, baby. It's just that too much time has passed."

Malika looked up at him, and lightly kissed him at first, then she got more aggressive and slipped her tongue in his mouth and kissed him with even more hunger.

Sin's body shut his mind down. He moved the thin strap of the baby doll and kissed her bare shoulder. He moved the other strap and the nightie fell around her hips revealing two big breasts with erect nipples. "Turn the light on," he requested. She did and Sin sighed. The tattoos were still there.

Sin attacked Malika's breasts like a man that crawled through the desert with no water for a year.

"*Oh, Sin that feels good!*" she moaned. Sin gave Malika's titties the proper attention then went further south. Malika kissed the top of his head as he licked her belly button. The half-carat diamond was a sexy touch.

After a short time contemplating, Sin pulled her panties off. Without the slightest hesitation he went down on her. He smelled the strong scent of strawberries. He stopped and looked up at her and laughed. "Oh, you just knew you were getting your pussy ate, huh?" he asked.

"Baby, *don't stop!*" she whined and pushed his head back down.

Sin started flicking his tongue across her clit and Malika looked as if she was having an epileptic seizure she was coming so hard. Sin held her down and continued the tongue-lashing.

"Baby, *stop!* I can't take no more!" Malika cried out after she got her most powerful orgasm, which was three nuts after the first. Sin kept going.

"*Oooh, shit, baby! I'm coming again! Oooh yeah, lick it, baby. Lick my pussy!*" she moaned.

When Sin was done he crawled up her body and kissed her. "*Mmmm, I taste good!*" she said. She then pushed Sin on his back and started trying to suck the life out of him.

"*Damn,* baby! You got major skills. I forgot how good this head was," he said as he gripped her head. He could only take it for so long. "Stop, I want to put this in the pussy," he said.

Sin moved behind Malika and stared at her little pussy, which was under her big round ass cheeks. He maneuvered into the tight wet opening then stopped. Malika had some good pussy. Sin knew from the past that you didn't rush in because it would be over before it started. He grabbed her hips and pushed in. It amazed Sin to see his dick disappearing in Malika. The way her ass moved when he was on the down stroke was sexy.

The only sounds coming from them were Malika's loud moans and Sin's stomach slapping against her ass. They were a hot sweaty mess by the time Sin felt his nut coming. When he busted off it felt as if Malika's pussy turned into a vacuum and sucked the nut out of him. Sin fell on her back.

"Damn, Sin that was so good, baby! I ain't got off like that since I was like 15," she said. Sin had to admit Malika had the best pussy he ever had. "Man, for real! Baby, we used to have it our way." Malika was quiet for a minute. She was thinking about Sin getting married and wasn't felling it at all.

Sin started falling asleep. Then outta no where he felt Malika rubbing her butt against him. Instantly he was hard again. She pulled him on top of her. Sin slid in her and they fucked like wild animals. After like an hour Sin felt his nut again. Malika had sucked on his neck and scratched his back up.

"Where you want to put it, in my mouth or my pussy?" she asked as she moved her hips.

"Your ass," he said.

"You have had my virgin pussy and my virgin head, now you want my virgin ass? I'll have to think about that," she said as she made her pussy muscles squeeze his dick causing Sin to bust off in her.

"Sin, please don't marry that girl. I'm not saying marry me, but give me a chance. I'm a good woman, a good mother, and a good friend. Baby, we have a chance to make right what went wrong," she said.

"Malika, it's been over thirteen years since we've seen each other. How can you ask me to put my happiness aside so you can be happy? You didn't think about my feelings when you got married," he angrily stated.

"Sin, I've been knowing you fifteen years. How long you been knowing this bitch?" she asked.

"I met her when I got home," he mumbled.

"So you mean five or six months? Nigga, get the fuck outta here with that bullshit!"

"What the length of time mean? I've been knowing you since I was fourteen and look at the shit you pulled!"

"Nigga, you stupid! What she do, suck your dick properly, fuck you right, and now you in love?" she asked.

"If it was just about a bitch sucking my dick and having some good pussy, why I ain't trying to marry you?" he asked.

"Nigga, because you stupid!" she said as she scooted to her side of the bed.

"I don't see why you acting like this. You let the next nigga raise *my* daughter," Sin said.

"Punk, you love that bitch so much, why your dumb ass ain't with her right now?" she asked.

"Because I'm with you, bitch, and you better watch your mouth before I beat your ass!" he said.

"*Bitch?* Nigga, you a *bitch*," she said and got up and snatched the comforter and a pillow off of the bed and went to Simina's room. Sin laid back and went to sleep.

Malika looked at the clock on the night table and saw it was 5:00 a.m. She picked up the phone and booked a flight to New Orleans for 9:30. She got up at 7:30 and came in the bedroom and saw Sin lying there naked. *I should get me some more dick*, she thought. She passed on it and went and got in the shower.

When she got out she put on a blue Nike sports bra, a blue thong and some blue windbreaker Nike sweats. She went in the bathroom and brushed her teeth then blew out her natural curls and put her hair in a ponytail. She put on the blue and white Nike T-shirt, some blue Jordan's, and the blue and white Nike jacket. She picked up her keys, purse and Sin's clothes and his keys and left.

Chapter Four

Making Things Right

When Sin woke up it was 9:15 a.m. He got up and went to the bathroom. He saw a wash rag, bath towel, and a new toothbrush sitting on the counter. He turned the shower on and got in. When he got out, he brushed his teeth and wrapped a towel around himself. He went through the house looking for Malika. When he saw that she wasn't there, he went back upstairs to get dressed. As soon as Sin got in the room and didn't see his clothes, he knew she took them. *This shit is classic Malika*, he thought.

He picked the phone up and called Lisa.

"Hello?" she answered.

"Lisa, I need you to go to my house and pick up some stuff. I'll have Davy get it ready," he said.

"Aight. Where are you?" she asked.

"In Dublin at the house you dropped me off at that time," he said.

"Some nigga named Bo came through about 20 minutes ago looking for you," she informed him.

"Aight," he said and hung up. Sin dialed the number to the house and told Davy what clothes to have ready. He then called Malika.

"Hello?" she answered.

"Where the fuck my clothes at?" he asked.

"In the trunk of my car," she said.

"Well where the fuck you at?" he asked.

"At Oakland Airport aboard my flight to Louisiana," she said.

"Malika, I'm going to beat your muthafuckin' ass!"

"Whatever, Simian. It ain't like you ain't beat it before. They just made the announcement to turn off cell phones. I'll see you when I get back later," she said and hung up.

Sin laid back on the bed and called information and got the number to B of A's regional office in San Francisco. He called and asked for Tiara. After going through the receptionist, an assistant, and her secretary, Sin was finally holding for Tiara.

"Thank you for holding. This is Tiara," she said

"Hey, this is Sin. Where do you want to have lunch at?" he asked.

"Are you out of the hospital?"

"Yeah, I left yesterday."

"How about Pier 29 in Alameda, say 12:30?" she asked.

"That's cool."

They made small talk for a while then got off of the phone.

When Sin checked his messages he had one from Bo, June, and Rod. He called back everyone but Bo. He ended up having a sale for 30 keys for June and Rod.

He went in the bathroom and put lotion on. Sin's phone rang and he looked at the caller ID and saw June's number.

"What up?" he answered.

"Meet us at my shop," he said.

"Aight," Sin said and hung up. The phone rang again. *Damn, this muthafucka ringing like a slot machine,* he thought.

"What up?" he answered.

"Cuzzo, I need to get at you. My peoples on some other shit," the voice said. Sin recognized the voice as being Hashi. Hash had from 25th and East 14th to Fruitvale and East 16th on lock.

"What's cracking?" Sin asked.

"I want you to put a couple of the turbo chargers (two kilos), on my cars," he said.

"Aight, meet me at June's shop on 80th. You straight?" Sin asked.

Hashi had been out of the Feds for three years, but Sin still looked out.

"Yeah, I'm cool. You know I'm about to open my clothing store," Hash said.

"That's cool, cuzzo," Sin said.

Sin heard a car pulling up and when he turned he accidentally dropped his phone in the toilet. "Damn!" he yelled.

He went downstairs and opened the door just as Lisa was about to ring the bell. She saw Sin standing there in the towel and blew out a breath

Lisa was wearing an eggshell colored Chanel tennis dress and matching Chanel sandals. She handed Sin the gym bag and the clothes that were on a hanger and covered in plastic.

"Kick back in the family room and I'll be down in a minute," Sin told her. He watched Lisa walk to the back and his dick got hard. He went upstairs and was about to get dressed, then he thought about Lisa again. He hurried and stripped the bed and put clean sheets on it. He then went to the top of the stairs.

"Lisa, come up here for a minute," he yelled down.

Lisa came upstairs into the room and asked, "Whose house is this? It's nice."

"It's my baby mama's house," he said.

"Ya'll must have been up in here getting ya'll freak on last night," she said sorta disappointed.

"I slept in here and she slept in our daughter's room," he lied.

Lisa gave him the "yeah right!" look.

"I need you to put lotion on my back," he said.

"Get it," she said.

He turned and went to the bathroom and she saw the scratches on his back. *Damn, he must have been killing somethin'!* she thought and shuddered at the feeling between her legs.

Sin came out of the bathroom ass-naked. When Lisa turned and saw this, she almost screamed. He handed her the lotion and laid across the bed. Lisa hiked her dress around her hips and straddled his back and lotioned him down.

Sin turned over on his back and Lisa saw how hard he was. "Now the front," he said.

Lisa felt herself getting wetter as she turned around and straddled him. She started massaging his shoulders and unconsciously started grinding herself on him. Sin rubbed his hands up her thighs all the way up to her hips and reached around and gripped her voluptuous ass cheeks.

"You really going to marry Shaunté?" she asked as she rubbed his chest.

"Nah, I can't trust her," he said as he moved his hips around.

Lisa turned around and massaged his ankles. Sin looked at her thonged ass and looked at the ceiling. "Lisa, please, baby. Just one lick," he begged.

Lisa sighed and backed her ass up to his face. Sin moved the fabric to the side and got busy. *"Ohhh, Sin!"* she moaned and started moving her hips. Lisa's face was directly over Sin's dick. She kissed the tip and rubbed her face with it before inserting it between her lips.

She ain't as good as 'Tay, but she's good, Sin thought.

"Sin, *please* don't do this to me!" she mumbled, but didn't stop sucking.

"Stop, baby," he said. Lisa did and rolled off of him. Sin got between her thighs and literally ripped her panties off. He then ate her pussy the right way. He had Lisa moaning and screaming out his name when she came.

"Please say you got a rubber," Sin begged.

"I don't have sex often enough to keep rubbers," she said.

"I'm going in raw," he said and took the tennis dress off of her and looked at her naked body and just shook his head.

"Why you looking at me like that?" she shyly asked.

"You are fucking gorgeous!"

"I don't look as good as Shaunté or Déja."

"Yeah, right. You look better than both of them," he said.

Sin looked at her then thought about her not really wanting to break her and Shaunté's bond. "You know what, baby? I'm not even going to hit it. I know you having conflict within yourself and I respect that," he said.

"Sin, I want you to. Come on, baby," she said.

Sin crawled between her thighs and slipped into her tight pussy.

"You feel good inside me," she said.

Sin took his time and made love to Lisa. When he felt the nut coming he pulled out and skeeted on her stomach.

While they were in the bathroom showering, Lisa dropped a bomb on Sin. "I know it may seem as if I'm hating, but I'm not. I've already had you. Chris went to Reno this morning, according to Déja," Lisa said.

"Is that right?" he asked. Sin knew he had to show Shaunté she was playing with fire. He had never really done any more than slap her in the past. He was going to kick her ass this time. *Bitch don't know who she playing with. I'm Sin Michaels. I ain't no soft ass nigga!* he thought.

"The only reason I told you this is because Chris is my ex, and Shaunté violated," she said.

"You didn't know she was fucking with ol' boy?" he asked.

"Not until last night," Lisa said as they stepped out the shower.

"Is that my baby?" Sin asked.

"Yes, it's yours. She didn't start getting loose until you stayed out all night on her and she went to Reno," Lisa said.

"Fuck her!" he said.

They dried off and lotioned down. Sin opened the bag and put on the blue silk boxers. He took the clothes out the plastic and hung them on the closet door. He sprayed on some Kenneth Cole then slipped on the cream Armani pants, the chocolate Armani button up, the butter soft chocolate brown Cole Haan shoes, and the Armani frames with the brown tint.

"I'm going to need you to run the business for me until I figure out what to do about the police. You could go on and shoot your half-ounce and under sales to Davy. Anything between a half-ounce and a key, give it to Terell. You don't sell nothing under a key. The fourth of July is next Wednesday. Thursday I'm flying out to Tucson. That following Monday I want you to fly out there so you can drive back with me," he said.

"Aight, bet. Look, Sin. I know you mess with a lot of chicks. That's how you get down and I respect that. So don't no feelings get involved, let's just keep it on the ponta tip. We can kick it when it's convenient," Lisa said as she put her sandals on.

Sin and Lisa cleaned up. When they were done there wasn't a sign that another female had been in the house. He grabbed his dope and the sheets that he and Lisa messed up and they left.

Sin knew two things were going to change. One, he was about to start backing up out the game, and two, he was going to settle down. Malika was looking like the top candidate. After today when he put the demo down on Shaunté, she would see that Sin was a vicious dude and not to be played with.

When Lisa pulled up on Sin's block he carefully scanned the street and didn't see anything out of the ordinary. He got out and hurried in. He heard voices in Davy's bedroom. He opened the door and saw Davy and a young chick from the block named Misha, lounging. He was in shorts and she was in panties and a bra. She made no move to cover up when Sin came in.

"Did she stay the night? That girl mama be on some calling the police type shit, and you know we don't need that right now," Sin said.

"Nah, bro, she came over about an hour ago," he said. Sin turned to leave.

"Hi, Sin," Misha said.

Sin nodded his head at her then went into his room and got his spare keys. He went to the garage and got in the Navigator and left. He went to the beeper shop and bought him and Davy both new phones.

Sin pulled up at Pier 29 at 12:45. He walked in and the host showed him to Tiara's table. Tiara frowned as he sat down.

"Sorry I'm late. The time got away from me," he said.

Tiara was sitting there in a blue pinstriped Donna Karan business skirt suit and a sheer white blouse, which enabled you to see the lace of her bra. *Hmm, sexy and still classy,* Sin thought.

"I was just about to leave," Tiara said angrily.

Man, this bitch better check her attitude, Sin thought. He looked at his watch and that set her off.

"You in a hurry or something?" she snapped.

"Did I say I was in hurry?" he snapped back.

"Hold up. *I know* you don't have the nerve to have an attitude! You had me sitting here for 15 minutes waiting for your ass," she said, eyes blazing.

"Look, I called your office and asked that you be notified that I was going to be slightly late. I don't have your cell number," he said angrily.

The waiter stepped to the table, making Tiara bite her tongue.

"I'll have the Shrimp Scampi, the pacific trout, rice, and a crab salad. I'll have iced tea for the beverage," Sin said.

"I'll have the Chicken Caesar salad, house dressing, and a White Zinfandel," Tiara ordered. The waiter walked away.

Tiara decided to squash the beef. "You look nice," she said as she noticed that the label inside Sin's jacket said Cole Haan.

"I know," Sin said with an attitude.

"Look, I apologize for copping an attitude with you. I'm a very punctual person and I expect the same from those I deal with," she said.

Sin and Tiara sat and talked for a while and he really started feeling her. She was genuinely a good person. She explained that she had serious clout on her job, and was like a daughter to the president of the Western Regional branches.

"I got a little problem," Sin said.

"What would that be?"

"I have a whole lot of money that I never reported to the IRS or banked."

"How much is a lot?"

"Something in the neighborhood of $300,000," he said.

"*What!*" she said loudly.

"Shhhh, keep your voice down!"

"Are you crazy? The first thing the Treasury Department will be talking about when they catch a black man with that type of money is it's from drugs."

"I just feel safer with my own money," he said as he sipped his iced tea. "We charge 200 a car. We average 30 cars a day on regular days, and 50 in the summer months," he lied.

They sat there silent for a minute. Tiara tried to size Sin up. She wondered if he sold drugs. She didn't discriminate if he did. She in fact used to be in an intimate relationship (fuck buddies) with a drug dealer. While they were not together, they did make time for each other one weekend a month, but that was a long time ago. She didn't have time for that now, and she had too much to lose.

"Sin you're not into illegal gains, are you?" she asked.

"I was, back in the day, but I caught a case and ended up losing my woman. When I got out of prison I still had money, but I lost the will to hustle. I ended up giving my brother 100 gees. He flipped it a few times."

"Is that where you got the 300,000?" she asked.

"No, the 300,000 is legit. From that I have 526,000."

They sat and talked about him opening a business and her bank giving him the loan, and him funneling his unaccounted for money through that. The waitress dropped off their food and Sin smiled at Tiara.

"Tiara, you help me get this thing right and I'll give you 20 gees," he said.

"Yeah right!" she said. "So that chick at the gym really wasn't your girl?" she asked.

"Nah, she was a friend. I'm single," he said.

They talked during their meal then Tiara paid the check.

"What're you about to get into?" Tiara asked.

"I almost said something. I'm going to go smoke some weed and ride," he said honestly.

"You don't need to be riding around getting high. You can come over to my house and smoke," she said.

When they got outside Sin took Tiara's hand. "We can take my car and I'll bring you back for yours," he said.

"I don't see your Lexus," she said as she looked around.

"That was a rental car. That's my car over there, hiding," Sin said as he pointed across the street to a hooptie 82 Honda Accord.

"Sin, I'm not trying to be a bitch, but I'm *not* riding in that shit. I'll drive my car. You're pushing your luck," she said as she started walking in the direction of her BMW.

Sin grabbed her arm and started laughing. "Damn, that Navigator is sweet! I wish I had one," he said.

When they got to her BMW he pushed the remote for the alarm and the Nav chirped.

Tiara looked at him and frowned. "You better stop playing!" she said and playfully pushed him.

"You should have saw the look on your face. That was classic," he said as he opened the door for her. When he walked around she leaned over and opened the door for him. That little move earned Tiara some brownie points.

"Tiara, what would you like to hear?" he asked.

"First, I don't call you by your government name of Simian, so don't call me by mine. Call me Tia. To answer your question, I would like to hear either Case, or 112," she said.

Sin picked up the remote and turned on 112. He boosted the stereo up to 6 and they pulled off.

"So you got a man?" he asked.

"Nah, and I'm not looking for one either. The last relationship I was in sucked."

As they were riding just for the scenery and it being a nice day, Sin drove up the Embarcadero. As they were talking Sin saw a for lease sign in front of what used to be one of the hottest clubs in the town.

"That building is owned by my bank," Tia said as she pulled her phone out and called her office and got the prices. "They want 25,000 down, 2500 a month. The lease has a purchasing option. If you do what I suggested I can have the keys in your hands by tomorrow at 3," she said.

"I'll be at your office tomorrow at 9." he said. Sin pulled off and made a left on Pleasant Valley Road and drove until it turned into 51st. He turned left on Shattuck. When he got to 46th he turned right and parked around the corner from the weed spot.

"I'll be right back," he said.

Tia looked a little nervous. "Sin, is it safe over here?" she asked as she looked around.

"Baby, you with me. I'm not going to let anything happen to you," he said as he walked away.

He walked back around the corner and went up the stairs and stopped at the second door and knocked.

Teesa looked out the window. She opened the door and Sin went in. "What up, Sin?" she asked.

Teesa was a bad muthafucka. She had a milk chocolate complexion, a short Halle Berry do, and gray eyes. She was a very pretty girl. Her body though, was off the Richter scale. Wide hips, a small waist, and a big sexy ass. She was stacked for real. Sin wanted to hit it bad, but she messed with his cousin, Shaqui on the low.

"Tees, let me get a half-ounce of that sticky," he said.

She walked out her house and went next door, came back and gave him a bag of buds. He gave her $200.00.

"Where my cousin at?" he asked.

"Probably with his girl. Sin, you gotta be careful. Them suckas could've killed you," she said.

"Aight, blood. I'll holla at you," Sin said and left.

When he got around the corner to the Navigator Davy was turning the corner in Terell's green and white 5.0, and Terell was following in his burgundy '87 convertible Iroc. They saw Sin and pulled over. "These my little brothers," he said as they got out their cars.

"Sin, them hoe-ass niggas Max and company came through Seminary," Terell said.

"What happened?" Sin asked.

Terell looked at him crazy. "What you think? I handled my business," Terell said.

"We'll holla about that shit later," Sin said.

"Damn, bro who is this?" Davy asked getting into the Navigator.

"Ask her, she talks," Sin said.

"What's up, boo? They call me B.G.," he said.

"I'm Tia. You are so cute," Tia said and smiled.

"So are you. Man, could you imagine what our kids are going to look like?" he asked.

"Whoa, baby boy! Pump your brakes! You ain't about to catch me a pedophile case no matter how fine you are!" she said.

"You have some pretty-ass legs. Get out so I can see all of you," he asked.

Tia got out and both Davy and Terell whistled. "You guys are off the hook!" she said while blushing.

"What you about to get into?" Davy asked Sin.

"I hope something sweet," Sin said as he looked at Tia.

"You need to pump your brakes too. You're not getting into nothing sweet on me on the first date," she said and blushed.

"We sideways. Davy, be home by ten," Sin said. He and Tia got in the truck.

They pulled off and made a left on Shattuck, and rode down to 63rd and made another left. They drove part way down 63rd and pulled over in front of Sin's mom's house. Malik was outside in front playing in the grass.

"Sin, is that your son?" Tia asked.

"Yeah, that's his little bad-ass," he said.

When they got out of the truck Sin saw Quesha coming down the street on her bike. "Daddy!" she screamed and skidded, dropping her bike. She ran to Sin and hugged him.

"What's up, princess?" he asked.

"Daddy, I want some new roller blades. Will you buy me some?" she asked. Sin pulled a meatloaf of money out and counted off five $20.00 bills and gave them to her.

"Oooo, Mama's going to get you! She said you can't have no roller blades because your stupid butt lost your other ones," Malik said.

Quesha pushed him. "What Mama tell you about calling me stupid?" she said.

"What I tell you two about always fighting? Go inside," Sin said.

Quesha took her bike in the back and Malik followed Sin and Tia in. When they walked in, Sin's mom and his niece, Shamika were sitting at the dining room table. "Why you ain't at school, Lil' Diamond?" Sin asked.

"Her ass got suspended again for fighting," his mom said.

Sin looked at his niece and shook his head. "Ma, this is Tia. Tia, this is my mom, Mrs. Michaels, my niece, Shamika, my son, Malik, and my daughter, Marquesha," he said. They all exchanged hellos.

"Mama, I need to borrow 140 gees," Sin said.

"Boy, you been smoking that reefer again?" she asked.

"Daddy, what's reefer?" Malik asked.

"It's weed, stupid," Marquesha said.

"Then why granny didn't just say blunts?" he asked.

Sin looked at Tia who was busting up laughing. "Take your little grown asses back outside!" he yelled.

When the kids were gone he gave his mom his sales pitch, and Tia reaffirmed what he said.

"So when will you give me my money back?" his mom asked.

"Right now. I got that in cash," he said as he went out to the truck and grabbed the gray Nike bag and came back in. He dumped the twenty-nine bundles of money on the table. Every bundle had one hundred $100.00 bills in it.

"You been riding around with that?" Tia asked amazed.

"Tell her where the best place for your money is, Lil' Diamond."

"Where you can see it," Shamika said.

Sin gave his mom 14 bundles. She went in her room and got her purse and got her banking info out and called her bank. Once that was done, she left and went to pick up the cashiers check.

"So who you been fighting?" Sin asked Shamika.

"One of them eleventh grade niggas grabbed my butt. I slapped him and he went and lied to his girl saying that I was trying to get at him. She ran up on me and caught a beat down," Shamika said.

"I'll have Davy come up there with Terell. Don't trip," Sin said.

Moms came back and gave Sin the check. He put the money that was left over in the bag.

"Lil' Diamond, when Tracy comes tell her I said to put this bread up for me," he said.

He and Tia left. He drove to her Moraga Hills home and was duly impressed. Homes in this area were starting at a million, easy. They went inside and Sin fell in love with her spot.

She escorted him to the family room. "Kick back and roll your *reefer*," she said and laughed as she disappeared upstairs.

Sin broke down a Dutch Master cigar and threw the tobacco in a paper bag. He then broke down a bud of the sticky kush and put it in the cigar leaf and rolled it. He walked through the house and looked around. He spotted a picture of some white dude kissing Tia. *So, that's how she get down,* he thought.

"Sin, will you please fire up the hot tub? It's through the door on the side of the bar," Tia said from the intercom on the wall.

Sin walked through the door and there was a whirlpool that could comfortably seat five. He turned the water on and sat and waited. Tia came down ten minutes later with her hair pinned up, wearing a robe. She was carrying a bottle of Hennessey and two glasses.

"You don't have shorts. You could get in in your underwear," she suggested.

"These drawers cost fifty bucks a pop. I don't think so. I'm not shy though," he said as he took his shirt and pants off.

Tia stared at Sin's ripped body and felt her juices flowing. She took off the robe and stood there in a sexy yellow bikini. Her titties and ass were begging for an escape. Tia saw the bulge in Sin's boxers growing. With no hesitation he dropped the boxers and got in the tub. *Goddamn!* she thought. She poured each of them a drink and got in.

Sin fired up the blunt and hit it a couple of times and passed it to Tia.

"I haven't smoked pot since my junior year in college," she said as she took the blunt and hit it.

They sat and got high and the next thing Tia knew, she was naked and she and Sin were fondling each other.

"Come on, baby. Just let me put the head in. I promise I'll take it out," he said.

"Sin, you're not going to want to take it out. I went through this same shit in High School," she said and laughed. She had to admit that she did want to feel that python inside of her.

He slid in just the tip and Tia stopped him. "That's enough," she whispered. Sin reluctantly pulled out.

"Come on, let's go work on your business plan," she said.

Sin looked at the clock and saw it was 4. "I can't right now. I got somewhere to be in the next hour," he said and kissed her.

They got out of the tub and went to Tia's room. They lotioned each other down and got dressed. Tia put on a gray thong, black Nike leggings, a black Nike sports bra, a white T-shirt and some black Air Max Nikes.

When they pulled up at Pier 29 Sin walked her to her car. "You're not mad are you?" she asked.

"Nah, baby it's all good. I'll call and check on you tomorrow," he said. He kissed her on the lips and left.

Chapter Five

You Played Yourself

Sin stopped and got some gas then hit Interstate 80 for the 3-½ hour, 224-mile ride to Reno. He lit a blunt and smoked.

He thought about Yvette and Simara. Before getting shot, he talked to them on the phone at least once a week and he spoiled his daughter from the moment the blood test came back saying he was 99.9% her father. With them living way out in Reno he didn't see her that often, but once a month he did come stay the night. *After I check 'Tay I'll go see my baby*, he thought.

Sin pulled up in front of Shaunté's sister, Destiny's house and saw the Lexus. He picked up his gun and slipped it under his shirt. He got out and went and knocked on the door.

Destiny opened it and got wide-eyed. That was all Sin had to see. As he stepped in, his stomach dropped. There was Chris sitting on the sofa. The expression on his face made Shaunté, whom was sitting across from him with her back to the door, turn around. She saw Sin and the color drained from her face.

It took everything Sin had not put his hands on her. "I knew something wasn't right with you. I'm cool on your scandalous ass, business or otherwise. Let this bitch-ass nigga take care of that kid," he said and turned and left.

Sin got in the Navigator and burned rubber away from the house. He slammed on the brakes when he remembered his keys. He put the truck in reverse and backed back down the street. As he approached the door he had the urge to kick it in. It opened and Shaunté came out with her purse in hand. Sin snatched it and grabbed her keys and took the keys to his house off the ring.

"Stay away from me, Shaunté. You're breathing on borrowed time as it is," he threatened.

"Nigga, what was you saying? This ain't your baby and you ain't fixing to take care of it?" she asked ignoring the threat.

"Tramp-ass bitch, that's exactly what I'm saying. That baby could be anybody's the way your hoe-ass be tipping," he said.

Shaunté looked at Sin for a second then looked away, and out of nowhere she pulled back and slapped Sin as hard as she could.

Sin was momentarily stunned. He didn't even think about what he was doing when he hit Shaunté in the jaw, it just happened.

A Little More Sin

Chris jumped out the chair and came running towards him. Sin pulled out the 9mm stepped back and shot Chris in the shoulder.

"I'm calling the police!" Destiny yelled. Sin contemplated shooting her too. He looked down at 'Tay.

"You played yourself," he said.

Shaunté touched her jaw and swore it was broken. She stood up and saw Chris lying there crying.

"Nigga, shut your bitch ass up! Sin, you bitch! You didn't even ask me what the fuck was going on. You just assumed the worse!" 'Tay screamed.

"Eat a dick, bitch!" he said and walked away.

Shaunté picked her purse up and pulled the Glock 40 out and let three rounds off at Sin.

Sin ducked behind the Navigator and pulled his gun back out. He let six off back at her.

Shaunté ducked back in the house and Sin got in the Navigator and tried to pull off. Shaunté unloaded her whole clip into the Navigator, busting the rear window and putting holes in the body. Sin punched the gas. He picked the phone up and called Yvette.

"Hello?" Simara answered.

"Sweetie, let me talk to your mommy," he said.

"Okay, Daddy" she said and handed Yvette the phone.

"What's up, Sin?" she asked.

"I'm on my way over there. I need to put my truck in the garage."

54

Yvette was still in love with Sin, but he wasn't feeling her like that. Too much shady stuff had happened between them, but Yvette still held her feelings.

"Okay, I'll open it now," she said.

"I'll be there in like 10 minutes," he said and hung up.

Sin drove the speed limit and was aware of the people staring at his truck with the blown-out glass and bullet holes. He pulled into Yvette's driveway and into the garage. As he was getting out of the truck she came out of the house.

"This is nice," she said only seeing the front of the truck. She walked down the stairs into the garage and walked around the Navigator. When she got to the back she saw the broken window and bullet holes. She looked on the passenger side and saw more of the same. "What happened?" she asked.

"Nothing," he said and walked in the house. He went to the family room and found his daughter laying on the floor in front of the TV watching a cartoon. Sin stood there looking at her and saw how much she favored him, Malik, and Simina.

His phone rang and he stepped out of the room. He saw Shaunté's number. "Bitch, you think I won't kill you?" he asked.

"You punk ass nigga! You must be driving real fast. I'm trying to catch you. You almost broke my jaw, bitch!" she said.

"Then I'm sorry, because I was *trying* to break that muthafucka!" he said and hung up.

Sin ended up staying at Yvette's until 8.

When he was preparing to leave Yvette cornered him. "Just stay the night and drop your car off at the shop out here and come back and get it," she suggested.

"I'm taking my shit to a shop at home," he said.

"Sin, are you going to keep acting like you hate me? I'm sorry for what I did. There's no more I can say. I know you want me. I can see it in the way you look at me," she said.

"So what you saying, Yvette? You want some dick or something?" he asked.

"Sin, *fuck* you! I'll see you next time you come out here," she said and turned to leave. He grabbed her arm and she blew on him. "Nigga, you talking about some *dick!* I ain't no ugly bitch. I can get dick from anywhere. I'm not on that material shit I was on before, and I ain't tripping on no man right now. This is Reno. I could find a high roller with a dick. I'm just showing respect for our child. *You* the one that's thinking about sex. *You* want to fuck *me.* I want you too, but I want more than sex."

"Baby, I can't give you that. You played me out of pocket, 'Vette. I was a straight sucka for you, and that's why you did what you did. I didn't expose you to my violent side. I'm proud of you though. You're a good mother and you got your life on the right track, but you ain't that ride or die chick I thought you were," he said.

"And what, that bitch, Shaunté is? That thug-ass bitch's cheating on you in your face. I fell weak because you weren't there with me. That bitch fell weak just *because.* I ain't trying to hear that shit about you rolled up on her with another bitch in the car and that's why she did it. I rolled up on you and Tracy fucking at the Marina. Did *I* leave? No, I didn't. Don't look shocked. I knew you were fucking her. I just loved you that much that I didn't trip. I just kept playing the position you wanted me to. Remember, look pretty and hold you down? You didn't give me the chance to do more than that, Sin," she said.

Sin pulled her to him and put his arms around her waist and hugged her tight. He let her go and kissed her on the forehead. "Me and you will do something special next time I come out here," he said.

"Don't think you getting no pussy," she said as she switched off.

"I'll see you later, Jell-O booty!" he said. He got in the Navigator and rolled out.

When Sin got home it was 11:30. He pulled the Navigator into the garage.

Davy was in the family room watching the wide screen and putting his rocks in 500 counts.

Sin went to his room and changed out of his clothes. His phone rang. "Hello?" he answered.

"Who the fuck you had in my house?" Malika asked.

"Punk, I didn't have nobody in your house," he said.

"Sin, the pillows smell like Dolce & Gabanna. I was wearing Tommy Girl yesterday," she said.

"I sprayed that shit on the bed to make you mad because you left me stranded. My daughter there?" he asked.

"Yes," she said.

He hung up and finished getting dressed. He put on some black Pelle Pelle jeans, a throw back Negro Leagues jersey, and some black and white Jordans. He went to the garage and got in the SS and hit 580 to Dublin.

Sin pulled into Malika's the driveway and parked next to her Tahoe. When he got to the door, an over-developed teenage girl opened it. Simina was a teenage version of Malika. You could tell she was Sin's daughter though. The light-brown eyes, the gap in her front teeth, the way she held her head, the high cheek bones, and the dimple in her left cheek all came from Sin.

Father and daughter smiled at each other and then they met in a tight hug. "Hi, daddy!" she said.

"Hey, baby girl," he said. They stood holding each other for what seemed like forever.

When Sin released her he closed the door. "Where's your mom, baby?" he asked.

"She's in her room. She don't want you to see the black eye that bastard gave her," Simina said angrily.

They went up the stairs and to Malika's room. When Sin saw Malika's face, his blood boiled. Her eye was black and her cheek was swollen.

She saw Sin and the anger in his eyes and started crying. Malika knew that if her soon to be ex, Joe was in Oakland right then, Sin would kill him.

"What the fuck's up with dude?" he asked.

"I don't know. What I do know is I'm going to have my brother, Mook beat his ass next week when he comes out here to get the Tahoe," she said.

"Nah, I'm going to beat his ass. Did you see him hit her?" Sin asked Simina?

"I always see him hit her. He hits me too," she said.

"Pumpkin, let me talk to your dad for a minute," Malika said.

"I'll be in my plushed-out room," Simina said as she walked away.

Malika looked up at Sin through swollen eyes.

"I'm going to kill this nigga!" Sin snarled as he sat down by her. Malika put her arms around his neck and hugged him and cried.

Sin went to Malika's dresser, grabbed a black gown, undressed her, and put the gown on her. "Lay down and relax. You ate yet?" he asked as he turned the covers back.

"I'm not hungry. Get Pumpkin something to eat," she said as she got in the bed.

Sin went down the hall to Simina's room. "Come on, baby we gon' go get some food," he said.

Simina put on her white and red Jordan's, and the red Jordan jacket and they went to the garage.

Sin took the garage door opener out of the Tahoe. He and Simina then got in the SS and left. When they pulled up at Denny's, Sin gave Simina a 50 and told her what to get him. After she placed the order she came back to the car.

"My Mama told me I have two little sisters and a little brother," she said.

Sin showed her the pictures he had of Simara, Quesha, and Malik.

"Is this their mom?" she asked, referring to Tracy.

"That's Malik's mom. Quesha lives with them though. Simara lives in Nevada with her mom," Sin said as his phone rang. He looked at the number and saw Lisa's. "What's up?" he answered.

"You coming over tonight?" she asked.

"Let me find out you whipped. I'll be there after I drop my lil' girl off at home," he said.

"Aight," she said and hung up.

"Mama told me you're about to get married," Simina said.

"I don't think so, baby," he said.

"So you going to get back with my mom?" she asked hopefully.

"Me and your mama got some bad history, sweetheart. I don't know if the shit we went through is repairable," he said as he got out of the car and went in and got their food.

When they pulled back up to the house Sin picked his phone up and called Malika.

"Hello?" she answered.

"I snatched you up a pancake breakfast. I'll be by here tomorrow," he said.

"You're not staying the night?" she asked.

"Nah, not tonight. Don't make any plans for tomorrow," he said and hung up. "You got some money?" he asked his daughter.

"Ten dollars," she said. Sin pulled a knot of money out his pocket and gave Simina $50.00.

"Joe took all my Mama's money," she said.

Sin counted his knot and came up with 6500. He peeled 500 off and slipped the rest in the bag with Malika's food. "I'll see you tomorrow," he said to his daughter and kissed her on the forehead.

Sin stopped at the gas station and filled up. As he was getting on the freeway he called Maria's.

"Hello?" she answered.

"Hey, I wanna apologize for putting my hands on you," he said.

"I was wrong and I deserved that," she said.

"I miss you, baby," he said.

"Nah, you miss the sex. Where you been putting in work at, because it ain't been here?" she asked.

"I just got out of the hospital. I'm on a come up. I don't have time for sex," he lied.

"So you don't have time to come sex *me*?" she asked.

"I'll be through there in a couple of days," Sin said as he took the 98th Avenue exit.

"You haven't called me about that other thing," she said.

"I'll probably call you tomorrow."

"Okay, well I'm about to get in the shower I'll talk to you tomorrow."

"Aight," he said and hung up.

Sin pulled up at Lisa's house and parked behind her Acura. He went to the door and knocked. Dante was one of the nicest streets on the Oakland/San Leandro border.

Lisa opened the door with a sheet wrapped around her body. Sin came in and they kissed. She led him to the bedroom and he undressed and got in the bed. They made small talk, and to Sin's delight, they went to sleep. Not that Lisa's sex game wasn't good, he was just tired.

Chapter Six

Let's Do This

The next morning Sin got up early and priced the equipment needed to open his club. He then went and picked Malika and Simina up and dropped the Navigator off at the shop where he got it painted.

The whole time they were riding around taking care of business, Malika was typing up Sin's business plan.

At 3:00 Sin showed up at his loan appointment and was approved, thanks to Tia. The loan was for 500,000. He immediately put the down payment on the property and took Malika and Simina to see it. He then took Malika home and Simina to his mom's house where she was treated like the golden child.

At 4:30 Sin's phone rang. He looked at his caller ID and didn't recognize the number. "What up?" he answered.

"Sin, this is Jamila. I met you on Bancroft when you was looking for your baby's mama, Kesha," she said.

"I know who your pretty ass is. What's up, you ready to get some paper?" he asked.

"Yeah, but that ain't what I called you for. That nigga, Max is back. I just saw him on 68th at that spot they got," she said.

"Aight. Where you at?"

"I'm at the Chevron gas station on 73$^{rd.}$"

"Meet me back there in a hour," Sin said and hung up.

He was just about to call Terell when he heard a car pulling up. He looked outside and saw his Hashi and Shaqui. He walked out on the porch and greeted them.

Hashi, Sin, Marco, Hasahn, Tariq, Tayshaun and Shaqui were all good friends dating back to high school. Hashi, Sin, and Marco actually went further than that, more like elementary. Hash's Father, A.B. was on the run with Sin's father. Hashi was the only cat that Sin fucked with real tough that wasn't Mad Circle.

As Shaqui and Hash came walking towards him he saw that Hash's boy, Kevin, and Sha's play-son, Dewan were looking at Shamika and Simina.

"What's up, cuzzo?" Hash asked and hugged Sin.

"What's up with you cats?" Sin asked.

"You know, trying to get this thang right," Hash said.

"I just got back from New York. Nigga, Hasahn doing it big out there." Shaqui said.

"You know I'm funking with them 61st Street niggas again," Sin said.

"Cuzzo, them nigga's bitches! I slapped that nigga, Tony Williams at Tariq's party a couple weeks ago. He went and got Max and J.B. Omar and Amir flexxed them niggas. We should've went on and killed them marks when they shot you," Shaqui said.

"You wanna go ride on them niggas or what?" Hashi asked.

"For sure," Sin said.

"Let me run down the street and get my Iroc from my mama's house. We can't roll over there in Hash's Camaro," Sha said and broke down the street.

Sin looked at how friendly the girls were being with the young cats. "I'm gon' tell ya'll now, they off limits. If I catch one of ya'll around my daughter or my niece, I'm killing you. Ya'll bring your asses in the house," he said to the girls.

"Bye, Kevin," Shamika flirted.

"I'm telling your daddy your ass out here being fast," Sin said.

"*Okaaay*, Uncle Sin! I'm going in," she said and went in the house.

"Mina, come on. We out," he said.

"Daddy, can I stay over here with my Grandma a little longer?" she asked.

"Yeah, I guess," he said.

Shaqui pulled up in his black 92 convertible Iroc.

"Man, this nigga tripping. I ain't fixing to go get at them niggas while we in a drop. We can take the Infinity, it's a rental," Sin said to Hash.

They told Sha what they were doing. They all got in the Infinity and went to 47th. Sha left the young cats and grabbed up some choppas (fully automatic machine guns). They then left to the east.

Sin pulled up at the Chevron gas station and saw Jamila looking fine. *Damn, why her ass gotta be on dope?* he thought. He parked at the gas pump.

"God damn! I'm at that," Sha said.

Sin stopped him. "It ain't that type of party. That's my folks," he said. He got out and walked over to Jamila who was wearing a short summer dress, displaying her sexy legs.

Jamila was a red bone who had a cool body. She favored a young Vanessa Williams, except Jamila's ass was bigger.

"What's up, lil' mama?" Sin asked.

"There's five of them around there. Two are on the porch, two in a convertible parked in front of the house, and Max is sitting in a brown Lexus truck parked across the street," she said.

"Aight look; meet me on Bromly at 7. You got some money?" he asked.

"I got about $20.00," she said.

Sin reached in his pocket and pulled a 20 out and gave it to her. "You stop getting high?" he asked.

"I ain't got high since we last talked," she said.

"Aight, I'll see you in a minute," he said.

She walked away and Sin stared at her ass. "Jamila, what's up with that?" he asked.

"This is all me, baby. You need to stop looking before you fuck around and get me killed. I did my homework on you. You mess with that bitch that got Seminary on lock; Shaunté," she said.

"I'll holla at you about that later. Say, was Kesha around there?" he asked.

"She had left in her Range Rover," Jamila said as she flagged down a cab.

Range Rover? That nigga must be sprung. Kesha did have some bomb pussy, Sin thought as he got back in the Infinity.

While coming down 68th, Sin saw that everything was just as Jamila said. He pulled up on the side of Max who was on the phone in the Lexus truck.

Sin pointed the MP5 at him. "So you like riding around looking mean, huh?" he asked.

The niggas on the porch stood up and started trying to make their way in the house.

"Man, I wish you niggas would!" Sha said as he pointed the AK-47 at them.

Hash looked at the dudes in the convertible 5.0 and sneered. "You niggas want to live to see tomorrow, right?" he asked as he pointed the M-16 at them.

Kesha turned the corner in a yellow Range Rover. She immediately saw what was going down and quickly got out of the truck. "Sin, what's going on?" she asked.

"That's what *I'm* trying to find out. Your dude been smashing through my spots looking at niggas crazy. What, you trying to see me, nigga? I gave you marks a pass when I got shot. You want a war?" Sin asked.

"Nigga, I ain't impressed with that speech. Yeah, nigga I want a war," Max said.

"You got that. Next time I see you I'm splitting your wig," Sin said. He put the Infinity in gear and pulled off.

Kesha looked at Max stupid. She slid into the Lexus truck.

"Why do you persist in trying to fuck with them? Sin ain't playing, Max! Them niggas in the car with him ain't no joke either. That was HB! He got the 20's on lock. That nigga is Big Omar's brother. The other nigga is Sin's cousin, Shaqui. He got spots everywhere. He's a fool too. I know you ain't no punk, daddy, but you don't want the problems them nigga's gon' bring. I also don't want this baby born without a daddy, or Quesha's daddy dead!" Kesha said.

●●●●●●

Sin pulled into June Bug's detail shop, called Top To Bottom as his phone rang. "What up?" he answered.

"Sin, this Pete. I wanna buy them three amps off you (3 kilos)," he said.

"I'm around the corner from your spot. Come through in about a half-hour. I want 495 (49,500)," Sin said and hung up. He called Lisa and told her to bring three amps.

Sin, Sha, and Hash all went into June's office. As they were all sitting in there smoking blunts with June, Lisa came. Sin called Pete and told him to come through. After the transaction was completed Sin stood outside talking to Lisa.

Yanna pulled in, in her gold Audi A8. Sin stepped away from Lisa and went to the car. "I'm ready," she said.

Sin pulled his phone out and called Maria. "I need to borrow fifty bucks (I need 50 kilos on consignment)," Sin said.

"Aight, meet me at that restaurant you took me to the first time I came out here to see you. Make it about ten," she said.

Sin looked at his watch and saw it was 7:00. "That's cool," he said and hung up.

"Man, you fronting with the dick. You gon' let me hit that again or what?" Yanna asked.

"Yeah, but I ain't had no time for no pussy, I been busy. I need you to make a run to Seattle Saturday. While we out there we gon' do it live," he said.

Sin noticed a big body Benz with four dudes inside pull in. A blue Suburban pulled in behind it. Yanna felt tension and pulled her Glock from under her seat and cocked it. A tall dark-skinned dude got out the driver side of the Benz. His squad got out behind him.

"Somebody tell June Bug that JB wanna holla at him," he said. June's main man, Kiaree went to the office.

"Block the driveway. Don't let nothing in," Sin said to Yanna as he walked away. He went to the office as June, Sha, and Hash were coming out.

"I'm going to tell you like I told these niggas. Don't trip out. I got this," June said. Hash and Sin looked at each other.

When they got outside, JB spoke to June Bug like he was the one that lost the first battle, when in all actuality it was a draw.

"Man, I suggest you get at your brother. That nigga shot one of my spots up not too long ago, and he smashing through my spot tripping on my brother behind a bitch," JB said.

"Nigga, who the fuck you talking to? You *suggest?* Nigga, fuck you and your suggestions!" June said.

JB noticed that June was standing with his cousin, Sha. Shaqui Michaels was a beast, with his hands or with a gun. JB heard when Sin got shot that Shaqui was the one who turned the heat up.

"And what the fuck you bring your muthafuckin' ass over here for, and why you ain't talking to my brother?" June asked.

"I don't know your brother, nigga," JB said.

"JB, you threatening my cousin, Sin?" Shaqui asked.

"Yeah nigga, and?" he asked.

Sin and Hash stepped out from behind the Infinity with the choppas.

"I'm gon' give it to you raw. Your hoe-ass brother robbed me. This shit is over that. Kesha brought me my shit and begged me to spare him. I squashed shit on the strength of her. Then niggas got at me, and I squashed that. Now him and ya'll boys rolling through Bromly looking stupid. Secondly, you ain't about to come in my brother's place of business like you can't be touched. Nigga, it's The Mad Circle. What!" Sin said.

"Your money ain't gon' support a war, nigga. So if this is what you want, it's what you got," JB said.

"Nigga, we done already dropped twenty of y'all. What, you gonna talk me to death? Get your bitch-asses up outta here while I'm allowing you to breathe," Sin said angrily.

JB looked behind him and saw Kiaree and Yanna standing there strapped. He knew that he fucked up by coming to June Bug's shop.

"This is your pass, nigga. Raise up," Sin said.

JB shook his head. "I'll see you again," he said.

"Bitch, you keep talking you gon' see the back of your eyelids," Sha said.

JB and his crew got in their cars and left quickly.

Sin looked at Lisa and nodded for her to follow them. She got in the Infinity and rolled off. Sin waited five minutes then called Lisa's phone to give her the play.

"Hello?" she answered as she pulled over at Sprewell's rim shop.

"Follow that nigga, and when he stops, flirt with him and hook up a date," Sin said.

"Aight, baby. He's looking at me now. I'll call you back," she said and hung up.

Sin walked over to Hash and June and they talked to Yanna.

"Cuzzo, what's up with you and 'Tay?" Hash asked.

"Not a God damn thang," Sin said.

"That must be why she's looking mad," Hash said.

Sin turned and looked, and saw Shaunté pulling up in her Yukon. She got out and walked over to them, and they saw the big ugly bruise on her jaw.

"You feel good about yourself, muthafucka? You nearly broke my jaw, punk!" she said.

"I feel bad, because I was trying to break it, tramp-ass bitch!" he said.

"You make me sick! Hashi, let me cop two of them thangs," she asked.

Out of all Sin's friends Hashi was the only one that Shaunté would fuck if she wasn't stuck on Sin. All that long hair, and them light eyes, and that buffed body, compliments of Lompoc's Club Fed, always had Shaunté hot and bothered. Not to mention the fact he was fucking both her twin cousins, Mia and Tia, and Déja. They all told her he had a big dick and a long tongue.

Shaunté knew not to mess with Hash. Sin would kill them both, and although Hash's baby mama, Angel wasn't as crazy as Shaunté, Angel was far from a punk, and she would bust her gun quick.

Hash looked at Sin after 'Tay made her request.

"Cuzzo, it's cool. Her money spend just like everybody else's," Sin said.

"Yeah, but my prices ain't as cheap as ya man's. I want 17-5, but I'll take 16-5 because we folks," he said.

When Sin didn't think the day could get any worse, here comes Simone and Malika pulling up in June's Vette.

"You messing with Simone again?" Sha asked June as he tucked a number he had just gotten.

"I never stopped. That girl got some booming-ass pussy. She does her thing and I do mine. I married Toya because she plays her part," June said.

"You some trifling niggas," Shaunté said.

When Malika walked up she recognized Shaunté from the picture Sin had in his wallet. "Where's Pumpkin?" she asked Sin.

"She's at my mom's with Shamika," Sin answered.

"Sin, you going to introduce me to your little friend?" Shaunté said, feeling slightly insecure.

"*Little friend?* Bitch, I look like a kid to you?" Malika barked on the shorter Shaunté.

Shaunté pulled back and slapped the shit outta Malika. Sin could have sworn that slap was heard on the East Coast somewhere.

It was on from there. Malika beat Shaunté's pregnant butt.

Shaunté broke away from Malika and went to her truck and grabbed the .45.

"Man, get her!" Sin yelled to Hash. Hash grabbed Shaunté and pulled her and the gun back.

"Tay, you tripping! Come on so we can handle our business," Hash pleaded.

"Bitch, your ass is mine!" Shaunté said as she let Hash pull her back to the Yukon. Shaunté pulled out of the lot fast.

"Is you stupid or something? That girl was fixing to blast your dumb ass!" Sin yelled.

"Nigga, ain't nothing changed! Who was that punk-ass bitch?" Malika asked.

"My ex-fiancée," he said.

"I wish I never came out here. You the same dog-ass nigga you always been!"

"*Dog?* Bitch, if I was a dog I wouldn't have given your ungrateful ass 18-5 on your spot, bought you furniture, or be being civil to you," Sin said in her face.

"I should take your daughter and go back to New Orleans," she threatened.

"I didn't ask your muthafuckin ass to come, *bitch!* Beat it!" Sin yelled as he went and got in Lisa's Acura.

He and Sha left. They went to the spot on Seminary and waited for Lisa.

Lisa pulled up and told him that she had gotten JB's number.

He got the prepaid phone out of the back of the Infinity and gave it to Jamila. He pulled a $1,000.00 out his pocket and handed it to her. "You going to Arizona with me tomorrow. I need you to carry a pound of weed," he said.

"It's all good. Can I get a ride home?" she asked.

"Lisa, take Sha to where he need to go. Cuzzo, you gonna be at the club tonight?" Sin asked.

"I don't know. Tenesha been tripping," he said.

"You still messing with the white girl, Erica?" Sin asked.

"Hell yeah. That's my B.M. (baby mama)," Sha said.

"I'll be at you," Sin said.

He and Jamila got in the Infinity after he stored the guns. "Where you stay at?" he asked.

"In 8-5 Village," she said.

Sin slapped in the Life After Death CD and rode. "You got a man?" he asked as he constantly sneaked peeks at Jamila's legs.

"Nah, I'm sadly single."

"How you end up on dope?" he asked.

"Damn, you don't pull no punches, do you?" she asked.

"That ain't my style, baby."

"I wasn't using that long. It was almost five months. The guy I was with got me on it," she said.

"Look, I'm taking you at your word. You said you ain't getting down like that. I'm not going to like it if anybody in my organization is dishonest. So if you still fucking around let me know. I'll still give you a job, but it'll be something else," he said.

"Sin, on my son, I'm clean. So besides going to Arizona with you, what else is my job?" she asked.

"Don't worry, I'm not going to have you dealing with no hard (crack). I'm going to have you getting on planes with the soft (powder cocaine)."

"What am I going to be making?" she asked.

"Every ten keys you take for me, you got 25,000 coming. If you get cracked keep your mouth shut! I got your bail and lawyer covered."

"Twenty-five gees, huh?"

"You know it."

"So what kind of dick benefi... I mean fringe benefits am I going to get?" she asked.

Sin laughed. He wasn't going to mix business with pleasure with this one. He already made that mistake with two chicks he relied heavenly upon to handle his business Yanna and Lisa. "I don't think any," he replied

"You think I'm a toss-up or something? Nigga, I ain't *never* fucked or sucked for dope. If I wanted to get high and didn't have it, then I didn't have it!" she angrily said.

"Hold on, baby!" he said and pulled over. "That shit you talking about never crossed my mind. I'm just not trying to have another woman hating me. I takes a woman through it. If at anytime I feel a chick ain't playing her position, I'm sideways to the next. I would feel more comfortable if we stayed in the friend zone," he explained.

"You can't live like that, Sin."

"Man, I just caught Shaunté, my *fiancée*, in Reno with a nigga she was seeing at one time. I can live however the fuck I want to," he said.

"Sin, I can see your logic. I've been through some shit too, but I'm not holding that against all men."

Sin pulled back into traffic. As they were riding he was thinking of 'Tay.

"Sin, the first time I fell in love was last year. I was 27 and that muthafucka got me on dope! I mean I loved this nigga so much that nothing else mattered. I came home from work one day, and finds this nigga butt naked in my bed with another bitch, fucking. He looked at me like no big deal, and she stuck out her hand to me to join them. I fucked them both up. All he had to do was ask me for a threesome, and I was so gone I would have said yes; but that was my fault, I settled for less. As soon as I saw that muthafucka hit that pipe I should have dumped him. What I'm saying is, I'm not holding a bad experience against the whole male species," she said.

Sin pulled up in 8-5 Village and a couple of dudes mean mugged him so he mugged them back. "We going to be doing it real big at Echelon later. Slide through," he said.

"I guess I can do that," she said and got out of the car.

Jamila's sexy butt and hips naturally rolled when she walked, and Sin was feeling that. He pulled off and was headed to Yanna's house when his phone rang. "Yo?" he answered when he saw Malika's number.

"What the fuck is up with you, Sin?" she asked heatedly.

"What the fuck you mean? Your ass got fly at the mouth."

"Nigga, I ain't talking about that! Why the fuck is Pumpkin and Shamika with your bitch?" she asked.

"Man, what the fuck is you talking about?" he asked.

"I'm talking about your baby mama taking my daughter somewhere without my permission!" she yelled.

"Malika, Tracy ain't going to hurt the kids," he said.

"Nigga, I'm not talking about Tracy! I'm talking about Shaunté! Tracy is here!" she yelled.

"Bitch, you yell at me again I'm slapping the fuck out you," he said calmly.

"Nigga, fuck you!" she said and hung up. Sin called 'Tay's phone.

"Hello?" she answered.

"Is you just trying to keep up a bunch of shit?" he asked.

"Look, just because me and you ain't clicking don't mean I can't see the kids, does it? I'm taking the girls shopping," she said.

"Where ya'll at?" he asked.

"Bayfair."

"Have them outside when I get to the Macys' side," he said and hung up.

Chapter Seven

Don't Bite the Hand That Feeds You

Sin got off of the freeway at High Street and got back on. He took the Marina exit in San Leandro and rode to East 14th Street where he turned right. There were all types of bad chicks out. Sin pulled his phone out and called June.

"What up?" June asked.

"So what we gon' do about them suckas? I say we hit them hard and get it over with," Sin said.

"Bro, we getting too much money to be out there on the front line getting at niggas. We gon' have our boys do the dirt," June said.

"Nah, I'm riding for my damn self. That's how niggas get them RICO charges. Cats get caught and get to talking about they were following orders, and then comes the Feds. I don't need that," Sin said.

"Well when you go I got some thorough niggas for you to take." June said.

This nigga ain't listening, Sin thought. "I'll see you later," he told June as he pulled into the mall. He saw

Shaunté sitting on a bench with Quesha, Simina, and Shamika. He pulled up in front of them.

"Bye, 'Tay," they all said and kissed her cheek. Shaunté looked at Sin and flipped him off as he pulled off. He made small talk with the girls all the way to North Oakland.

As Sin parked in his mom's driveway, Malika came out with an attitude. "So you going to stay with your daughter tonight? I'm trying to hit the club," she said.

"Let her kick it with your folks tonight," Sin suggested.

"I'm not going over there," Simina said and poked out her lip.

"You gon' do whatever the fuck I tell you to do!" Malika said.

"Except go over there," Simina mumbled.

Malika's hand came up fast as she slapped Simina in the mouth. Simina looked at her shocked. "Your spoiled-ass grown now?" Malika asked.

Sin exploded inside. He wasn't going to have her doing his daughter like that. "All of you, go in the house," he said to the kids.

Simina cried as she was led into the house by Shamika.

"Don't you ever do her like that in front of other people. What if I slap the shit outta you and embarrass you in front of people?" he asked.

"Sin, first of all, you're not going to slap me. Second, you don't tell me how to chastise my daughter.

You ain't been around for birthdays, sick days, or no days."

Sin's temper started rising fast. He snatched Malika by her shirt.

"Nigga, you better let me the fuck go!" she commanded.

"Ask yourself why I missed them days. It was because your bitch-ass let me," he said as he pushed her against the car.

"I'll say it again. Sin, let me go," she said.

Sin slung her away from him.

"Nigga, you a punk! You always trying to bully somebody. Bully one of them niggas in the street!" she said.

Sin collared her again. "Bitch, who the fuck you talking to? The streets know how I move. Any nigga in the street that got nuts big enough to see me got action," he said as he pushed her away again.

Malika came walking back up on Sin. He knew she would try to put on a show for the people looking out of their windows by getting off on him.

"Sin, you bet' not hit that girl!" his mom said from the porch.

"If she hit me I'm knocking her ass out," he said.

"You know what, Sin? Fuck you! I hope something happens to you!" Malika said.

That cut Sin deep. With the life he led and what he'd just been through, you didn't say things like that. "You know what, smart ass? Meet me back in Dublin.

You can take your ass to your folk's house. I'm taking the spot unless you got 18-5 for me for what I spent on that muthafucka," he said.

He jumped in the car and went to 48th. He saw Davy posted. He hit the horn as he stopped. He rolled the window down. "Come on. I need you to go drive the SS to Dublin for me," he told him.

Davy went and stashed the dope he had and then came and jumped in the car. When they got to the house, they got all their stuff and put it in the cars then left.

They got to Dublin at 8 and saw Malika in the garage putting a few boxes in her Tahoe. Sin directed Davy to park in the garage. He got out of the Infinity and took his stuff upstairs to the master bedroom. Davy put his stuff in the downstairs bedroom. As Sin was making his way to the Infinity he saw Malika open her door and hit the SS.

"Malika, my paint cost five gees. Don't let your attitude get you fucked up!" he said. She looked as if she wanted to say something but didn't. She got in her Tahoe and left.

Sin went upstairs and called Maria.

"Hello?" she answered.

"Where you at?" he asked.

"I'm just coming over the Altamont," she said.

"Take the Broder exit when you get in Dublin," he told her, and gave her directions to Malika's house.

Sin jumped in the shower and washed up. When he got out he got dressed and then sprayed on some Issey Miyake.

A car pulled into the driveway and Sin looked out the window and saw Maria's Expedition. He went downstairs and saw her getting out of the truck looking extremely sexy in the tight low-rise blue jeans and a brown halter.

There was a Mexican dude with her. Sin looked at dude and remembered where he knew him from. He was the cat that was on the videotape eating Maria out. Her cousin's baby daddy.

Maria opened the lift gate. Sin grabbed the boxes and stacked them in the garage. As soon as he and Maria started in the house he pushed the button on the wall closing the garage door just to be funny.

Davy was coming out of his room and saw Maria and stopped in his tracks.

"Who's this?" Maria asked.

"My young folks," Sin said.

"Hey, young folks," Maria said as she rubbed his cheek as they made their way upstairs.

Davy's eyes were glued to Maria's butt. They went in the master bedroom and Maria closed the door. Sin went to the closet and grabbed a box containing his money. He took twenty $10,000.00 stacks out and put them into a backpack and handed it to Maria.

"What you doing tonight?" she asked.

"Going to the club," he said.

Maria unzipped his pants and stuck her hand in and grabbed his dick. "Let me pick out something for you to wear," she said as she went to the closet. She pulled out some loose fitting black leather pants and an all black fitted T-shirt. She looked down at the Kenneth Cole's and nodded. They went back to the bed and Maria saw something in the chair. "Who's house is this?" she asked.

"Mine," Sin replied as he took off his shirt.

"So I guess these are yours," she said as she picked up the pink panties that were in the chair.

"That shit belongs to the previous occupant," Sin said as he took his jeans off.

Maria sat at the foot of the bed and pulled him to her. She pulled his dick out the slit of the boxers and teased him with her tongue. "So when you going to spend some time with me?" she asked. She took all of him down her throat.

"Damn, baby you ain't right!" he sighed.

"When, honey?" she asked.

"As soon as I get back from Seattle," he said.

A few licks later and Maria stopped. "I have a doctor's appointment tomorrow morning. I want to see you tomorrow afternoon. Fuck when you get back!" she said.

Sin finished getting dressed. He walked Maria down the stairs and to her truck.

"Tomorrow, Sin," she said and hugged him. She got in and left.

Sin went in the garage and grabbed the boxes of dope and put them in the Infinity. He went back in and got his gun and went to the family room. "Come hang with me," he said to Davy.

They went and got in the car and he called Lisa and told her to meet him at Oakland airport.

●●●●●●

"Cuzzo, hit your boy, Sin. We need some more product," Marv said.

"Man, that nigga be straight having me on hold," Bo said as he picked up the phone and dialed Sin's cell number.

"What up?" Sin answered.

"Sin, this is Bo. What's up?" he asked.

"What's up, my nig'?" Sin asked.

"I need to get the whole thing done, plus I want it like last time," Bo said. "Aight, meet me at BP at the Mall." Sin said and hung up.

Bo thought about calling the police instead, but figured he may as well get all the money he can before it was too late. "Cuzzo, if that nigga wasn't around we would be getting better money," he said.

●●●●●●

Sin turned in the Infinity at the rental agency and rented a Suburban. When Lisa came, she brought him his money. He took two keys out and gave her the other forty-eight. He then left.

When they pulled up at the BP station, Sin saw a bad chick pumping gas into a red Mitsubishi Montero. She looked at Sin and waved. He rolled his window down. "What's up, boo?" he asked as he noticed all the activity going on in the gas station.

"What's up with you, daddy?" she asked.

"You know, doing me. What's your name, sexy?"

"Keena, what's yours?"

"Simian, but you can call me Sin."

"Hmmm, I bet!"

"So what you about to get into?"

"Me and my lil' sis going to Roscoe's then I'm going home. I have to work in the morning."

"So can I have breakfast with you in the morning?"

"Where?"

"In bed," he said.

"Whoa, baby boy. I don't get down like that," she said.

Keena had medium length braids, chinky eyes, full lips, and an over all cute face, and had a video girl's body. She had average titties, wide hips, a small waist, and a nice size ass. It wasn't the size of Malika's, but it was bigger than Shaunté's.

"Baby, I just want to see what it feels like to wake up next to an Angel. We ain't gotta do nothing," Sin said.

"Get out so I can see what the rest of you looks like," she told him.

Sin pushed his gun under the armrest and got out. He walked over to where Keena stood. A younger version of Keena stuck her head out the window.

"Who in the truck with you?" the girl asked.

"My little brother," Sin said.

"Tell him to get out so I can see him."

"Go over there and holla at him, Tiny," Keena said.

When the girl got out of the truck Sin was stuck. *Why in the fuck do they call this girl Tiny? It ain't nothing tiny about her but her feet,* he thought. "You got the wrong nickname," he said.

Tiny looked exactly like her sister, except she was shorter, and where Keena was a cinnamon color, Tiny was a shade or two lighter. Tiny's body was off the chain. Her titties were at least a 36DD and she had a bigger ass than her sister did.

"My real name is Tanya," she said as she walked towards the Suburban.

"BG! Nigga, you owe me big for this!" Sin called out.

Davy got out the truck and Tiny smiled. "I know you. You play basketball for Fremont, don't you?" she asked.

"Yeah, I remember you too. You cheer for Oakland High. How old are you?" he asked.

"Seventeen. I graduated last week. What about you?" she asked.

"Seventeen," he lied.

"Nigga, quit lying. You played for the freshman team last season," she said.

"What my age got to do with us?" he asked.

"Nothing. You lying for nothing," she said.

Sin and Keena stepped away.

"So what's really going on?" Sin asked as he took her hand.

"I'm down to come by your house, but I ain't fucking," she said.

"That's cool, baby," he said as he wrote his phone number down. "Call me when ya'll get done eating and I'll meet ya'll back here," he said as he noticed Bo and Marv pulling up in a blue '97 Honda Accord. "Baby, don't fake," he said.

She reached in her purse and got her Kaiser Hospital ID and gave it to him. "Does that reassure you?" she asked.

"Yeah, for sure," Sin said as he pocketed the I.D.

"Tiny, come on you'll see him later," she said to her sister. They got in their truck and left.

Sin walked over to the Suburban as Bo walked up. Bo handed him a bag containing $33,000. Sin handed him the two keys.

"Man, this shit will be gone by tomorrow. I'll call you as soon as I have your 16-5," Bo said.

"I might not be around. If I'm not, don't spend my money with nobody but Rod, Shaqui, or Hashi," Sin said. He got in the Suburban and left.

●●●●●●

Bo was steaming as he got back in the car. "I don't know who that bitch-ass nigga think he talking too. Cuzzo, I gotta put you up on something. The Task Force ran up in my house talking about Twit getting burned up and they found three keys of hard," he said to Marv.

Marv didn't like where this conversation was going. "Man, if they caught you with three keys of hard, then you got a Fed case, not to mention attempted murder for Twit," Marv said.

"I dropped a dime on Sin and his broad. You was there with me when she killed them niggas, Jeff and Alonzo," he said.

"Nigga, is you out your muthafuckin mind! Them Mad Circle niggas will kill our whole family behind this shit! We don't even know for sure if that was Shaunté that killed them niggas," Marv said.

"Nigga, quit acting like a bitch! We fixing to use this nigga, Sin to the fullest. I'm not going to turn him in until around Christmas. We gonna keep getting work from him and taking it down south where they paying 20 a key. We gon' get our weight up, and when I turn him in we'll be set to take over Oakland as well as everything else in the Bay. You with me or what?" Bo asked.

"Nigga, you my blood. I'm with you right or wrong. I just hope you know what you doing," Marv said. Marv knew in the back of his mind that shit was going to get real ugly. The Mad Circle was the deadliest crew in Northern Cali.

Sin, June, Tayshaun, Rod, Sha, Hasahn, Amir, Marco, and Scatter were the inner Circle. Scatter had caught a Fed case for tax evasion and a gun the year before. Marco had caught a murder in '86, when he was only 15. It was Scatter's vision that started the Circle, but it was all of their gangsta that made it.

Marv looked at Bo as he drove. *Stupid muthafucka! I'm going to stack my paper and get the fuck away before the shit falls apart,* he thought.

Bo knew he probably should not have told Marv about his ratting, but he needed to keep somebody he trusted behind him. If and when the shit fell apart, Bo knew without a doubt that Marv would bust his gun with him.

Chapter Eight

Turn It Up

Sin and Davy went to the hills and dropped the rest of Maria's money off then went to Manny's. There was really nobody there so they went to Café Echelon. When they pulled up it was packed. Sin saw Hashi arguing with his baby's mama, Angel. He parked and he and Davy got out. Hashi's little brother, EJ was parking lot pimpin'. Everything top notch that went by he was at. Sin spoke to them and kept it moving.

"Any of these broads ask you how old you are, tell them 19," Sin said to Davy.

Sin was greeted by many cats and a bunch of chicks. Every dude that wanted to get at him on business who wanted anything less than a key he shot them to Davy.

When they got to the door Mick the bouncer stopped them. "Sin, the young cat can't get in," he said.

Sin slid him a $100 bill and told him, "He ain't drinking," and they went past. They got to the dude with the hand-held metal detector, and the dude scanned Davy. When he attempted to scan Sin, he stopped at the look Sin gave him. The manager, Carmen saw what was going on and rushed over.

"Carm, when you gonna let me suck up on that thang, baby?" he asked.

Carmen was a big, plus size girl. She was pretty than a muthafucka, but she was *big*. Sin always flirted with her. "You know I'm married, Sin. Plus your girl ain't no joke, and I like breathing," she said as she nonchalantly grabbed his dick as she walked away.

Sin and Davy saw June, Simone, Hasahn, his girl Brianna, and Malika at the back tables. Some cute chick stopped Davy and asked if he wanted to dance. Sin went and sat down and a waitress came over.

"Bring me a bottle of Louis," he said and pulled his money out and gave her 1600.

Sin noticed Malika cut her eyes at him as he and Hasahn talked. He felt someone tap him on his shoulder, and turned and looked, and it was Anita.

"What happened to your finger?" she asked. Sin looked at his hand.

"Nothing," he said.

"Then why haven't you used it to call me? Let me talk to you for a minute. Excuse us," she said to the table. She and Sin walked to her table. "Why you playing with me?" she asked as she got in his face.

"How am I playing with you? You the one playing games," he said.

"How am I playing games? I haven't done nothing but jock you since the other night."

"Baby, if we were at my house and my ex came banging on the door while we were fucking you would have thrown a nutty."

"First of all, when we met and you asked, I told you I was kinda seeing someone. I told you it wasn't nothing serious. If it was, you never would have gotten in me. Then I told you not to leave. And who is that girl over there with the tight eyes that keeps looking at me like she wants to kill me?" she asked.

"That's my oldest daughter's mom," Sin said as he looked at Malika.

"Oh, my bad. I ain't trying to get you in trouble."

"I ain't up in here with her. I'm out. I'll talk to you Monday," he said as he attempted to walk away.

Anita stepped in front of him. "Look here, Sin. If you wanna keep playing games, just lose the number," she said and walked away mad.

As Sin was going back to his table he saw Terell and Lil' Walt grooving with some broads. As he approached the table a chill went up his spine. He turned and looked just as Max and some other nigga was coming toward them, reaching under their shirts.

Everything seemed to be going in slow motion as Sin dove over their table knocking Simone and Malika down just as the first shot rang out. Sin pulled his gun out and stood up, busting. He saw that there were about five cats shooting at him and the crew. He hit one of them and ducked back behind the table as bullets whizzed past his head.

Terell and Lil' Walt started getting at Max's boys from behind. Sin, Hasahn and June started getting off.

Max and the two cats left standing with him made a break for the door. There were too many people running around so Sin couldn't get a clear shot. Sin pulled a hysterical Malika up.

"Who the fuck was that?" Hasahn asked.

"Them 61st Street niggas," Sin said as he looked around for Davy. Once he spotted him he nodded for the door.

"Oh it's on. I'm killing all them niggas! What, that nigga JB ain't learn the first time, yo?" Hasahn asked sounding like he was from the East Coast.

"Let's lift. We'll handle this shit tomorrow," June said.

As they were leaving Sin pulled Carmen by the arm. "I got 5 gees for that security tape. Call me in the morning," he said and hurried out.

As they got outside they saw two bodies on the ground, and one of them was Max. Sin spat on him and ran to the Suburban. As he was getting in with Malika and Davy the police came speeding into the parking lot. Sin pulled out like everyone else.

As they were getting on the 880 Freeway Sin's phone rang. He looked at the caller ID and saw Shaqui's number. "What up, cuzzo?" Sin asked.

"Cuzzo, Shaunteezy (Shaunté) is a fool. Ol' dude and his boy came up outta there getting off. I started getting at them. Your girl and her potna pulled up in that Lex and dropped both them niggas. That was some straight gangsta shit!" Sha said.

"Blood, them marks was at ya cousin something cool. Get in touch with the fam and lets link up at the spot where we put the Circle together, in the morning," Sin said as his line beeped.

"Aight," Sha said and hung up.

Sin saw it was Shaunté. "You aight?" he asked.

"Yeah, I'm straight. I saw who that was running out after I heard the shooting, and knew you and Davy was up in there. I know his boy is all the way out the game (dead), but he may not be," she said.

"Good lookin' out, boo," he said.

"Don't trip. You my baby's daddy, I gotta lookout. Once you learn who gon' go to hell and back for you, maybe a bitch can get the props she deserves," she said.

"I'm going to call you tomorrow. Be careful."

"You too," she said and hung up.

Sin pulled up at Simone's house and walked Malika to the door. "You gon' be aight?" he asked.

"Sin, I just saw four dead bodies! No, I'm not going to be alright. Will you stay with me?" she asked.

Sin was tempted. Malika was looking extra good. "Nah, I'll see you tomorrow," he said and went and got back in the Suburban.

"Nah, we wasn't there. We went to Town and Country and shot some pool." Davy was on his cell phone, and he mouthed Keena's name to Sin to let him know who he was talking to. "Ay, we on our way to the gas station," he told her, and hung up. He then told Sin, "She say they heard about that shit when they were coming out of Roscoe's."

Sin fired up a blunt as he pulled off. He was way past mad. He wanted to go kill Max and JB's mama. That was a no-no though. There was an unwritten rule that you never, ever went after a dude's family. That was a death sentence if you were part of the Circle. Sin passed Davy the weed. *I'm killing that fool!* Sin thought.

When they pulled up at the gas station, Sin scanned his surroundings as he pulled up next to Keena's truck. He picked the gun up off the seat and put it in the console.

"BG, don't be riding crazy, that heater's in here," Sin said as he got out. Tiny got out of the Montero and got in the Suburban with Davy. Sin got in with Keena and reclined his seat back some.

"Baby, hit 580 going East and go to Dublin," he told her.

"So Sin, where do you work?" Keena asked, knowing perfectly well that he was a hustler. He had to be, as much bling as he was rocking.

"I manage my brother's detail shops right now. In a couple of months my business will be off the ground," he said.

"What kind of business?" she asked.

"I'm opening a club."

"I see you doing it big. Staying in Dublin and shit."

"Nah, baby, this house we going to ain't mine. I'm house sitting for my potna."

"You ain't no broke ass nigga. I'm not at you for no money, I got my own. I just like guys that are doing their thang, whether it's legal or illegal," she said.

"Well, I guess I'm ass out, because the jewels are fake, the Suburban is rented, and the only thing I'm having is nice clothes," he said.

"Are you serious?" she asked.

"As AIDS!" he said.

Damn, this nigga was almost perfect! she thought.

Sin gave Keena the directions to the house. When they got there she pulled in the driveway and Davy pulled in next to them. They went inside and Sin took his jacket off and hung it in the hall closet. He turned and looked at Keena and laughed.

"What's so funny?" she asked.

"I lied, Kee," he said.

"About?"

"Everything. The only part that was the truth was the truck being a rental, and this not being my house," he said. They went in the family room and he explained to her about Malika, past and present.

"Where's your bedroom?" she asked.

"Upstairs, double doors at the end of the hallway." Keena went to her car to get an overnight bag, and then went upstairs.

Sin went to the Suburban and got the money he got from Bo. He took it to Simina's room and hid it with his other money. As he was coming out he heard Davy and Tiny arguing about him going out to make a $300.00 sale.

Sin went in his room and scanned through the numbers in his phone until he found the one he was looking for. He called the number.

"Yeah?" the voice said.

"Carlos, this is Sin. I got 25 racks ($25,000.00) for you," he said.

"Who, where, and when?" Carlos asked.

"I'll up you on it tomorrow. Meet me at Choppy's at 9:30," Sin said and hung up.

Sin took off his jewelry, pants, and shirt. He put on a wife beater and some blue Fubu shorts, and laid on the bed and smoked a blunt of kush. *Damn, 1998 is almost over. If I can go on a good run all the way to New Years 2000, I'll have like three mill,* he said to himself.

Keena came out of the bathroom a half-hour later dressed in a long T-shirt. "Mmmm, that felt good!" she said as she straightened out her work uniform. She set the clock for 6:30 and laid across the foot of the bed facing Sin.

"So you ain't got no dude, do you? I wouldn't want a nigga to be sitting at home wondering where you at," he said.

"No, if I did I wouldn't be here."

"Is that right?"

"Fuh sho. When I have a man I'm overly faithful. It's only about him. What about you? Why a good looking, level-headed brother like you don't have a woman?" she asked.

"I don't trust ya'll," he said, and gave her a brief rundown of him, Yvette and Shaunté.

"Are you sure those are your kids?" Keena asked.

"I had the DNA test for Simara and she's damn near 100% me. When this new baby comes I'll do the same," he said.

"Damn, I thought I had been through some bullshit. I was hopelessly in love with a wannabe pimp who tried to get me to hoe up. Don't get it fucked up. I'll do what I have to and play my position so we can have thangs, but at the time we were doing cool. His potna is K-Red, and you know K is Pimp of all Pimps. This nigga was trying to be like K. Nigga, pimp all you want, but I'm wifey. If I want to hoe up, let me bring it up, not you," she said.

"I feel you. I take whatever money. I don't turn my nose up to hoe money or dope money, but I can't send my wife. I guess that's why I ain't no pimp. K go hard in the paint. He'll send whoever," Sin said.

Keena scooted closer to Sin, so close their noses almost touched. "So when you coming back from Arizona?" she asked.

"July 3rd," he said.

"You gon' call me?" she asked.

"Fuh sheezy, boo. I'm feeling your vibe," he said as he pulled her even closer.

Keena put her leg over Sin's hip, and he grabbed her butt and pulled her so close that for him to be any closer he'd have to be in her. That's how they slept.

Chapter Nine

Rocked to Sleep

When JB got to the hospital Max was in surgery. Kesha saw the look on JB's face as he approached. He spoke to his mom and dad and then pulled Kesha to the side.

"I'm killing your boy. That nigga about to feel the wrath!" JB threatened.

"My girl, Joesette was there. She said Max, Merl, Link, and Henry came into Echelon shooting. I know Sin. He ain't going to fire the first shot unless it's all out war," she said.

"You sound like you taking that nigga's side, bitch!" he said. Kesha got in JB's face.

"Nigga, you lucky I'm pregnant! Because you going through some shit, I'm going to pretend you didn't just say that. Now, if Sin wanted to kill Max, he could have killed him and the boys earlier. Then I found out some bitches in a Lexus in the parking lot shot Max and killed Link," she said.

"What color Lexus?" he asked."

"Black. JB, lets be realistic. Max set this shit off. He was the first to pull a gun. After I got this shit squashed, he rolled through Seminary. Then he let off the first shot at the club.

JB started thinking that maybe kicking the war off was a bad move. When he and June were at war a couple years before, he lost seven soldiers, and June only lost one. The Circle was deep, and they had somebody that was hooked up with them on almost every block. So far Sin hadn't lost anyone, and he and Max lost Link, Henry, and Newt.

JB hated what he was about to do, but he had no choice. "Kesh, do you think you can get this shit squashed?" he asked.

"I'll try, but you know Max and Henry were shooting at Hasahn too," she said.

"Awwww, fuck!" JB said. Kesha pulled her phone out, called Sin, and left a message on his voice mail.

● ● ● ● ● ●

The alarm went off waking Sin and Keena. She reached across him and turned it off. Keena got up and went to the bathroom and washed up. Sin saw his phone blinking. He unhooked the charger and looked at the one number that was on there four times. He didn't recognize the number so he didn't call back. He went to the dresser and took out some white silk boxers and went to the bathroom and stripped and turned the shower on. Keena slapped his ass as he was getting in.

"Okay now!" he said.

"I wish I had time to get in with you," she said.

"You ain't about to let me have it my way," he said as he showered.

Keena opened the shower door and saw Sin standing there naked and had a good mind to call in sick. "You are fine than a muthafucka. We might have to have some alone time," she said.

"Yeah, yeah," Sin said and took his shower.

Keena went back in the bedroom and he got out and dried off, and lotioned down then put his boxers on. He went in the bedroom and Keena was putting on her shirt. The room was clean and the bed was made.

"I'll make you some breakfast," she said as she finished buttoning her shirt.

"Don't worry about it, baby. I'm having breakfast with my homies," he said.

Sin put on some blue denim Sean John shorts, a white Jordan T-shirt, and his red and white Jordan shoes. He grabbed the white do-rag and put it on

By the time Sin and Keena got downstairs it was 7:30. Sin went and opened Davy's bedroom door to wake him up. Davy was up, and he was banging Tiny out. Sin pulled the door closed.

"BG, I'm gone!" he said.

"Aight," Davy said.

"Let me tell my sister something," Keena said just as Sin's phone rang. Keena opened the door and saw Davy hitting Tiny from the back and gasped. Tiny screamed and covered herself. Sin laughed as he answered his phone. "*Yo?*"

"Sin, why you ain't call me back?" Kesha asked.

"I just woke up, Kesh. What's up?" he asked.

"JB wants to talk to you," she said.

"Yeah, right. That nigga can talk to these hot ones (bullets)," Sin said.

"Sin, for real! This shit has to stop. It ain't good for no one if ya'll have a war. Shit, Max done got shot up, the paper says ya'll's boy, Fred got shot. JB will meet you wherever you choose," she said.

"Kesha, my kids will be there. If some shady shit jump, I'm killing you first. Jack-In-The-Box on 45th & Telegraph at 3:00," he said and hung up.

As Keena and Tiny were going word for word, Sin called Janine in Tucson.

"Hello?" a female answered.

"May I speak to Janine?" he asked.

"She's not here right now. May I take a message?" she asked.

"Will you tell her Simian called?"

"Sin?" the chick asked.

"Yeah, who dis?" he asked.

"This is Sonia. We didn't get to meet when you were out here for my grandmother's funeral. I was too messed up to attend. Auntie speaks highly of you," she said.

"Sonia, will you let her know that I'm leaving tonight, and I should be there by early morning. I'm bringing two little ones, more than likely three mid-teens, and my cousin," he said.

"Damn, all them your kids?" she asked.

"Just, three of them. Mine is a thirteen-year-old girl, a ten-year-old girl, and seven-year-old boy. My niece and little brother's coming. She's fourteen, and he's fifteen."

"I'll have something for them to do. Mario's daughter, Ebony is fourteen. She'll be here. My daughter Jessica is eleven. She'll be here. Mario's nephew, John Jr. is sixteen, and he'll be here also," she said.

"That's cool," he said as he became aware of Keena staring at him frowning.

"Bring some of that green stuff you gave auntie," Sonia told him.

"Oh yeah, baby that's mando (mandatory). I'll see you later on," he said and hung up.

Keena rolled her eyes at Sin and walked out through the garage.

"What's wrong, baby?" he asked.

"How you gonna be on the phone with a female while I'm right here?" she asked.

"Man, you tripping. We had a cool night, don't fuck it off behind some insecure shit," he said. He walked her out to her truck and tried to kiss her. She turned her head. Sin looked at her stupid and walked back in the garage and got in his SS and started it. The moment that Keena backed out and left he went back in the house. He snatched 10 gees and left.

When Sin pulled up at the apartments where Scatter's mom used to live he saw June's black S600, Rods beige CL600, Shaqui's gold drop 69 Camaro, Hasahn's blue Range Rover, Amir's blue drop SL500, and a couple of other cars of cats that weren't original members.

They discussed the demo that the 61st Street niggas put down. Sin let them know he was going to put a hit on JB as soon as they finished this meeting. After everything was agreed upon they all left.

Sin pulled up at Choppy's and called Yanna while he waited for Carlos.

"Hello?" she answered.

"Wash your pussy, I'll be there in an hour," he said.

"Nigga, my pussy stay washed. You coming over here to suck my clit?" she asked.

"For sure, you know my work. What you got on?" he asked.

"You know I sleep naked. For real though, baby I don't want you to give me any head. I want some of that big-ass dick you packing," she said.

"You gon' cook after we finish?" he asked.

"If you do your thing right I'm going to do whatever you say. Now hurry up," she said.

"Aight," he said and hung up.

When Sin looked to the passenger side somebody was standing there. He got spooked and was about to reach for his gun until he saw it was Carlos. He popped the lock and Carlos got in. "Man, you better quit sneaking up on niggas before somebody blast you," Sin said.

"You better quit slipping. You at war with them 61st Street niggas whose turf ain't but fifteen blocks up," he said.

"Yeah, you right," Sin said and dapped him.

"So who you want killed?" Carlos asked.

"That nigga, JB"

"I owe that sucka one anyway. He killed my sister's husband. When you want it done?"

Sin pulled his phone out and called Lisa.

"What's up?" she asked.

"Call that nigga, JB on the three-way and set up a date at that pool spot in Concord," he told her. Lisa did as told and clicked over. Sin heard the phone ring three times before it was answered.

"Hello?" JB said.

"JB, this is Linda. I met you at the rim shop yesterday," she said.

"Oh yeah, what's cracking, boo?"

"I was trying to see if you wanted to kick it tonight, on me."

Sin knew JB was feeling that. If a chick wanted to kick it and was talking about footing the bill, then she wasn't gold digging. Sin knew pussy was man's downfall. He vowed right then to stop fucking with so many bitches.

"Yeah, I'm with that. What you trying to do?" he asked.

"I was thinking of going to this little under pool hall in Concord, and maybe going to the mo-mo (motel) next-door. They got hot tubs," Lisa said.

"Yeah, like that?" he asked.

"Yeah, baby just like that," she purred.

"I'll be there by 9. I know where it's at" he said.

"Okay, I'll see you then," Lisa said and hung up. "You coming over, because we need to talk. Your girl called me, talking about she saw your car in my driveway last night night," she said to Sin.

"I'll be by there later," he said and hung up. Sin gave Carlos the 10 gees. "Dawg, don't let anything happen to my girl," he said.

"I got you, man. Say, why don't you keep half this loot and give me some cream (dope)?"

"Man, if you get off that shit I'll help you get some real money," Sin said.

"I am off of it. I been getting money in Berkeley on 8th Street. Ask Terell. I been spending with him," he said.

Sin picked his phone up and called Terell.

"What up?" he answered.

"Hit Carlos off with 16 zips (ounces). I got the money from him already."

"Tell him to meet me on 48th at 12. Bro, your girl on some scando shit. You know she up in here fucking with her cousin's baby's daddy," he told Sin.

"Fuck that bitch! Handle your wax. Meet me on 4-6 at 2:30," he said.

"Aight," Terell said and hung up.

"Sin, take me to the little hooptie spot on 45th and Market," Carlos said.

As Sin was pulling off, his young rapping homeboy, D9 pulled up. "Sin, come check this out," he said.

Sin got out of the SS and walked over to D9's Expedition and saw the TV's in the headrest and the one in the dash. "That shit *like that!* Where you get it done at?" he asked.

"That beat shop on Shattuck, around the corner from your mom's house."

"I'm shooting my Navigator up there," Sin said.

"Let me buy 5 zips," he said.

"Call T. I ain't selling nothing today," Sin said and got in the SS and pulled off, bumping Makeveli's "Hit em up".

They pulled up at the lot, and Sin saw a clean '79 Caprice Classic for Davy. He got out and found out they wanted two gees. He bought it and called Davy.

"Hello?" Davy said out of breath.

"Damn, nigga you still hitting that? Ay, I bought you a car. Come to my mom's house."

"Aight, I'll be there in a few minutes," Davy said and hung up. Carlos put 5 gees down on a 300ZX.

Sin drove to Yanna's house in the 2000 Lake Shore high-rises. He parked and called the dude, Mark at the paint shop and told him he wanted the truck done expediently. Mark told him that he put Bondo on the bullet holes, and resprayed the truck since he had saved some of Sin's original paint.

"Nigga, I don't be fucking with Bondo. Just get me a new lift gate and windows," Sin said as he got out of the car.

"You were still going to need some Bondo for the holes in the quarter panel. I got the back window, and the truck is under the lights now. Sin, I'm telling you, you can't even tell where the bullet holes were at," he said.

"So when am I going to be ready?" Sin asked.

"I been working on your shit all night. It'll be ready by five tonight."

"Damn, nigga you must be off that meth," Sin said.

"Nah, I'm off that 7 gees I'm fixing to charge you. Holla!" he said and hung up.

Sin went into the apartment building towards the elevator. As he was getting on the elevator he called Yanna.

"Hello?"

"I'm here, baby. I'm getting on the elevator now," he said.

"I'll meet you at the door," she said and hung up.

Sin went to the 19th floor and got off and made his way to the right. When he got to 2904, Yanna was standing in the door, butt naked. He walked in and closed the door.

Yanna stripped him at the door. She jumped up and wrapped her arms and legs around him. He gripped her ass-cheeks as she guided him into her wet pussy. He pressed Yanna against the door and served her for 15 minutes. Sin felt his nut coming and stopped. He reached for his pants and put a rubber on. He guided Yanna to her couch, bent her over, and hit it from the back. Yanna started moaning and bucking, which let Sin know she getting off. He wasn't too far behind her.

"That's what I'm talking about, baby!" she said and leaned back and kissed him. Sin noticed then that she had gotten her eyebrows and hair done. Yanna was actually a pretty girl. They went and got in the shower and washed up, and the sucking and eating started.

As they dressed, Sin's phone rang. "What's up?" he asked.

"Sin, I'm at your mama's house," Davy said.

"I'll be there in a minute," Sin said and hung up. He watched as Yanna put on a cream-colored Versace dress, with no panties, no bra.

"Sin, you ain't no joke with that tongue. You gon' make a bitch fall in love," she said.

"Your pussy just has a one of a kind flavor to it. Make sure you meet Lisa in an hour so you can get the stuff. Call the airport and make flight arrangements. Then call me and let me know what time you'll be ready," he instructed her. They finished dressing and left.

At 3:00 Sin was parked in the Jack-In-The-Box parking lot waiting for JB. Simina, Quesha, and

Shamika were inside eating. Sin's phone was on speaker. JB and Kesha pulled up in a black BMW 850. A black MPV pulled in behind them.

"We on them," Terell said over the phone.

JB pulled along side the Suburban. Sin held his MP5 tight.

"Tee, my kids inside. Make sure that if them niggas start busting, they all die," Sin said before he rolled his window down.

"Say, man what we gonna do? This shit ain't worth it," JB said.

"It ain't worth it for me either, playboy. Next time it can be me that gets killed," Sin said.

"Well it's squashed on my end," JB said.

"Where's my baby?" Kesha asked.

"She's inside with her sister," Sin said

"Sister?"

"I'll tell you about it some other time," he said as he tapped the horn. The girls came out and Kesha talked to Quesha. She kept looking at Simina and frowning at Sin.

"Tell Kesha bye," Sin said.

●●●●●●

At 6:30 Sin's Navigator was done. He picked it up and dropped it off at the beat shop. He then loaded the kids into the Suburban and hit the interstate with Jamila.

● ● ● ● ● ●

At 9:00 Carlos was sitting in a black Toyota Supra in the pool hall's parking lot when he saw Lisa pull up in her Acura. He was glad Sin insisted that they meet each other so there would be no mistakes.

Ten minutes later, JB pulled up in a Green Viper. Carlos slipped out his car and crept up on the unsuspecting JB, who was busy talking on his phone. Carlos walked right up to the window and let the silenced fully automatic MP5 spit. He dropped a whole clip into JB's body.

Carlos wanted so bad to keep the gun, but Sin gave him strict orders to leave it on the scene. He tossed the gun on JB's lifeless body and walked back to his car, cautiously looking around. He got up outta there without a problem. He pulled the phone out and called Sin to let him know the deed was done.

"Yeah?" Sin answered.

"It's a wrap," Carlos said.

"Aight, I'll have my girl get at you," Sin said and hung up.

Chapter Ten

The Get Back

Sin pulled into Janine's ranch at 4:30 a.m. Janine came to the door in her robe. He woke the kids up and took them to their rooms. Sin then went to Mario's guest cottage. He got undressed and got into the bed. Sin had no idea that in the next room laid a naked woman.

The next morning Sin woke up and felt that someone was in the room with him. He turned over and saw an Angel. *I must be dreaming,* he thought.

"Hey, sleepy-head" she greeted. She was the same color as Sin. She had high cheekbones, and black hair that was in six braids that came to the center of her back. She was a dime for real. Her ass looked like two halves of a basketball. If Sin had to pick a star she looked like, he would have to say the sexy R&B chick, Claudette Ortiz.

"You must be Sonia," he said as he got up. Sin's dick was making a tent in his boxers. He walked into the bathroom and closed the door.

It's on and poppin'! Auntie said he was cute, but this nigga is fine than a muthafucka! Sonia thought.

Sin jumped in the shower. When he came back in the room wrapped in a towel, Sonia was still sitting there. "I hope you don't mind," she said and pointed to the bed which was made and had an Ecko shorts set sitting on it, along with a pair of boxers.

Sin picked up his shaving kit and boxers and went back to the bathroom. When he came out he was shining and smelling extra good. As he got dressed he and Sonia talked.

"Did you bring some of that weed?" she asked.

"Yeah, let me go and get it," he said. Sin walked out and went down the path until he got to the guesthouse. He knocked and Jamila came to the door in a white and red stripped bikini top and shorts that were unbuttoned.

"God damn!" Sin said. Jamila's body was like that. He grabbed the weed. "I may have to make a housecall!" he said.

"I ain't fucking with you. You fixing to go get high?" she asked.

"Yeah," he said as he kept looking at Jamila's titties.

"I see I gotta put these thangs up," she said as she pulled on a red Polo shirt. She sat down and put on red and white Nike slides, and they both went to where Sonia was and got high.

Sin pulled his phone out and called white boy Tommy.

"Yo?" he answered.

"Tommy, this is your boy, Sin. I'm out here and I got some of that sticky," he said.

"I'm trying to get on line with that," Tommy said.

"You got a scale?" Sin asked.

"Yeah, I got one at Gina and Sandra's spot. Meet me there in a couple of hours," Tommy said and gave Sin the directions.

Sin and the girls left out. The whole time they were getting high, Jamila was giving him fucked-up looks.

"Sonia, go on ahead. I need to holla at 'Mila," Sin said as they stopped by the Suburban. Sonia went in the main house and Sin looked at Jamila. "What's your problem?" he asked.

Jamila put her hands on her hips and rolled her eyes. "The way you and that bitch was staring at each other!" she said angrily.

Sin looked at her and frowned. "Pump your brakes, blood. I ain't got no woman. I can look at who the fuck I want to, anyway I want to. I told you from jump that I wasn't fucking with you like that, and this is one of the reasons why," he said.

"Yeah, nigga? We'll see about that!" she said and went in the house.

When they got inside the house, Jamila was blown away. Sin led her to the dining room and everyone was there.

"It's about time. We can't start without you all," Janine said.

Sin was introduced to the kids. He noticed that Davy was really feeling Mario's daughter, Ebony. This threw Sin. He thought that Davy and Shamika liked each other. He laughed because the kids were trying to throw him off.

"Daddy, sister's going to take us horseback riding," Quesha said.

"Bro, this place is tight as fuck!" Davy said,

"What you say, boy?" Janine asked.

"Excuse me, Miss Janine," he said.

They all had a buffet-style breakfast and talked.

Sin left the table with some sugar cubes and a couple of apples. He took Malik, and they went down to the stables. They fed Heart Breaker, and Malik wanted to ride her. Sin wasn't going for it. All he needed was for the temperamental horse to hurt Malik. Tracy would kill him.

At 11:30, Sin and Davy pulled up at Sandra's house. Sin got the weed, and they went to the door. He knocked, and Gina answered it. "What's up, Sin?" she asked.

"What's cracking, G? Where your girl at?" he asked.

"In her room. She's pissed off that you never called her. She said she didn't want to see you," Gina said as she gave him a digital scale. Sin gave Davy the scale.

"Make fifteen 28 gram ounces. Which room is hers?" he asked.

"The one upstairs on the left," Gina said.

When Sin opened the door to Sandra's room he found her lying across her bed watching TV. When she saw Sin her blue eyes blazed. "What, do you want?" she asked.

"Damn this!" Sin said and turned and walked out. He went back downstairs. "Gina, let me get sixteen sandwich bags," Sin requested.

"I told you she was mad," Gina said.

"Fuck her! She can stay mad," Sin said.

Just then they heard stomping coming down the stairs. Sandra came in the room wearing a long Phoenix Suns jersey. She walked right up in Sin's face and threw a nutty. "Who the fuck do you think you are to have me chasing behind you? I don't need this shit you pulling!" she yelled.

"Chasing? I didn't ask your ass to chase behind me. I had to do my thing. I don't do nothing halfway. Me and you hooking up while other shit was in the works would have been some halfway shit," he said.

"No, what it was, was you couldn't get from under your Mexican bitch's thumb for a minute," Sandra said.

"I don't fool with her no more. Plus, don't nare bitch dictate my program, and I don't know who the fuck you think you talking to. I ain't one of these poot-butt ass niggas you be fucking with. I'll slap the shit outta you!" he said. Sin knew you had to be aggressive with aggressive broads or they wouldn't respect you.

"Fuck you!" she said and stomped off.

"Finish that shit," Sin said to Davy and followed Sandra. They both entered her room pissed. "I ain't feeling that fucking screaming you doing!" he yelled.

"Oh muthafuckin' well!" she yelled.

Sin pushed her and she pushed him back. He was about to hit her, but instead he pulled her to him and kissed her.

Sandra responded just as rough. She pulled his T-shirt over his head and unbuttoned his pants. Sin pulled her jersey off and then her panties. Sandra kissed on Sin's chest as she dropped his pants and boxers around his ankles. She pushed him back and straddled him. Sin's dick-head had just passed the entrance to Sandra's pussy when he thought about a rubber.

"You know what, you motherfucker?" she asked as she bit his shoulder.

"What?" he asked as he flipped her over on her back and put her knees to her shoulders.

"You gonna lick me first next time," she commanded.

"You ain't said nothing," he said as he worked her pussy.

"God damn, your cock is good!" she moaned.

Sin knew he had to serve the pussy if he hoped to get it again. After thirty minutes he pulled out and busted on her stomach. Sandra had some good pussy, and Sin couldn't wait to hit it again, but unfortunately he had things to do.

Sandra went into the bathroom and got a soapy rag and cleaned Sin up then went and got in the shower.

Sin pulled his clothes on then went back downstairs. As soon as he got to the room Tommy, Gina, Davy and some Asian chick were laughing.

"Man, you was up in there tapping that ass for real!" Tommy said.

"I'm jealous," the Asian chick said. Sin looked at her and saw that she was a dime.

"This is Sandra and Gina's girl, Jae," Tommy introduced.

"You got a brother or cousin or something?" she asked.

"Yeah, my brother is right there," Sin said, nodding towards Davy.

"I'm tempted, but he'll have me in jail. He's too young," Jae said.

"Baby, age is a state of mind. My money's grown though," Davy said.

Sin sat down and helped Davy bag the rest of the weed up.

"Let me get four of them," Tommy said.

"Give me 2500," Sin said. Tommy and Gina went to her bedroom.

"Sin, let me get one," Jae asked.

"Give me 450, but don't tell Tommy," he said. She hurried and gave him the money.

Sandra came down wearing shorts and a wife beater.

Sin and Tommy concluded their business and they all smoked.

"I went by Pedro's today. We looking right, homie. I ain't waiting until the 4th. I'm picking my shit up today," Tommy said.

"Me too," Sin said as his phone rang. He looked at the caller ID and saw a number he didn't recognized. "Hello?" he answered.

"Sin, the fucking DEA ran up in Rods' house and got two-million-dollars! Then they ran in Auntie's house and got another five-million. Three of that was mine," June said.

"You ain't got nothing at your house or mama's do you?" Sin asked.

"Nah. Where you at?" June asked.

"I'm in..."

"Don't say it over the phone! Them muthafuckas may be listening," June said.

"I'm in Arizona. You already know where."

"I'm on the next thing smoking. Scoop me up from the airport?" June asked.

"Aight," Sin said and hung up. *Somebody's talking,* he said to himself.

Sin called Hasahn and wasn't able to find out anything.

He then called Tariq and found out that there was indeed someone talking. The police had run up in his brother, Eddie's house.

Sin called Lisa and told her that somebody was running their mouth, and not to do anything until he got back.

When they got to the paint shop they went in and found Pedro, and were led to the back storage room where the completed jobs were waiting to be paid for.

Pedro had car covers over two cars. He took the cover off of Tommy's SS first. The car was candy wine burgundy with a black base. The car could look black, brown, or reddish depending on the lighting and what angle you looked at it. He had a black top and burgundy cloth interior. Tommy went all out for his car, spending over 10,000 just on paint and interior. The new 454 engine that had the racing cam, pop up pistons, and the transmission with the shift kit, and the Flow Master dual exhaust came to another 10. The gold Daytona rims came up to another 3500.

Pedro lifted the cover off of Sin's SS Chevelle and Sin fell in love. The car was white with a powder blue pearl, powder blue Rally stripes on the hood and trunk, powder blue top, and the same color leather interior. The car was immaculate.

"Damn, Sin, that shit is tight!" Davy said.

Sin pulled his money out and gave Pedro another 500.

"I didn't do your car. My cousin Louie did it. I'll give this to him," Pedro said.

"I want to meet him," Sin said.

Pedro handed him his keys. Sin got in and started the SS and the Flows had it growling. He let the top down and pulled out.

"Louie, come here," Pedro said in Spanish. A short stocky Mexican guy came over.

"Homie, you did a good job on my car. I may need you again," Sin said. They exchanged numbers, and Sin pulled out. He gave Davy the Suburban keys and left.

At 2:00 Sin was outside the South West terminal waiting for his brother. June came out looking agitated. Sin tooted the horn. June came and got in the Suburban and they pulled off.

"Man, them muthafuckas ran up in my house looking for dope. Toya called me before I got on the plane," June said.

"Shit, they ran up in Eddie's house too. I talked to Tariq earlier," Sin said as his two-way chirped. Sin got scared. The only people that had his two-way number were his mom, Shaunté, Tracy, Malika and Yvette. They all knew to only call if there was an emergency. Sin opened it and saw the message was from his mom. It read:

> *"The Feds just came in my house looking for drugs, money, and guns. They also told me that they were looking for your brother for questioning. Something about the death of a Federal informant. They didn't mention your name, but you know that don't mean nothing. Be careful. I'll talk to you when you get back.*
>
> *The Queen.*

Sin handed the two-way to June Bug to read. He pulled off and went to the ranch.

"What the fuck are they talking about? I ain't killed nobody!" June said.

"You better get a lawyer," Sin said. They pulled up to the gates and Sin pushed the remote.

"This is cool. How did you come up on it?" June asked.

"This lil' broad that I used to holla at, her mama lives here," Sin said. He didn't want to let June know that Maria was his connect just in case he went bad.

When they got to the front of the house June was blown away. "This is what I need. This is a mansion! How many bedrooms?" he asked.

"Nine bedrooms, and four guest cottages," Sin said. He parked in front of the garages and they got out. As Sin was going into the main house his phone rang. The caller ID showed Kesha's number.

"What's up, Kesh?" he asked.

"Sin, you wrong!" she yelled.

"What now, man?" he asked.

"Why did you do that? I thought you guys agreed to let the shit go. You didn't have to kill him!" she cried.

"Whoa, hold up! First of all, you outta pocket for talking like that on this phone. Second, who got killed?" he asked. Sin wanted to laugh badly.

"Don't play stupid with me, Sin! I'm talking about JB," she said.

"Girl, I'm in muthafuckin' Arizona. I left about an hour after I saw you," he said.

"Yeah, right! If your ass in Arizona, you flew there after the shit happened. I don't even think you there. JB got killed around 9:00," she said.

"Muthafucka, I'll prove where I'm at. Your phone got caller ID?" he asked.

"Yes," she said.

Sin hung up. He walked into the family room where Quesha and Jessica were watching TV. He picked up the house phone and called Kesha.

"Hello?" she answered.

"Hold on," he said and passed Quesha the phone. "Hello?" she asked.

"Hi, honey!" Kesha said excitedly.

"Hi, Mom!"

"Where you at?" Kesha asked.

"In Tucson. Mom, they got horses, and my big sister took me riding. My daddy got a horse named Heart Breaker," Quesha said excitedly.

"When did you go there?" Kesha asked.

"After I saw you yesterday. It took a long time to get here. We passed through that place that had all the lights where grown people lose their money," Quesha said.

"That's Las Vegas, baby. I love you, honey. Let me speak back to your daddy," she said.

"Okay, I love you too," she said and gave Sin the phone back.

"Look, I just proved that I didn't have nothing to with that hoe-ass nigga getting served. They try to ride on me or any of my people, I'm killing every last one of them!" Sin said and hung up.

Sin took June outside to the pool area, and that's where the teenagers and adults were.

Sonia was in the pool. She swam to the side where Sin was. "Come in, the water's fine," she said.

Sin was loving the way the yellow swimsuit was fitting her curvaceous body. "*Talvez alrato. Tengo que llevar a mi hermano por ropa.* (Maybe later. I need to take my brother to get some clothes)," he said in Spanish.

"You speak Spanish. So what's on your agenda for later?" she asked.

"Nothing really. What you want to get into?" he asked.

"Let's go out to eat. Then we can go to this new club that opened downtown."

"That's cool," he said. Sin looked across the way and saw that June was talking to Janine. He got his attention and they left. As they were pulling out the gate Sin's phone rang.

"Yeah?" he answered.

"Hey, what's up? Where are you?" Maria asked.

"In Arizona. I came out here to pick up my car."

"I'm flying out Saturday."

"I'm driving back Friday"

"I wanted to tell you this in person. I'm late on my period."

"How late?" he asked.

"About a week."

"Don't go jumping to conclusions," he said as he fired up a blunt.

"Sin, what if I am pregnant?"

"First thing you want to do is figure out who's it is."

"You said that like I'm fucking a lot of other people."

"Baby, I don't know *what* you doing. I *do* know you fucking your cousin's baby's father," he said.

"Who told you that, Sonia?" she asked.

"It don't matter who told me."

"I was drunk, Sin. It only happened once."

"Muthafucka, you was with that sucka the other night when you came by my house!" Sin yelled.

"So fuckin' what! You think I have to put a baby on you? I ain't never fucked him without a rubber. If I'm pregnant it's yours!" she yelled and hung up.

Chapter Eleven

Cousin Got Some Freak In Her

Sin and June went and shopped then came back to the ranch. Sin was bone tired. He went to the guesthouse and went to sleep. He slept until Sonia woke him up at 8:30. He went and got in the shower and let the cold water wake him completely up. He got out and rubbed lotion on his body then put on a pair of tan silk boxers.

He saw that the housekeeper had pressed his clothes to perfection. He put on the dark blue Pelle Pelle jeans and the black Kenneth Cole shoes with the buckle. He then went in the bathroom and shaved his head. When that was done he put cocoa butter on it and rubbed it in until his head was shining. He went back in the bedroom and slipped on his black long sleeved Marc Buchanan shirt leaving it open. He put on his ice and was good.

As Sin was sitting in the living room rolling a few blunts and waiting for Sonia to get ready, June came in. "What time you sliding?" he asked.

"I'm going to dinner then I guess we'll be up there around 11:00 if this woman hurries up!" he said loud enough so that Sonia would hear him.

"If I take your rental, what you gon' drive? June asked.

"Come on, I'll show you," Sin said. They went outside and Sin went to the garage door that Janine's red 97 convertible Corvette was parked in front of, and opened the door.

June saw Sin's SS Chevelle and grinned. "Your shit's like that. Wait until you see what I bought for the 4th. I'll be the first nigga in the town with one," June said.

What you get?" Sin asked.

"I flipped a cinnamon brown Azure," he said.

"A Bentley?" Sin asked.

"I figured it was time to let niggas know that I was still on top. Now I wish I didn't buy that muthafucka. I damn sure can't afford it," he said.

Sin looked at his brother and thought about how he carried him when he was locked down, but he also thought about all the shit June Bug did for him. June put Sin in the game back in the day. He taught Sin most of the game, and he basically was Sin's male influence. That made Sin decide what he was going to do.

"When we get home I'm going to loan you 100 gees, and front you 10 birds. When you get right, just give it back. I can't see you liquidating your stuff," Sin said.

"Damn, you got it like that?" June asked.

"I got like 800,000. I get off like 80 keys a week being the middleman for my hook-up. They give me a free key off every 15 I get off. They don't have to do nothing, and they don't have to meet nobody. I'm taking all the risk," Sin said.

"Damn, your folks got it good!" June said.

"One day I'll up you on it," Sin said.

Jamila came out in a white slip dress. The dress was short and showed thigh, and dipped at the neckline. It was also tight on her hips and molded to her ass.

"God damn!" Sin and June both said in unison. They were both having the same thoughts of going up in Jamila.

"You ain't going out in that dress," Sin said seriously.

Jamila looked at him like he was crazy. Inside she was smiling because the dress had the desired effect. "Fool, I'm 28 years-old. A grown woman. I'll wear whatever I want to," she said.

"Fuck it! If you want a cat to be looking at your panties every time you sit down, then that's on you," he said.

"Sin, ain't nobody going to be looking at my panties."

"How you know?" he asked.

"Two reasons: One I don't carry myself like that, and two, I don't wear them," she said as she went and got in the Suburban.

"You hitting them or something?" June asked.

"Not yet, but I will be," Sin said.

Sin went back in the house and Sonia was ready. His mouth dropped. He could not believe his eyes. Sonia was wearing a short green dress that had a patch of the silk material cut out exposing her right hip, navel and sexy abs, and matching open-toe four-inch heels. Her hair was up in curls and she was looking good. Sin was glad his pants were loose fitting because he was super hard.

"Put this necklace on me," she said. She handed him the thin platinum chain with the two-carat diamond pendant. She turned her back and backed up.

Sonia opened her eyes wide when she felt Sin's erection poking her. *Damn!* she thought. He fastened it on her and she picked up her clutch and was ready.

Sin went into Mario's closet and got two Glock 40's. They left the house and he gave June a gun. He put the other in the small of his back and covered it with his shirt.

Sonia and Sin went in and got the keys to Janine's black S500.

"Daddy, can we go to the skating rink?" Simina asked.

"What Janine say?" he asked.

"She says she don't care, but she ain't taking us and picking us up," Shamika said.

Sin went and found Janine, Quesha, Jessica, and Busy all watching a cartoon. "Janine, will you let my brother and Jamila use a car? I'm going to let the kids use my Suburban to go to the roller rink," he said.

"I need to talk to you. Come upstairs for a minute," she said and led the way. Sin's eyes were on the tight jeans.

When they got to her room Janine closed the door. *If she tries to holla again, I'm going to give her some dick,* he thought.

"So how do you like Sonia?" she asked.

"I think she's only trying to holla at me to get back at Maria," he said.

"Give her a chance. I think she likes you," Janine said.

"You and me got issues to resolve," he said.

Janine kissed him lightly on the lips, and said, "We don't have any issues. I was wrong to put you in that position."

"Nah, I was wrong. I should have put you in a position while I had a chance."

Janine laughed and hugged him. "I would have turned your young ass out," she said.

"You seen how I get down," Sin said as he popped her on the butt.

"Yes, I have," she sighed. They both laughed and went back downstairs.

Sin grabbed the keys to Janine's Lexus truck. "Princess you be good, and don't give Auntie Janine any trouble," he said.

"Yes, Daddy," Quesha said and kissed his cheek.

Sin, Sonia, and the teenagers all went outside. He tossed June the Lexus keys.

"Look here, it's 10:15. When I call this muthafucka at midnight, ya'll better be here. No drinking, no smoking, and no stupid shit," he said to Davy and John, Jr. Since John, Jr. (or JJ as they called him) was the oldest, he gave him the keys. He gave Ebony, Simina, and Shamika $50.00 apiece.

"Shamika, no fighting," June Bug said and kissed his daughter. Everyone got into their vehicles and left.

After Sin led the kids to Skating World, he took Sonia to the restaurant. They missed their reservation. "We can go somewhere else," he said.

"Baby, noooo! I want to eat here," Sonia whined.

Sin slid the Hostess a $50.00 bill and they were seated. Sonia leaned over and gave him a big kiss on the mouth. "Thank you," she said.

"I meant to tell you that you look pretty sexy tonight," he told her.

"Thank you. You looking pretty good too. I almost said to hell with going out," she flirted.

They had pretty good conversation going on throughout dinner, and no matter how much Sin tried to resist Sonia, he couldn't.

At 11:15 they pulled up at the Oasis and it was packed. They blew a blunt then got out of the car.

Sin wasn't into standing in lines so he took Sonia's hand and led her to the front. When they got to the door they saw two big bouncers. Sin stepped close to one and whispered in his ear. They looked over the clipboard, and Sin dropped a 100 on it.

"Enjoy your evening," the bouncer said as he handed Sonia and Sin two VIP passes.

They slid in and saw that there was another dude scanning guys for any metal they had on them, but not girls. Sonia put her arm around Sin and discreetly took the Glock 40 out of his back and put it in her bag. Sin was scanned and they were let in.

When they walked past the velvet ropes to the VIP, Sin saw Sandra giving her number to a short dark-skinned dude that was wearing a lot of jewelry.

Tommy saw Sin with Sonia and nodded his approval. They saw June at the back talking to a pretty, petite white girl. They sat down and June popped a bottle Möet.

"Let's dance," Sonia said.

As they were making their way out to dance, Sin and Sandra made eye contact. He and Sonia went to the dance floor just as LSG's cut, *My Body* came on. Sin and Sonia held each other tight.

"So what we gon' do when we get home?" he asked.

"Count how many positions you can get me in," Sonia said and kissed his neck.

"You using me to get back at Maria, huh?" he asked.

"At first that was my plan, but after hanging out with you, I guess I'm digging you," she said.

"Girl, your ass high," he said.

"As a muthafuckin' kite, and horny! I never fuck on the first night, but that weed, the ack, and your fine ass got me wet," she said.

Just then Sonia frowned, and Sin felt the tap on his shoulder. He looked and there stood Sandra, looking right at him.

"May I?" she asked Sonia.

"Hell nah! Get somewhere!" Sonia said, and pulled Sin closer.

"Sin, I'll be ready in a little while," Sandra said and walked away shaking her ass. Sandra was wearing a red waist-length leather coat zipped down far enough to expose her cleavage, a short red micro mini that would show everything if she moved wrong, and thigh-high red leather spike heeled boots.

Sonia pushed Sin away and made a sour face. "Ewww! You sticking your dick in that hoe?" she asked loudly.

"Sonia, stop being loud," he said.

"What? Sin, I hope you used a rubber on that..."

Sonia never finished her sentence, because Sin walked away. He went up to the VIP. "Ay, I'm gone. Ol' girl acting stupid," he said to June.

"Sin, who's your friend?" Jae asked as she came over in a sexy black dress.

Sin wondered for a minute if he could fuck her and Sandra.

●●●●●●

Maria was sitting in her family room, fuming. Across from her were Terell and Cynthia acting all lovey-dovey. Maria knew that Terell was in love with Cynt, and it wasn't just a fuck thing with him, so she started letting him stay over.

She picked up the phone and called Sonia's house for the umpteenth time, and still got no answer. She called her mom, Janine.

"Hello?" Janine answered.

"Mama, I can't get in touch with Sonia. You talked to her lately?" she asked.

"Yes, baby. She's out here. Her and Simian took his brother, Erick and cousin Jamila to that new club Downtown," Janine said.

"Oh yeah?" Maria asked.

"Baby what's wrong, you sound sad?" Janine asked.

"I'm pregnant."

"Please don't say it's Mark's."

"It's Sin's."

"Maria, I'm not going to have you bringing shame to this family!"

"God damn, Mama! What part of what I said did you not understand? I said it's Sin's!" she yelled.

Janine took the receiver away from her ear and looked at it. "Girl, I will beat your ever lovin' ass if you *ever* talk to me like that again!"

Maria hung the phone up and called Southwest Airlines and found the last flight to Tucson was leaving in the next 45 minutes. She gave them her credit card number then ran upstairs and got her purse and keys. *This bitch is trying to take my man!* she thought.

"Cynthia, I'm going to mama's. If Mark comes, *don't* let him in," she said. When she got outside the only cars there were the Expedition and the 'Vette. Since Cynthia wasn't allowed to take the 'Vette Maria took it.

When Maria got to the long-term parking lot she left the 'Vette. She just barely made her flight and sighed a breath of relief.

Chapter Twelve

She Got What She Wanted

Sin and Sonia left the club at 12:00. When they got back to the house Sonia went to her room. Sin slipped back out, and as he was leaving out the gates his phone rang. Davy's number showed on the caller ID. "What's up?" he answered.

"Sin, I'm about to have some drama with these niggas up here," Davy said.

"I'm on my way," Sin said. *I knew I shouldn't have let them bad muthafuckas go. I bet you Shamika's crazy ass started all this shit*, he thought as he hung up.

Sin pulled up at the skating rink and saw a crowd. He got out of the car, and when he pushed his way into the crowd he got pissed off. The people that were surrounding the kids were either 18 or older.

"Bitch, you was talking all that big shit, why you need your home girls?" Shamika asked. The kids hadn't seen Sin yet. He wanted to see how they handled themselves.

"It don't matter anyway. Muthafuckas jump her I'm stomping them out!" Davy said.

"Who the fuck you and these stuck up bitches suppose to be? Nigga, it's Jordan Park over here!" an older dude said.

"Who the fuck you calling *bitches?* If my daddy was here he'd kill your punk-ass," Ebony said.

Sin saw that the kids held their own, but he was going to make an example out of somebody. He stepped forward and the kids saw him. "What's up with this shit?" he asked the girl that Shamika was into it with.

"That little bitch was trying to talk to my man," she said, pointing to 'Mina.

"Bitch, please! Your ugly-ass dude was trying to talk to *me*. When I told him I was only 13 he said he didn't care. When my cousin called him a molester he came and got you," Simina said.

"How old are you?" Sin asked the girl.

"Nineteen."

"What about you?" he asked the dude that was talking shit to Davy.

"Twenty-one."

"So basically ya'll are all adults, right?" Sin asked.

"Yes, and your point is?" the chick responded smartly.

"These are my kids. They range from 13 to 17," Sin said.

"And?" the girl repeated. Simina hit her right in the mouth and started kicking her ass. Shamika hit the other girl in the face. Davy and JJ both jumped the 21 year-old dude.

"Bitch don't you ever talk to my daddy like that!" Simina screamed as Sin pulled her off the girl. Other people in the crowd acted like they were going to get in it.

"Anybody get in this gotta see me!" Sin said.

"Nigga, what you saying?" another dude asked as he pulled a chrome .25 automatic out of his jacket.

Sin lifted his shirt and pulled out the Glock. "Nigga, what! My shit already got one in the hole. What you trying to do?" he asked. Everybody went silent.

Simina and Shamika beat the shit out of the two older girls. Sin stopped them. "Y'all get up out," he told them.

"Nah, these niggas gotta see me and Davy," JJ said.

"Man, later for this. I ain't trying to go to jail. Catch these marks another time," Sin said.

JJ, Shamika, Simina, Ebony, and Davy walked over to the car.

Sin pointed his gun at the dude with the .25, and the dude almost pissed on himself. "Let me get that up off you, *playa*!" he said.

The dude handed Sin the gun and backed up. With no warning Sin turned and hit the dude that was the cause of the drama. Ol' boy's jaw shattered, and he hit the ground like a dead weight.

"If any of you niggas *or* bitches ever disrespect one of my kids again, I'm killing you," Sin said as he pulled the clip out homeboy's gun and threw it over the roof.

"And don't you be pulling no guns on muthafuckas if you ain't going to shoot them," he said as he gave dude the gun back and walked off.

"It's 12:20. Ain't ya'll suppose to be somewhere?" he asked the kids. They got in the Suburban and pulled out. Sin got in the S500 and pulled off.

When Sin pulled up at the club he saw his brother, Jamila, and Jae. He parked and got out. While walking he saw Sandra talking to some dude. He kept it moving. He saw cats trying to get at Jamila and she was shooting them down.

"You ain't trying to get your freak on?" Sin asked.

"These ancient-ass niggas ain't on my level. The white boy's flyer than these suckas!" she said.

"Bro, why don't you drop Jamila off. I'm going to be putting some work in," June said and looked at Jae.

"Let's go," he said. They went to the S500 and got in.

Sin rolled up on Sandra and rolled the passenger side window down. "What's up, you with me?" he asked.

"Give me a minute," she said and resumed talking to ol' boy.

Sin and Jamila looked at each other then Sin hit the gas. "That bitch got me fucked up. *Give me a minute? Who she think I am, Lonnie Lunch Meat or some shit?"* Sin asked.

Jamila was cracking up. "You wrong for that. That's what your ass get for fucking with that white bitch," she said.

"Yeah, whatever," he said.

Sin and Jamila got high all the way to the ranch. As they were getting out the car, Jamila's dress rode up on her hips. "You sure is making it hard on a nigga," he said as he followed her up the walkway, staring at her ass.

Jamila flashed her ass and hurried into her cottage. Sin was going to follow. The only thing that stopped him was Sonia opening the door to their cottage. She was wearing a sheer pale blue baby-doll, and nothing else. Sin detoured and went in.

"I thought you went to rendezvous with that bitch," Sonia said as she closed the door.

"What's really going on, baby? You trying to use me for get back, because your cousin's fucking your dude?" he asked.

"I told you at first I was on that type of time. Then after we kicked it today, I started feeling you. You on the same level I'm on. We just trying to get with that one, and be on top of the world. I'm not trying to use you. Sin, I've been with five guys in my 28 years of life. I have never been a loose bitch, like Maria. I like you and I want to pursue something with you," she said as she walked into his comfort zone and kissed him.

Sin went to his room and stripped to his boxers. He then went to the living room and scooped Sonia up in his arms and carried her to her room. He laid her on the bed and kissed every one of her toes, her heel, and her ankles. He lifted her legs and licked behind her knees while looking at her pussy. He let her legs go and licked between her thighs. When Sin got to her pussy it was on. Sin sucked Sonia's clit and she grabbed his head.

"Oh shit, Sin! Yeah, baby! Get it like that" she moaned. When he was done, he put her legs over his shoulders and slid up in her.

"Sin, don't come in me. I'm not trying to get pregnant right now," she said.

Sin worked that pussy until he was about to bust. He stopped and pulled out for a couple of seconds. "Turn over," he said. Sonia got on her hands and knees with her ass facing him. He slid back in and he fucked her hard. Sonia didn't throw the pussy like Maria did, but it was still good. He felt that powerful nut coming and busted off on her ass-cheeks and back.

"You wanna take a shower with me?" she asked once they caught their breath.

"Yeah, go run the water."

When Sonia got up Sin admired her body. He followed her in and they showered.

"So where do we go from here?" she asked.

"I'll come out to visit you when time permits," he said.

"My dad lives in Modesto. I was thinking of moving out that way," she said.

"You sounding like you want to kick this thing up a notch."

"You have that effect on me. I feel good about you," Sonia said.

"Nah, you feel good about how I freaked you," he said. Sonia playfully pushed him. "For real though, I do big biz with Maria, and if I started seeing you it would surely mess that up," Sin said.

"You have business with Mario, not Maria. All she's doing is overseeing the business. Mario's connect is our fathers. If you making them money, they ain't about to cut you short because of her," Sonia said.

When Sonia and Sin got out of the shower they lotioned down. Sin put on his boxers and shorts and went to check on the kids.

He went into the main house and went upstairs to check on Quesha and Malik first. He then went to check on Simina and Shamika. Neither of them were in their room. He went downstairs to the family room. Sin saw the French patio doors open and heard Shamika's voice outside.

"I wore that bitch out!" she said.

"Nah, I wore that bitch *I* was fighting out. Man, I thought my daddy was going to kill them niggas!" Simina said.

Sin looked out the door and saw Simina, Shamika, Ebony, JJ, and Davy smoking weed.

"Sin is cool as fuck. He kicked it with me the whole day of my great grandma's funeral," JJ said.

"He thinks I like you," Shamika said to Davy.

"I would never mess with your crazy-ass. I'm sprung on Ebony," he said.

"Nigga, save the drama. You don't even know me," Ebony said.

"I don't have to. I knew I was sprung on sight," Davy said seriously.

"You gonna have to break her off some money," Shamika said and laughed.

"I don't need no nigga for his money. My daddy, grandfather, and my Auntie Maria got long money," Ebony said as she hit the weed.

"I ain't paying no way! Shit, Sin and June got top notches on the team, and they ain't paying," Davy said.

"Shit, my daddy just bought my brother's mama a brand new Range Rover, and Uncle Sin gave Auntie Tracy 13 gees for furniture for her new apartment," Shamika said.

"He gave my mama 9500 on our house too," Simina said.

"He kicked her out too. We live there," Davy said.

"She ain't tripping. She knows she'll get it back. Auntie Malika ain't tripping on no money. She stayed down for Uncle Sin when he didn't have shit," Shamika said as she hit the weed.

"Nah she don't want no money. She wants my daddy back," Simina said.

Sin took that opportunity to step out. "Baby girl, you out here getting loaded?" Sin asked. Simina, Shamika, and Ebony all got scared.

"Daddy, please don't tell my mama!" Simina begged.

Sin took the weed and hit it and gave it back to her. "Ya'll be up and ready to bone out at 11," he told them and went back to his and Sonia's cottage.

●●●●●●

When Maria's plane landed she went and rented a convertible Mustang. The whole time she was enroute to the ranch she was thinking of Sin fucking Sonia.

When she got to the gate she pushed her remote which she kept with her. She sped down the road and pulled up at the garage. She looked towards her cottage and saw all the lights off.

Maria got out of the car and went to her door and used her key. When she got inside, she went to her room and turned the light on. She saw that Sin wasn't there, but he had been by the clothes in the chair.

"Fuck it, if they fucked, they fucked! I ain't got time for this shit!" she said as she undressed and got in the bed. *I wonder where this muthafucka at*, Maria thought as she cut the lights off.

●●●●●●

Sin got up at 9:00. He washed up and put on his boxers and shorts.

Sonia woke up and smiled. "You something else," she said.

"What, you thought I was a rookie or something?" he asked as he walked out and went to Maria's.

When Sin walked in he didn't pay any attention to the women's leather coat on the sofa or the black Cavallo's sitting by the door. When he walked into the bedroom he saw Maria lying in the bed, uncovered.

Maria had on a cream colored bra and thong set. *Shit!* he thought as he quietly walked in the closet and got his blue Phat Farm shorts, the gold and blue Lakers jersey with Kobe's number 8 on it. He snatched up the white Air Force One's and went into the bedroom.

As he was getting his socks and drawers he felt Maria looking at him. "You going to say something or are you just going to stare?" he asked without turning around.

"Where you been?" she asked.

"Out," he said as he went to the bathroom and got dressed. He came out and sat on the edge of the bed and put his Nike socks and his shoes on.

"So you just saying fuck me, huh?" she asked.

"I'm not saying anything. You made a decision. I was outta pocket for mixing business with pleasure in the first place, but I couldn't resist you. I was also outta pocket for not using a rubber," he said.

"Sin, I don't want it to end like this. I love you," she said.

"Baby, it ended when you popped fly out the mouth. Then last night you lied to me about fucking Sonia's baby daddy. You lied about the fool, Donny too," Sin said as he looked at her angrily. He saw the sadness in Maria's eyes as he was leaving out. *Fuck her!* he thought as he walked back to his and Sonia's hideaway.

When Sin stepped into the room, Sonia was stepping into a pink sundress. "Maria's here," he said.

"Did you tell her?" Sonia asked, not caring one way or the other.

"No, she didn't ask," Sin said as he put his chain, watch and ring on.

"Sin, she's going to ask," she said as she put on her D&G sandals. Sin didn't reply. "We can just deny it. To throw her off, I'll act as if I don't like you," she said.

"Nah, just act normal. I ain't trippin'," Sin said as he left out to go to the main house.

As he was walking down the path Jamila was coming out her bungalow. She was wearing a light-blue bikini top and a matching sarong around her hips. "You can fly back today if you want to," Sin said as he openly admired her body.

"I'll leave with ya'll," she said.

They walked in the house and the girls were dressed and ready. Sin's phone rang. He looked at his caller ID and saw Tommy's number. "What up, Teezommy?" he asked.

"I need to get three more of them," he said.

"Aight, meet me at the mall," Sin said and hung up. He sat down and had breakfast with everyone. Sonia came in a few minutes later.

"Janine, I need you to cut the kids loose in a car," Sin said.

"Psss! No you don't!" she said.

"I'll let them take my truck. Bro, you can push the drop," Sin said to June. He gave JJ the Suburban keys, and June the keys to the Chevelle.

"Daddy, I want to go with ya'll," Quesha said.

"It's only the big girls today, mama," he said. Quesha put that sad look on her face that always got Sin.

"Don't worry about it, pretty. You can go shopping with me and Jes. Then we're going to the movies," Sonia said.

"Guess who Busy's going with?" Sin said as he looked at Davy and JJ.

"Aww, bro come on!" Davy begged.

"Quit hating on a player. If I can't go, ya'll ain't getting the truck. Right, Dad?" Busy said.

"You know it," Sin said.

"It's cool. His little crazy butt can go," JJ said.

Maria walked in and kissed her mama, niece, nephew, and little cousin. She then kissed Quesha on the head.

"What, about me?" Busy asked, looking at Maria like she was crazy.

"I didn't forget about you, lil' daddy," she said as she walked over to Busy and gave him a big hug and kiss.

"That's Maria, ya'll," Sin said.

She looked at Simina and tripped on how much she looked like her daddy. "You must be Simina. You are very pretty. You look like your daddy spit you out," Maria said.

"That's my big brother, Erick, his daughter, Shamika, and my cousin, Jamila," Sin said as he pointed them all out. "Ladies, lets get sideways." He and the girls all got up preparing to leave.

"Wait! I have to tell ya'll something," Maria said.

Sin looked at her. "Man, don't start," he said knowing that she was about to announce that she was pregnant.

"*Anyway!* Mario's going to call at 2. He told me to make sure you, Eb, and JJ are here," she said.

Sin let the girls into Janine's Benz then went to the guest-house and grabbed three ounces of weed and two blunts. As he was walking out Sonia was coming in.

"So what's on the agenda for later?" she asked.

"I was thinking we could ride up to Scottsdale and get a suite at one of the plush hotels, and pretty much get our freak on," he said.

"Yeah, I'm definitely feeling that. I'll see you later on," she said and kissed him. Sin popped her on the ass and left out.

Before he got in the car June came out of the house. "Man, I'm wore out," he said.

"Shit, as good as Jae look I bet you are. I'll get the 4-1-1 when I get back," Sin said.

Sin got in the car and slid his Cartier's on and left. Once they were off the property he lit a blunt. "Look, I'm fixing to lay some real shit on you," he said to Simina whom was sitting in the front. "I don't care what you do as long as you respect your mama, me, and your grandmother, take your ass to school, and don't get pregnant. Never ever tell our business, and don't do wrong in front of your little sister and brother. You too

Shamika and Ebony," he said as he passed his daughter the blunt.

"I'm going to tell ya'll something else. This shit is for real so listen. Dudes ain't shit. I got four kids and two on the way. All by six different women. Shamika, your daddy has ten. The only two by the same woman is the twins. What I'm saying is, don't let a muthafucka tell you he loves you and you have sex with him. I've done that shit a million times, and only meant it three times. I loved Malika to death. I would have died for her if I had to. I loved Tracy too, and I still love Shaunté. Malika was my first, and the one who hurt me the most. She's the reason I dogged chicks out and don't trust them fully," he said as Ebony passed him the blunt.

"Uncle Sin, what did Auntie Malika do?" Shamika asked.

"Me and Malika had our apartment when we were 15. Her mom gave us permission to live together as long as she went to school every day and she didn't get pregnant. To make a long story short, she got pregnant and got sent to New Orleans to live with her grandmother. I didn't know whether she had my baby or got an abortion. I went to her mom's house one day to raise hell, and Tina told me Malika had a miscarriage. I was hurt beyond belief. All this time I'm thinking Malika said the hell with me, and wasn't trying to get in contact with me, but she was." he said and paused "My mom was intercepting the mail because Tina said she'd have me arrested for statutory rape if I got in contact with Malika. She could have got in touch with me if she really wanted to. Thirteen years later, here she comes telling me I have a 13-year-old daughter," Sin said.

"That's why I hate my Mama's mama," Simina said, frowning as she hit the blunt.

"Don't hate her. She was just protecting her kid, like my moms was protecting me," he said as they pulled into the mall.

Sin saw Tommy and pulled on the side of him. They got out their cars, and Sin gave Tommy the weed and Tommy gave him the money. Sin gave each one of the girls $500.00.

Sin bought him a few things and got a few numbers. He loved how the white girls looked walking around in their short-shorts. White girls with sista asses were as common as CocaCola now. They were at Sin something serious. He ended up seeing Davy, Busy, and JJ. At 1:30 he caught up with the girls and they left.

When they got back to the ranch, Sin saw Maria and Jamila sitting by the pool getting high. He went into the house and poured himself an iced tea. The phone rang as he was putting the tea back in the fridge. "Hello?" he answered.

"I have a collect call from Mario. Will you except the charges?" the operator asked.

"Yes," Sin said.

"What up, my nigga?" Mario asked.

"You know, doing my thang."

"I'm about to get out! They found some shit on the cop that bagged me," Mario said.

"You lying, cuzzo!" Sin said excitedly.

"Real talk, blood!"

"Oh yeah, we gon' kick it."

"You ready to get some real paper?" Mario asked.

"Nigga, for sure!"

"Don't tell Maria. I want to surprise my mama and Charmaine," he said.

"So what day you touch down?" Sin asked.

"July 10th," Mario said.

"I'll be out there to snatch you up." Sin paused. "Man, your sister says she pregnant. I ain't calling her a hoe or nothing, but she been fucking other muthafuckas," Sin said.

"She *is* a hoe. I already know about her and my cousin Sonia's baby's father. Look, that shit's between you and her. You my nigga, Sin. I trust you more than most of the muthafuckas in my fam. You like my brother, so don't trip," Mario said.

When Sin and Mario finally got off of the phone, Sin leaned against the counter.

Sonia came in and kissed him. "So is she pregnant by you?" she asked.

"I don't know. I did hit them a few times without a rubber," he said.

"Then nine times outta ten it's yours," she said angrily.

Sin frowned at her. "Nah, nine times outta ten it's your boyfriend's," Sin said as he walked away.

"Sin, this conversation ain't over. We will be talking about this tonight," she said.

"I got some good news though," he said and proceeded to tell her about Mario.

As Sin and Sonia were coming out the house, June was pulling up in the Chevelle.

"What up?" he asked.

"Nothing," Sonia said.

"Bro, let me put a bug in your ear," he said. Sin walked over to June. "Malika's husband's suppose to touch down tomorrow morning. Dude called her and spooked her," June said.

"Fuck her!" Sin said.

"Cut it out. The only chicks you ever messed with that was worth a damn is Shaunté, Tracy, and Malika. You ain't about to let nothing happen to her," June said. Sin knew June was right.

"You gon' watch the little ones?" Sin asked.

"Yeah. When you leaving?" June asked.

"Now," he said and walked over to the pool and whispered in Sonia's ear. Maria watched with distaste. "Something came up and I gotta jet back to Oakland," he said.

"I had my heart set for tonight," she whined.

"I want you to go with me."

"When we coming back?"

"Tomorrow night or early Tuesday morning."

"I'll go pack," she said and got up and left.

Sin pulled his phone out and called Malika. He was surprised she didn't call him herself.

"Hello?" she answered.

"What ol' boy talking about?" he asked.

Malika started crying. "He said he was going to kill me and 'Mina. Sin, I'm scared. That nigga really is crazy," she said.

"Malika, what the fuck did you marry the muthafucka for then? Now I gotta come take care of this shit," he said.

"I told you I married him because I needed help!" she screamed.

"I'll be there in the morning," he said and hung up.

Sin walked over to Jamila, who was lying on her back. "'Mila, go pack, we out," he said.

Sin went and talked to Simina and told her what was happening. She said she wanted to go, and asked if Ebony could go. Sin said it was cool, then cleared it with Janine.

When they arrived in Dublin it was midnight. Everyone went in the house and crashed. The next morning Sin called Malika and found out what time she was picking her husband up.

Chapter Thirteen

Too Much Going On

At 10:35 Malika pulled up to the United Airlines terminal. She saw Joe coming out with a twisted look on his face. As soon as he got in the truck he slapped the shit out of her. Malika screamed out.

Joe was tempted to go to her ribs. "Bitch, where's my daughter at?" he asked.

"She's at my cousin's house," Malika said as she pulled off.

"I'm killing your hoe-ass when we get back to 'Nawlins. Go get her so we can get the fuck on the highway, you punk-ass bitch!" he yelled. Malika rubbed her cheek and nodded her head. *Yeah, nigga you gon' get yours soon enough!* she thought.

Malika made a right turn on Seminary and saw Sin and Terell sitting by Sin's Navigator talking. Simina was standing on a porch across the street talking on a phone.

"You just let her ass come out here and run wild," Joe said as he observed Simina wearing a short Guess skirt, midriff T-shirt, and she had her long tresses down. They both got out of the truck.

"Bring your little hot-ass here and get in the car! You going back to the South!" Joe yelled.

"I ain't going nowhere!" Simina said as she came off of the porch and went and stood next to Sin.

Joe looked like he was about to blow his top. He snatched Malika by her arm and pulled her to within five feet of Sin and Simina. "Girl, you done lost whatever little bit of mind you got? I will beat your..." Joe at that moment really looked at Sin.

Malika snatched her arm out of his grip. "This is Simian, Simina's father," she said.

"Baby girl, go back in the house," Sin said as he noticed the red mark and swelling on Malika's face.

Simina looked at Joe and walked away. She stood in the doorway and glared.

"Nigga, you like beating up on women?" Sin asked.

"Why the fuck you worrying about how me and my bitch get down?" Joe aggressively asked.

"Bitch, you better change your tone! I ain't her, I'll smother your punk ass! Fool, this ain't your bitch, nigga. This my woman for life, pimpin'. We went through some shit and that's how you ended up with her. Nigga, she only got with you to use you as a stepping stone. You just ended up getting pussy whipped," Sin said, trying to get a rise out of Joe.

"I ain't tripping, man. Best believe I rode this bitch out," Joe said.

"Fool, who you think taught her all that shit? Any treatment you got, I got about a hundred times," Sin said.

Terell noticed a blue four door Delta Eighty-Eight coming down the street. As the car got closer he saw that there were four dudes inside. "Sin, who is these..." he never finished his sentence because shots rang out.

Sin pushed Joe in front of the car's window. He flung Malika between the parked cars, and brought his gun up. As he dove over Terell's Iroc, the windows exploded.

Terell stepped in front of the car and started busting his .45. He hit the passenger in the head, but the dudes in the backseat started getting off.

Sin knew he couldn't leave his boy for dead, so he stood up and started getting off. The driver punched the gas.

"That was for J.B., bitch!" someone yelled out as the car shot down the street.

Sin saw that Terell was cool. He stepped between the cars and helped Malika up. "You aight?" he asked.

"Sin, where's my baby!" Malika screamed.

Sin turned and looked, and saw Simina standing in the door on the porch. She ran out of the yard and came to Sin and Malika. Sin looked back at Joe's bullet-riddled body. "Ya'll gotta get up outta here," he said as he tried to shield Simina from seeing Joe. She looked anyway and screamed. Sin hurried them over to his Navigator. "Who's name is your truck in?" he asked.

"Mine," she said.

"Take my truck, and give me your keys. Go to Simone's and stay there until I get there," he said as they exchanged keys. Malika got in the Navigator and sped off.

Sin and Terell went down the street to the spot and hid the guns and looked out of the window as the police came. "Jump the fences and run over to Lina's and tell her if the police knock on her door to say she ain't seen shit," Sin told Terell.

Terell ran out the back door and jumped the five fences to Lina's. Sin looked down the street and saw that Malika's truck was blocked in. *Fuck! All I need is for the police to get this nigga's ID and see that he's from New Orleans, and that the truck has Louisiana plates,* he thought.

He opened the door and went out and proceeded down the street where the cops were. "Excuse me, officer? I need to get to work. Can you let me through?" he asked.

"Did you see what happened out here?" the cop asked.

"Man, I heard shooting and hit the floor. I don't want to be no accident," Sin said.

"Where's your car?" the cop asked.

"The burgundy Tahoe," Sin said and pointed.

"Go ahead," the officer said as he told the other cop to move the car. Sin exhaled a breath of relief as he was starting the truck. When he got to the corner and was about to turn left he saw three Task Force cars turning down the block. The last car had a female Task Force officer inside. Sin couldn't see her face but something about her looked familiar. As she turned her head, Sin saw her face. *What the fuck?* he thought as he turned the corner before she saw him. The Task Force officer was Anita.

Sin was spooked as he drove to Simone's. Once he parked he started thinking about how he hooked up with Anita. *This bitch got on my line the same day I noticed that the police was following me. Shit! I gotta disappear for a minute,* he thought.

As he approached the door, Malika opened it. He walked in and hugged her. Sin was truly scared. He didn't know what was going on.

"I want you to go trade that truck in today. Get whatever you want, and I'll pay the difference. I also want you to move back into the house tonight. Don't go there *until* tonight. When we get back from Arizona, baby, have all that done. Now where is my daughter?" he asked.

"In her room."

Sin walked in Simina's room, and she stood and came and hugged him. Sin held her at arm's length. "Baby, I know that shit scared you. It scared me too, but it's over. Don't repeat what happened to no one, okay?" he asked.

"Yes, Daddy. Dad, I thought you got shot. I watched the whole thing," she said with tears in her eyes.

"Look, are you going to be okay to go back to Arizona, or do you want to stay here?" he asked.

"I'm going with you," she said.

"You aight?"

"Yeah, I just never saw a dead body before."

"How do feel about that?" he asked. Sin did not need for her to be traumatized by seeing the man that raised her getting killed.

"I hated how Joe treated my mama and me, but I didn't want that to happen to him, but I rather it be him than you," she said.

●●●●●●

I hope he didn't see me, Anita thought as they pulled up at the murder scene and got out of the car. Anita and Perez walked up to the body where Jones was standing.

"Looks like your boy struck again," Jones said.

"Last I heard he was in Arizona," Anita said.

"Well from what our informant tells us, this is his turf," Perez said.

"You said 'again'," Anita said to Jones.

"Everyone knows that The Mad Circle and 61st Street are at war, and your boy had something to do with J.B Ramsey getting killed. We also know through *you* that he was at the club the night Max Ramsey got shot," Jones said.

"Jones, all that shit is coincidental. I've sat and talked to Sin for hours, and I'm 100% sure he's clean. All he talks about is starting a business and being there for his kids."

Jones looked at Anita like she was crazy. He knew for a fact that Simian Michaels was a high-ranking member of The Mad Circle. Even if Bo Andrews was stalling them to stack some money, Jones knew that if he caught Sin, then there was a chance he could finally get Sin's cousin, Shaqui and Hasahn and Amir Williams on a conspiracy. Jones hated The Circle and everything it stood for, especially Shaqui Michaels, whom he suspected was sexing up his ex, Teesa.

"Anita don't let this muthafucka cloud your judgment! He's dirty. Please don't say you falling for this scum bucket muthafucka," Jones said.

"No, my professional judgment says he clean," Anita stubbornly replied. "If you can prove he's dirty, fuck him! If not, I'm not going to put him out there or have any part of your bullshit set ups, and you know how you do it!"

Jones pulled a phone out and dialed a number. He waited as the line rang. *I can't believe Anita's getting feelings over this asshole. She won't even give me the time of day,* he thought.

"Hello?" the voice said.

"Andrews, your time is up. Call your boy and hook some-thing up," Jones said and hung up.

"You'll have your proof soon enough," he said to Anita and walked away. *Sin, please don't be involved in this shit, or I'm going to have to bust you,* Anita thought.

● ● ● ● ● ●

Bo hung the phone up. *Shit! I need just a little bit more time,* he thought as he dialed Sin's number.

"What up?" Sin answered.

"Hey, this is Bo. I need to see you. I got 65 for that car," he said.

"Bo, I ain't selling that car until the 10th," Sin said and hung up. *Cool*, Bo thought. He dialed Jones's number and relayed the message.

Chapter Fourteen

Everybody Ain't Ya' Friend

The game had changed for Sin in the last three months of Mario being home. Mario dropped a hundred keys of raw coke on June and Sin, and they put a cut on every one they sold to make them a key and a half. They moved the dope in less than a month. Sin had stacked 2.5 million dollars.

With Tia's help he opened his club called 'Sin'. By there not being any cool clubs for cats to chill at in the town or in the Bay Area for that matter, Sin was a huge success.

June turned the game up in a real way. He stopped messing with all the in-the-way cats, and started messing with thorough cats in The Circle. June also left all the hood rats alone and devoted more time to his wife, LaToya. He still crept to Arizona to see the Asian chick, Jae, but he cut off all the other strays.

The war with the Mad Circle and Max and his crew was uglier than ever. What really made Sin mad was the fact that Kesha always called him talking mess when he retaliated against Max and his boys. Shaqui was putting in much work on the 61st Street cats.

It was a trip how things started coming together perfectly. The whole Circle was eating well and it was because of Sin, June, and Mario. Everything was too perfect to Sin. He felt deep down that something bad was going to happen soon.

Sin's phone rang and he rolled over and saw that Malika was gone.

He grabbed the phone and looked at the screen. He saw Bo's cell number and smiled. He was getting so much dope from Mario that he started fronting Bo twenty-five keys at a time. Bo would leave five on the block with his cousins, Marv, and Nitty and take the rest down South and move them for 20 a brick easily. Sin was charging Bo 12-5 a key. He knew if Bo was calling he had 310,000 for him.

"What up, blood?" Sin answered.

"Cuzzo, I got that. I need the same thing and I want to spend 375," Bo said.

"Aight, I'll meet you at Rod's Cafe" Sin said and hung up.

Sin got up and went to the bathroom and tended to his business, and then got in the shower. When he got out he looked outside and saw that it was going to be a dreary day.

He went to the closet and took out the tan Kenneth Cole Khaki's, a white T-shirt, and a Burberry short-sleeved button up. He slipped the cranberry Lugz boots on, and the tan leather three-quarter length coat.

Sin went to the garage and saw that Malika had taken her Tahoe. He got in his Grand National and left. As he was pulling into the gas station he pulled his Nextel out and called Shaunté.

"Hello?" she answered.

"Lil' mama, I need you to meet me at the club," he said.

"Aight, I'll be there in a minute," she said and hung up.

By the time Sin pulled up at the club, Shaunté was there in her root beer brown Range Rover. He got out of his car and went in the club.

He went into the basement and moved a few things and pushed in on the dartboard on the wall then pulled down on it slightly. The hook in the wall triggered the hidden door. Sin heard the hiss of the air lock, and a section of the wall slid in and to the left. He walked in and got Bo's order. He put it in two boxes, took them to 'Tay's truck one by one, then closed and sealed the hidden room and put boxes back in front of it.

Sin told Shaunté where to meet him, then got back in his car and pulled off.

As he drove he thought about asking Malika to marry him. She was playing her part well, but he still couldn't forget all that time that passed without him knowing of his daughter.

Then there was Tia who he was falling for. Tia knew about Malika and let it be known from jump that she wouldn't be intimate with Sin while he was with Malika. It was hard being around her and not hitting it.

They laid in her bed on weekends with her in nothing but panties and a gown or T-shirt.

● ● ● ● ● ●

The Oakland Drug Task Force and Berkeley Task Force were geared up and waiting for the signal to strike. Jones and Perez were so sure that they were going to catch Sin dirty that they had a KTVU News crew standing by.

Anita was having mixed emotions. On one hand, she wanted to uphold the law she was sworn to, but on the other hand, she had a soft spot for Sin, and as much as she didn't want to believe that he was selling dope, she knew he was.

"I gotta use the bathroom," she said as she got out of her car and went into the Thrifty's where they were keeping surveillance on Rod's Cafe. The minute she got in the bathroom and closed the door, she dialed *67 to block her number, then Sin's cell number.

● ● ● ● ● ●

"Hello?" Sin answered as he got off the freeway on 51st and made a left onto Shattuck.

"Sin, I hope I didn't make a fool out of myself by believing in you, but just in case I did; if you on your way to Rod's Cafe to meet Bo Andrews, don't go. He's trying to set you up. He's been working for the police for the last eight months," Anita said.

"How do you know this, Anita?" Sin asked, acting as if he didn't know she was the police.

"I can't tell you that right now, but trust me on this. I'll call you later," she said and hung up.

This bitch ass nigga! I brought this punk-ass muthafucka from standing on the block to supplying damn near everybody in Berkeley, Sin thought as he dialed Shaunté.

"Hello?" she answered.

"Don't go there! It's a setup, baby. Where you at right now?" he asked.

"I'm just approaching Jackson liquor's," she said.

"Go to my mother's," Sin said and hung up.

When Sin got to his mom's, he did what he had to do then got in the Range with Shaunté.

"Baby, I told you that nigga wasn't cool. He trying to fuck off everything we've built. We need to be going to handle that nigga," Shaunté said.

"Oh, believe me, we will!" Sin said.

Shaunté reached over and grabbed Sin's dick. "You put me to sleep yesterday, Daddy," she said as she noticed that they were going up Shattuck in the direction of Rod's Cafe. "Where you going?" she asked.

"To Rod's," he said and told her his plan.

Anita saw Sin and Shaunté pull up and get out of the Range Rover. *What the fuck is wrong with this nigga? He must be trying to go back to jail! Fuck it, I did what I could,* she thought. She watched Shaunté and Sin go in the breakfast spot and be seated. As she watched them eating through her binoculars, the team got ready.

As Shaunté sat at the table eating, Sin felt as if his world was crumbling. *I wonder how long this bitch-ass nigga been trying to get me caught up? It ain't no doubt that if I get out of this shit I'm going to have to shut this shit down or hit another state. One thing's for sure, two things for certain: I'm going to kill this bitch-ass nigga!* Sin thought.

As he looked at Shaunté Sin thought about all the shit they put each other through. "'Tay, I love you, baby," he said as he grabbed her hand.

"I know you do, Sin. What I don't know is why you do me like you do. I love your dog-ass like my next breath. I would do whatever for you. Since we broke up I've only been with one dude, and it was only a few times," she said with tears in her eyes.

"I'm saying, 'Tay. You had a nigga straight bugging. I never even wanted another chick until you pulled that one move," he said as he rubbed her cheek.

"Nigga, quit lying. Your ass was already in Seattle when I decided to go to Reno. Them muthafuckin' twins were slobbing on your dick when you wasn't answering my calls!" she stated angrily.

"I'm sorry, 'Tay. Baby, I got sidetracked. I know I was outta pocket for carrying you like that. I let this money shit get to my head. For real though, it's like I said a long time ago. If it wasn't for you, I wouldn't have it like I do," he said and kissed her on the lips. "If I get through this punk-ass shit I promise I'm going to do right by you."

Shaunté got a funny feeling in her stomach when she saw the sincerity in Sin's eyes. *Damn, I love this nigga!* she thought. "Sin, you only got one more time to fuck over me. I've shot muthafuckas for much less than what you be doing. You do me wrong again though. I don't want nothing other than our daughter and business to do with you. Baby, I'm serious as AIDS," she said.

Sin pulled his phone out and called Maria and had her call Mario on the threeway in case his phone was being tapped

"What's up. Sin?" he asked.

"Bro, one of these suckas done twisted me with the dicks. I ain't knowing how the cards going to drop. My rider will be at you. She got the same program as me, so look out for her," Sin said. He and Mario talked for another minute then hung up.

"I wish I could beat that pussy up real quick," he told Shaunté.

"Yeah, I could use some of that turbo tongue you working with too."

"Come on, baby, let's do this!" Sin said.

They walked out and got in the Range Rover, and Shaunté fired up a blunt. As they smoked, Sin saw a Berkeley police car pull up behind them.

"It's about to go down, baby," he said.

Shaunté pulled out her Glock 9mm, took the clip out, slid it in her purse, and put the gun in the glove box and locked it. They saw another cop car pull up in front of them.

Sin hit the blunt a couple of times. All of a sudden two vans screeched up, and out jumped the two city's elite.

"Out of the God damn car, now!" one of the cops said.

Sin leaned over and kissed 'Tay again, and they got out. The police rushed them and threw them both up against the Range, and cuffed them. Just then Sin saw the KTVU news crew. *These muthafuckas were super confident*, he thought. Sin looked at Anita feining surprise. She turned her head in disgust. *She probably thinks that I'm super stupid for still showing up*, he thought.

"We've been after these two for a while," Jones said to the news reporter.

Perez pulled the 9mm out of Shaunté's glove box.

"That's registered to me, and you didn't ask permission to search my vehicle!" Shaunté yelled.

Jones grabbed Sin and pulled him to the back of thr Range Rover and opened the rear door. The news crew focused in on the two duffel bags. When Jones opened them, his eyes got big as saucers. He went through both bags like a cyclone. The cameraman focused in on the clothes which Jones tossed all over the place.

"Man, what is you looking for? Better yet, don't tell me. Call my lawyer right away!" Sin demanded.

Jones snatched Sin by his collar and slammed him against the truck. "Where's the dope?" he yelled.

"Let him the fuck go!" Shaunté screamed as she tried to break away from Anita and another female cop.

"What dope?" Sin yelled back.

Jones roughly moved Sin over to where Shaunté was standing.

"You muthafuckas always trying to get bad when niggas' in cuffs. I bet you won't uncuff him and do that shit!" Shaunté said.

These muthafuckas thought they had me dead bang. I can't believe they actually brought a news team, Sin thought. "Nah, he ain't going to uncuff me. It would be a shame to get his ass beat *and* get fired on the same day," he said.

The hatred in Jones' eyes was unmistakable. If it was late night and he had Sin by himself he wouldn't hesitate to put a bullet through Sin's head. He'd done it before to others. "You know what, bitch? We about to see just how bad you are," he said as he snatched Sin and slammed him on the hood of a squad car and uncuffed him, totally forgetting about the news crew.

"Kick his muthafuckin' ass, baby!" 'Tay said.

"Somebody come get this bitch!" Perez said and pushed Shaunté to another officer, causing her to fall.

"Muthafucka, she's pregnant!" Sin yelled and pushed Perez into the wall. The cops mobbed on Sin and got him in a chokehold, causing him to lose consciousness. All the while the news crew was filming this.

When Sin came to, he was in the paddy-wagon with a sore neck and a big lump on the back of his head.

When the wagon stopped they were at Oakland Police Station.

The doors opened and one officer was standing there. "You okay, Michaels?" he asked.

"Nah, I'm fucked up. What happened to my baby's mother?" he asked.

"They brought her here in a separate car. That was bullshit what they did to you. You had every right to try to protect your girl and unborn child. I know one thing; some very important people want to see you," he said.

Sin stepped out of the wagon and the officer uncuffed him. They went through a door and Sin was handed off to the jail staff.

Just then Perez and Jones came in. "Why the fuck is he not in cuffs! I want this piece of shit cuffed, now!" Jones yelled.

"Wait a God damn minute! I don't work for you. You don't run shit up in here, officer. Now I suggest you stay away from this man, and those are orders from the Chief!" the jailer said and bogarded past Jones and Perez and went to a hallway.

"Michaels, I have to put you in cuffs because we're about to ride on a civilian elevator," the jailer said and cuffed Sin in front.

They got on an elevator and rode up to the 4th floor. The jailer turned Sin over to another cop that had sergeant's stripes on his uniform. Sin was then taken to an interrogation room. He sat in that room for over three hours. He knew there were people on the other side of the tinted glass, because one of their stupid asses lit a cigarette and he saw the flame out of the corner of his eye.

Ten minutes later, Jones, Perez, an Internal Affairs officer, the Deputy Mayor, the Chief of Police, the Police Commissioner, and the Task Force captain, all came in.

The chief slid Sin a piece of paper. "Sign it and you're free" he said.

"I'm not signing shit, and I ain't saying shit else without an attorney present," Sin said.

"If that's how you want it. You're being charged with assault on a police officer, threatening a police officer, and resisting arrest," the Chief said.

"Well, let's do this. I need my phone call to call my lawyer and to make bail," Sin said.

"I don't think so. You see Mr. Michaels, you neglected to register with our police station upon you getting out of that prison in Georgia and coming to Oakland," the Police Chief informed him.

"Negative, Chief. First of all, that's a condition of parole. I didn't get out on parole in Georgia. I served my whole sentence. Secondly, you only have to register if you have a sex or narcotics case. I had a gun charge."

"If you sign this paper all of this will go away. You'll have a license to do as you wish," the Commissioner said.

"Ain't nuttin' happening. Now what about my legal right to a phone call within three hours of being arrested?" Sin asked smugly.

"Have it your way. Book him and the girl. I want her charged with double murder for the killing that took place at Roscoe's," the Chief said.

"You do that, then you're going to have another lawsuit on your hands. I'll make sure she sues you for not having probable cause to search her vehicle, assault on her and our unborn child, and filing false charges. Now that your boys here done used excessive force, and you know I'm going to file a civil suit *and* win, you wanna try to pin some shit on my baby's mom. Shit, I can probably get Johnny to take this case," Sin said.

The District Attorney came in and sat next to Sin. "Mr. Michaels, I'm Sam Neil, District Attorney. Shaunté Rogers will be released in the next hour. I assure you that the events that took place today will not go unpunished. However, you putting your hands on Officer Perez will also be punished. If I was in your position, I would have done the exact same thing, but the law is the law," he said.

"I accept that. I'll be filthy rich by the time I get home," Sin said and smiled at the Deputy Mayor.

"Book him and charge him with assault on a police officer," the deputy Mayor said.

The sergeant that led Sin into the room escorted him out.

When Sin went to court three days later, he was arraigned. Ayanna Gates, who was one of the top lawyers in the country, represented him. Ayanna was born and raised in West Oakland. When her man, Tariq told her about the case, she jumped at it. The D.A. met with her and told her that because of the events that took place, he was only going to ask that Sin receive a year and a day. That would make Sin automatically have to go to prison. California law prohibits any inmate being sentenced to anything over a year to serve their sentence in a county jail.

Later on that night Sin was sitting in his cell reading and thinking about what was going on in the streets.

"Michaels, you have a visit," the deputy said over the intercom.

Sin looked at his celly, Mark. "Man, these muthafuckas about to try to kill me," he said as he got up. When his door popped, he stepped out and went to the unit's exit and waited. The deputy mechanically popped that door, and Sin went to the control bubble.

The door opened and Sin saw it was Deputy Greer. Deputy Greer was a bad broad. She looked a lot like that chick that plays Lynn on "Girlfriends", Persia White. She said, "I could get in serious trouble for this, but I know you got done wrong, and she's a good friend of mine. Plus, I know you gon' tell you folks to give me a permanent VIP pass to your club."

"You got that," Sin said.

"Tell her ya'll only got an hour," she said.

Sin went and stood by a door that led to the visiting area. When it opened, he stepped through and went up the stairs. He looked in all the behind the glass visiting cubes on both sides and didn't see anyone. He looked in the contact visiting room, which was only used for contact visits with attorneys, and saw Anita. The door buzzed and he went inside. They both just stared at each other with different thoughts on their minds.

Damn, I know he's mad at me, Anita thought.

This girl saved my muthafuckin' ass. If she didn't give me the heads up, they would have me on some serious shit, Sin thought.

"Let me say what I have to say then you can cuss me out if you choose to," she said.

Anita was looking good as hell to Sin. She was wearing a medium length green dress and sandals.

"Sin, we got that guy Bo Andrews, and he gave us your name and Shaunté Rogers' name. He even said that she killed those two low lifes at Roscoe's and you were right there. Me meeting you at that light was planned. After we kicked it at Mexicali Rose that night, I had doubts that you were a drug dealer. To be sure, I put surveillance on you, and you showed no illegal activity. Shaunté showed none either.

"That night you left me hanging at my house, I called Jones and told him I thought he was wrong about you. I called and told you it was a set up just in case I was wrong. I fucked around and caught feelings for you. Your arrogant ass still went to the meet. Then Jones, being just as arrogant but at the same time stupid, had the news people there."

Sin just stood there staring at her. She had no idea that she saved him. "Anita, I'm not mad at you, baby. All you did was your job. I'm in this shit because I went to that meet even after you warned me. This ain't your fault, baby. I already knew you was the police. I saw you that day on Seminary when that dude got killed.

That shit sorta made me mad, but after you risking your job for me, how can I be mad?" he asked.

"I know you were at war with Max Ramsey, and ya'll had a shootout at the club, because I was there. I just want you to be honest. Did you kill his brother, J.B.? This is off the record."

"Come here, baby," he said. Anita walked into Sin's arms. He looked down at her. "When that cat got killed, I was in Arizona. My baby mama messes with Max. She called me accusing me of that shit. I was at a truck stop in Arizona getting gas when dude got killed. I got receipts and everything, and I paid for the gas and other things with my Visa," he said.

Anita looked in Sin's eyes and felt he was telling her the truth. She also knew that Sin wouldn't tell her if he did do it. She kissed him. "Come sit down. I brought you something to eat," she said.

Sin sat down and sat Anita on his lap. "Food ain't what I'm trying to eat," he said as he ran his hand up her leg.

"You better eat your food," she said as she opened the Styrofoam container that contained a cheese steak sandwich. As Sin started eating he felt his dick getting hard. Anita must have felt it too, because she turned and looked at him.

"I'm breaking the law by doing this, but here," she said and gave him a blunt and a lighter.

"Since you already breaking the rules..." he said and rubbed his hand between her thighs. He felt the heat coming from her before his hand rubbed up against the crotch of her panties.

"Sin, I..." she never finished, because he moved the wet panties aside and stroked her. He moved the stuff on the table to the side and laid Anita on it. He pulled his jail pants down and ripped her panties off. Sin gave Anita head the first ten minutes then went up in her. He had to put her panties in her mouth to keep her from screaming so loud. He pulled out at the very last second and busted off in a napkin.

As Anita was preparing to leave, she looked over at Sin.

"So, you gon' come visit me in the pen?" he asked.

Anita smiled. "For sure. I'm going to go home and write you so that you will have my address," she said.

They kissed and she left. Sin went back to his unit and into his cell.

"So who was that?" Mark asked.

"Homie, you wouldn't even understand," Sin said and tossed Mark Anita's ripped panties. Mark inhaled Anita's scent as Sin fired up the blunt and leaned into the toilet blowing the smoke down with every flush.

The next morning Sin called Malika and Shaunté one by one and told them he was going to take the deal.

"You only going to be gone for a minute. I'll get the marriage license," Shaunté said.

Malika started crying and told him she was going to hold everything down for him.

Chapter Fifteen

I Threw Up Wit' Dat Nigga Grew up Wit' Dat Nigga

On November 18, 1999 Sin was sentenced. He saw his cousin, Shaqui, and his potnas, Tayshaun, Hashi, Hasahn, Tariq, and Amir in the courtroom. He looked at his brother whom was standing with Mario and nodded to Sha. Mario balled his fist up and tapped his chest. Sin looked at Malika who had tears in her eyes. He decided right then that he was going to do right by her. "I love you," he mouthed.

"I love you more," she mouthed back.

Sin was then taken out of the courtroom and led back to the North County jail. Later that night he was transferred to Santa Rita jail where he would await the prison chain.

On December 1, 1999 Sin got off the bus in San Quentin. The first person he saw standing off at a distance was Marco.

"I'll be by West Block to see you after you get processed in. My potna up in R&R got some shit for you," he yelled. Sin nodded his head. Marco had grown in every aspect. He was 5'10" and weighed 230 pounds of muscle. He was brown-skinned, brown eyes, and had a bald head.

Sin and Marco hadn't seen each other in over 13 years, not since that day in the courtroom. Sin went in the Receive and Release building.

"Ay, which one of you cats is Sin?" some huge light-skinned cat asked.

"Me," Sin said.

"What's up, cousin? I got a gang of shit for you from your brother, Marco," he said and gave Sin four clear plastic bags. "If you need anything, fam let me know. My name is J.C.," the big dude said. He and Sin gave each other the ghetto hand shake and hug combo.

Three hours later Sin was stripped, issued the orange reception center fit, finger printed, photographed and interviewed. Once they gave him the TB skin test, and he answered the medical personnel's' questions, he was issued his bedroll and taken to West Block.

When he got to his cell, he looked through the bars and saw that his celly was this dude called Slo Moe. His real name was Maurice, and he was from 96th Ave and Birch Street.

Once Sin had his bed made he looked in the bags that Marco had sent. There were a brand new pair of black and white Air Max, magazines, shower shoes, books, two bags of food, a bag of hygiene supplies, two cartons of Newports, and about twenty books of stamps. Sin put that stuff away and got up on the top bunk and thought about the tragic night that caused Marco to be sent to prison when they were only 15…

August 1985

Sin and Marco were at the Eastmont Mall buying the new Adidas tennis shoes when Sin's pager went off. He looked at the number and didn't recognize it. He walked out of FootLocker and went to the phone booth and called the number back.

"Hello?" a female answered.

"Who paged?" Sin asked.

"Hold on," the girl said and passed the phone.

"Sin, I'm at Rhonda's house, and them Funktown niggas outside posted. They don't know I'm here, but I gotta leave before her moms get home, and they right outside the building where I'm parked," Corey said.

"Man, you trippin'! I told your ass to stop going to that bitch house. Have her meet you somewhere," Sin said.

"Man, miss me with that! I know I fucked up! Just come get me!" Corey said.

"We'll be there in a minute."

Sin went back to FootLocker and paid for his and Malika's shoes, then he and Marco left. When they got to Marco's four door '74 Impala, they threw their bags in the trunk. Marco gave Sin an Uzi.

When they pulled out the mall on 68th and Foothill, all eyes were on them. Marco's car was a rust color, peanut butter leather top and interior, and sat on

Star Wire rims and Vogue tires. Marco threw Too Short's *Blow job Betty* in the deck and the four 12" E.V. woofers and Zap eq. had the car pounding as they rode. When they got to 98th and East 14th Marco pulled over.

Sin called Corey back. "C.B., when you hear shots look outside. If ain't nobody out there go get in your car and cut," he said and got back in the car, and put his burners (gloves) on, and wiped the gun down.

When Marco rode past 98th and Walnut, they saw about six dudes on the corner. Marco rode up a block and made a U-turn. Sin cocked the Uzi and rolled the window down.

When they got close to the dudes, one of them recognized Marco's car. "Watch out!" he screamed. Sin started letting off shots. He didn't hit anybody, but he did notice the niggas in front of Rhonda's building come running towards the corner.

Corey heard the shots and looked out the window and saw the dudes out there running towards the corner. He grabbed his gun, kissed Rhonda, and ran outside and got in his gray four door '79 Caprice. He busted a U-turn and went the other way. He went straight to Seminary where their spot was located. As he was pulling up, Marco and Sin were getting out of Marco's car.

"C.B., man, you better quit going out like that. Have somebody bring that bitch over here," Marco said.

Malika pulled up in the Maxima Sin had bought for her. He walked over to her car and pulled her five-month pregnant body out. "Where you been? I called you hella long ago," he said.

"I took your little sister to Berkeley and dropped her off at her friend's house," she said.

Sin led her across the street to his '69 convertible Cougar. They got in, and Sin opened the console and grabbed the paper bag of money and gave it to her. "Count that shit when you get home. I think its 10 gees. If not, it's over 10," he said. Malika pulled two ounces out of her bra and another two out of her panties and gave them to Sin. "Put that money in the Fila box in the closet. Don't mix it with that other money that's in the Nike boxes," he said.

"What you want for dinner tonight?" she asked.

"Stop at Lady Esther's and get me an oxtail dinner with greens and mac and cheese, and a banana pudding."

"Okay. I love you."

"I love you too."

"I know you do," she said and leaned over and kissed him.

"We gon' do some freaky shit tonight?" Sin asked.

"Like what?" she asked.

"Like... you know."

"If you talking about me sucking your dick, I already do that every night. You gonna lick me?" Malika asked.

"If that's what you want."

As they got out of the car, a champagne pink four door '82 Caprice pulled up. Inside the car were LaShaye AKA Lay, Angelique, Marie, and Tyisha. Lay was Sin's best friend and part of the Mad Circle. Angelique was Hashi's girl. Tyisha messed with Tayshawn, and Marie messed with Hasahn..

Malika frowned when she saw Lay. She stayed accusing Sin of messing with her. "Your girlfriend's here," she said.

"Man, don't start that shit. I'm not trying to hear it," he said.

"You know where you sleeping tonight," she said as she got in the Maxima.

"You keep talking that shit it'll be in the next girl's bed." Sin said. Malika started the Maxima and drove off.

Sin walked over to Lay's car and leaned against it. Lay handed him a wad of cash. "That's the 2500 I owe you," she said.

"I got two more for you."

"Are they already cooked?" Lay asked as she stepped out the car.

"I'm going to twist them now."

The other girls got out of the car, and all except Lay, and Angelique stayed outside.

Sin cooked all four ounces and Lay cut and weighed them into grams. Each gram would go for $100.00. After they bagged them he slid 56 of them to Lay.

"3500 me, 2100 you," Sin said.

"That's cool," she said. Lay stood and started walking away.

"LaShaye, where you get that from?" Sin asked.

"What?" she asked.

"All that ass."

Lay was 15, the same age as Sin. She was light-skinned, had light-brown eyes, long sandy brown hair, dimples, full lips, and a very pretty face. She had above average titties for a girl her age, wide hips, and a big butt.

"From letting your little cousin, Shaqui hit it doggie style. You could have still been hitting it, but you let that bitch fuck your head up," she answered.

"Whatever, blood. My head wasn't fucked up when I ate your pussy and had you crying," Sin said.

"Lay, you ain't shit! You didn't even tell me that, and we suppose to be girls," Angelique said.

"Angel, you need to stop that shit. Hash told me how you be getting when he licks on you, with your fat booty self," Sin said.

"Yeah, but this is Hashi's fat booty!" she said and slapped her soft ass.

The girls walked out and Sin grabbed the other 56 grams and went outside too. The rush was exactly what he needed, because he started thinking about Malika and wanted to get home. He sold out within an hour as did Lay and Marco.

"It's raining too hard out here. I'm going to see my little man then go home," Lay said as she gave Sin the 3500.

Sin and Marco called June and told him they needed some more dope before he closed up shop for the night. "Just get the whole key from June and I'll give you my half tomorrow," Sin said.

"Aight. Don't you still got some dope?" he asked.

"I got like five zippas (ounces) left. You fly me six gees you could get them," Sin said.

"I'm with that," Marco replied.

"You gotta go to my mama's house and get it from Kim. My girl tripping. I'm going home," Sin said. He called his little sister and told her where the stuff was and to give it to Marco.

He ran across the street and got in his Cougar and pulled off knocking UTFO's *Roxanne Roxanne*.

When Sin got to his and Malika's Adams Point apartment he parked in the underground garage next to Malika's Maxima. He set his alarm and got out.

As he walked towards the elevator he had his .45 out. June taught Sin some of the game, but this chick that used to stay on the block named Lottie laced him with *all* the game. One of the most important things she taught him was to always be aware of his surroundings. He pushed the elevator call button and scanned the garage. When the elevator came he got on and went to the third floor. He got off the elevator and went to number 306. He stuck his key in the door and went in. He walked down the hall and looked in the dining room and saw Malika doing her homework. He went to the bedroom and emptied his jacket and all his pants pockets onto the bed.

Sin pulled all six shoeboxes out the closet and looked in every one of them. Every box contained ten gees. He counted the money he had dropped on the bed. There was the 2500 that Lay had given him when she got on the block, the 3500 she made on the block, and the 5600 he made himself. *Damn, I got 11,600 today, and Marco got 6 more gees for me. He can just keep it and I'll give him another 3500 for my half of the key*, Sin thought. He took his new Adidas out of the box and put five gees in it. He put all the boxes back in the closet and then took Marco's 3500 and put it to the side. He put $100.00 on his dresser for pocket money for the next day and 3,000 on Malika's nightstand for her go buy her and the baby some stuff.

Once Sin did what he did with the money, he sat down and did his homework. As soon as he was done he laid back.

"Malika, come back here!" he called.

Malika came to the bedroom door. "What" she said with an attitude.

"I'm sorry I said that shit to you. I'm just tired of having this same argument with you everyday. Me and Lay been friends for ten years. She messes with Sha anyway, and even if she didn't, I don't want Lay, I want you, baby," he said.

"Well you don't act like it, Sin," she stated.

"What do you mean? Everybody I fuck with is calling me a sucka. I spent $16,000.00 on your car, 2,500 on your school clothes, and 5,000 on your watch, chain, ring, earrings, and bracelet. And I don't love you?" he asked with a frown on his face.

"Sin, I told you before. The money don't mean nothing to me. You don't spend no time with me. As soon as Marco, Hashi, Scatter, Hasahn, Tariq, or June calls you leave."

"Baby, come here" he said. Malika laid next to him. "If I don't hustle, how's the rent going to get paid? How are we suppose to eat? If me and you both had jobs we wouldn't make enough to pay the rent."

"Sin, you missing the point."

"Aight, I'll quit the game. Tomorrow we can go find some jobs."

"No you won't," Malika said not believing him.

"For you I would."

Malika knew that Sin would do anything for her, and if he said he'd quit for her then he would. "Nah, you don't have to quit yet, but I want you to start spending more time with me."

"You done with your homework?" he asked.

"Yeah. I was done when you got here."

Sin and Malika laid back both thinking of how good they had it. Then the phone rang.

"Hello?" he answered.

"Sin, I got Rhonda and her cousin, Danielle over here on the block. Danni is bad than a muthafucka!" Corey said.

"Aww, nigga, if it's that much money I'm on my way!" Sin said to throw Malika off.

Malika looked at Sin like he was out of his mind. "So you just going to leave after we just finished talking about this same shit?" she asked.

"I'm going to take care of some business real quick," he said.

"Baby, please don't go. I just want you stay home with me."

"Baby, I'm only going to be gone for a minute, I promise." Sin said.

Malika had a funny feeling in her stomach. Something was going to happen, and she felt it. She started crying as she got off of the bed. "I'm leaving then," she said as she went to the closet and got her suitcase.

"Where you going?" Sin asked as he put his shoes on.

"Back to my mother's."

"Whatever, man!," he said as he grabbed his black leather bomber with the fur around the hood. Malika fell to the floor crying, and Sin felt bad.

"Get up," he said.

Sin picked Malika up and laid her on the bed. He then went and ran them a bubble bath. He led Malika to the bathroom and they stripped and got in the tub. When they got out they put lotion on then went to the kitchen and ate. After they finished they put the dishes in the dishwasher and went and got in the bed.

●●●●●●

"Where your cousin at, C.B.?" Danielle asked Corey.

"That nigga probably got caught up," he said as he passed Rhonda the weed.

"Baby, I want to go to Great America on Halloween. You going to take me?" Rhonda asked.

"If that's what you want to do," he answered.

A car turned the corner. Corey looked in his rear view mirror and saw the head lights and figured it was Sin in his Chev. "Here that nigga come now," he said.

When the car pulled up on the side of him, Corey looked and saw it wasn't Sin, but it was too late. Guns started blazing from the front and back passenger side windows. Corey reached for his gun as the girls ducked. Just as he was pulling the 9mm up, an AK round hit him in the back and a .38 slug hit him in the neck. The driver of the car hit the gas.

Vickie, a fiend on the block, and her husband, James came out.

Rhonda sat up and looked at Corey, who was slumped over. "Corey!" she called out. When she shook him and felt blood on her hands she screamed.

●●●●●●

Malika was laying in Sin's arms asleep when the phone rang. "Hello?" she answered.

"Malika, is Sin there? It's an emergency!" Lay cried. Malika thought about hanging the phone up, but didn't because of how Lay sounded.

"Baby, wake up. Sin wake up, telephone," she said as she shook him.

Sin woke up and took the phone. "What?" he answered.

"Sin, Corey got shot!" Lay cried.

"What!" Sin yelled and sat up.

"He's at Highland Hospital and they don't think he's going to make it."

"I'm on my way!" he said and hung up.

"Baby, what happened?" Malika asked.

"Corey got shot," he said as he got up.

"I'm going with you," she said.

Sin put on his blue wind breaker Adidas sweat pants, a blue T-shirt, his blue and white striped suede Adidas shoes, and the blue bubble puff coat.

Malika put on a white Fila sweatsuit, all white Fila shoes, and an orange Fila puff coat.

Sin grabbed his gun and his keys and they left. When they got to the garage Sin used his keys to get into Malika's Maxima and they pulled out quickly.

Since they only lived ten minutes from Highland, Sin got there in five. As soon as he pulled up at the hospital, he jumped out, leaving Malika to park. When he got off the elevator in ICU, Sin saw everyone crying, and a few people trying to console Corey's mother.

June came up to Sin with a tear in his eye. "He's gone, bro!" he said.

Sin backed away from him. "Nah, nigga, he ain't gone! Fuck that, June Bug! I'm killing all them niggas!" Sin cried. Corey, Marco, Sin, and Lay were all like family.

Sin walked over to Corey's mama, Denise and hugged her. "Mama Niecey, I *swear* who ever did this to Corey is going to catch it!" Sin said.

"Sin, please let the police handle it. I don't want to lose you guys too," she said.

Sin and Marco pulled Rhonda to the side to find out what happened.

"We was on Bromly waiting for you to come. A Chev turned the corner coming from Seminary and Corey thought it was you. When they pulled up on us we saw it was that nigga Rich that be on 5th Ave. Corey, Hasahn, and Tariq stomped him out at the movies last weekend. I saw that nigga with my own eyes, Sin," she informed him.

"Let's go get these niggas," Marco said.

Sin made eye contact with Hasahn and Tariq, and nodded to the elevator. They all made their way to the elevator. As it opened, Malika was standing there, and when she saw Sin's face she knew Corey was dead.

June turned looking for Sin and saw him as the elevator doors were closing. "Sin, no!" he yelled.

They all got off of the elevator and walked out of the hospital.

"Where did you park at?" Sin asked Malika.

"Across the street."

Just then Shaqui pulled up in his hooptie LTD. He got out of the car and saw that everyone had tears in their eyes. He started crying too. Corey was his boy. He was the only one that didn't treat Sha as if he was a kid.

Sin walked Malika over to a cab. "Give me my keys," he said to her.

"Sin, please don't go do nothing," she begged as she handed him his keys.

"Take her to 330 Adams Point," Sin said to the cabby and threw $20.00 into the cab. He looked at his little cousin. "Sha, go home," he said.

"Nigga, I'm riding! Corey was my folks too," he said. Sin didn't have time to argue with him, because June and his right-hand man, Kiaree came running out.

"Ya'll know where to meet me," Sin said and ran to Malika's car. He got in and pulled off. He was the first to pull up at Lay's house. Raindrops were hitting the Maxima hard as he sat there thinking.

Sin had never killed anyone, but he had shot quite a few. He knew that tonight he was going to get blood on his hands. Lay pulled up, followed by Hasahn, Marco, Tariq, and Shaqui. They went to Lay's back yard and got the choppas (assault rifles) they had stashed there.

As they were leaving, June pulled up in a '74 four door Delta Eighty-Eight. He and Kiaree got out. "I knew ya'll was over here," June said as he popped his trunk and pulled an M-16 out. Kiaree grabbed the AK-47.

"Sha, you ain't going," June said to their little cousin.

"Nigga, you crazy. I'm going!" Sha said as he pulled an Uzi out of his car.

"Fuck it! When shit get hot don't start crying," June told him.

"Big cousin, you got *me* fucked up! I ain't scared of shit!" Shaqui said.

"Tariq, you and Hasahn ride with us," June said.

Marco, Sin and Lay got in Sha's car. They all took off.

"When we get there, let Lay drive," Sin said.

They drove passed 5th Avenue and Foothill and saw about ten niggas outside the corner store. They drove around the block and parked. Everyone got out of the cars.

"This how we gon' do it: Kiaree's going to drive me and Hasahn around the corner. When we start getting at them niggas, they'll start running this way. Ya'll get off on them when they get here. That way we got them in a cross fire," June said.

"Lay, follow June," Sin said.

Lay pulled off behind Kiaree. Sin cocked the Mac-10 and went to the corner of the building they were on the side of, and peeked around the corner. He saw the niggas in front of the store posted up talking. He looked down the street and saw June Bug turn the corner. He looked at Tariq, Sha, and Marco and nodded.

June leaned out the window and started letting off with the M-16. Hasahn let loose with the pistol grip shotgun. Just like June said, the guys ran towards the corner. Sin, Sha, Marco, and Tariq stepped out and lit them up.

Sin saw the dude, Rich running to a Chev that was parked across the street. Sin ran after him. When he got to the car, he raised the Mack-10. Rich looked at him and knew it was over. When Sin pulled the trigger, the gun jammed. Rich tried to reach under the seat for his gun. Sin swung the Mack and busted the driver side window. Rich ducked and got his hand on his gun, but when he looked up, Sin was coming up with his .45. The last thing Rich saw was a flash. Sin's first bullet went into Rich's eye and exploded out the back of his head. His next bullet hit him in the throat. The rest of the clip Sin dumped into Rich was a waste of ammo.

Sin looked across the street and saw Shaqui shoot a cat running for the store. Shaqui then ran up on him and emptied the rest of the clip into the dude. Lay skidded up and Sin and Sha both jumped into the car. Lay did 80 down 5th Avenue.

When Lay crossed East 18th, the police got on them. Tariq took Shaqui's Uzi and leaned out the window and sprayed the squad car. The police car went out of control and jumped the curb and went through someone's fence and straight into their living room.

"Go to that Shell on Broadway Terrace," Sin said. Lay did, and Sin filled a gas can up with gasoline and called a cab. He drove Shaqui's bucket up two blocks and doused it with the gasoline and threw a lit match in it.

When the cab came, they had the driver drop them off on 65th and Bancroft, where they walked the block to Havenscourt where Lay lived.

Whey they got there, Sin wiped the Mack-10 and the .45 off and gave them to Marco. "Get rid of that shit," Sin told Marco. He and Sha got in the Maxima and went to North Oakland. Sin's Aunt Barbara lived in some Housing Authority apartments on 46th Street.

"Don't mention this shit to nobody, cuz!" Sin warned.

"Come on, blood. You act like I'm stupid. Come through after school. I need to re-up," Sha said.

Three Weeks Later

Sin and Marco were at McDonald's on 68th sitting on June's Benz which Sin was driving that night. They were getting at some top-notch broads when Lay and Angelique pulled up in Hashi's green Chev. They got out of the car and walked over. "Why ya'll always talking to these rat head bitches?" Lay asked.

"Bitch, who you calling a rat head?" the girl Sin was talking to asked.

"You the only rat head I see, bitch!" Lay answered.

"Well if you see a rat head, beat a rat head," the girl said.

Just as Lay was about to hit the girl, five OPD cars pulled into the parking lot. Sin hid his gun in the console of the Benz and rolled up the windows up and locked the doors. Marco slid over to his Mustang and locked it up.

"Hey you! Come here!" one of the cops said.

"What, man?" Marco asked.

"That your car?" the cop asked.

"No, sir. I ain't never seen that car in my life."

"Okay, Mr. Smart Ass. Get against the car," the cop ordered. He searched Marco and found three gees. He stuck that in his pocket and handed Marco off to another cop who put him in a police car. The cop looked in Marco's convertible '66 Mustang and found a gun.

From inside the McDonald's door, Sin saw that the gun was the nickel-plated .45 he used to kill Rich with. Sin almost had a heart attack right then. *This nigga didn't get rid of the gun! Fuck, fuck, fuck!* he thought.

Once the cops hauled Marco off, Sin hot-wired the Mustang and had Lay take it to Marco's mama's house. He stayed at Marco's house until he called three hours later.

"Man, what was you thinking about?" Sin asked.

"Don't trip, bro. I'm going to ride this one out. I need you to look out for my mom. Look out for Tara too. She's about to have my son. You know where my scratch (money) at. Put it on a lawyer for me."

"I got you," Sin said.

On May 20th, 1986, Marco pleaded guilty to manslaughter. He was sentenced to juvenile life, which meant he would be in Youth Authority until he was twenty-five unless he caught some more time. He did, for shanking three white boys when he was nineteen. The judge gave him another five years, and committed him to State Prison.

Marco was a straight rider in the pen. The OG's from different gangs tried to recruit him, but Marco wasn't for it. He stayed solo and didn't fuck with anyone who was affiliated with a gang. To him the weak joined prison gangs for protection. He had heard that a lot of weak dudes were getting up under the Mad Circle too. He would be out in June 2000, and every fake-ass nigga in The Circle was going to get dealt with. His inner circle was the only ones to look out for him and his family. Sin, Shaqui, Tariq, Hashi, Scatter, Hasahn, Amir, and June Bug kept it real.

Tariq, Scatter, and Sin all put up money to buy Marco's mother a house down the street from Tariq's in Lafayette. Sin gave Marco's mother money every other month in the sum of $10,000.00. Shaqui made sure Tara and Marco's son, Marco Jr. were straight. Even though Tara was stripping at a club in Pleasanton when Sin asked her not to, they still looked out.

Present

"Michaels, step out!" the 2nd tier C.O yelled.

Sin stepped out of the cell when the door opened and saw Marco coming down the tier with another bag. "How did you know I was coming today?" Sin asked.

"Somebody called Shaunté, and she called Déja. Déja told me when I called her this morning," Marco replied. He and Sin hugged and held each other for a minute.

"Blood, I missed you," Marco said.

"I missed you too. Damn, nigga, what you doing, hitting everything on the weight pile?" Sin asked.

"Shit, I was way bigger than this. They took the weights. Now all I do is pull ups and dips."

"That's what I do in the streets, bro. Pull up on suckas and dip on marks," Sin said.

"Nigga, I heard you out there killing them in the streets. They're like, when the droughts come, you and The Circle are the only ones out there with dope."

"Maniac, I'm going to keep it all the way clean with you. I'm in with some muthafuckas that got everything. I got damn near all of Northern Cali sold up. Nigga, the money I got put up for you is close to a mill ticket. You don't need no loot do you?"

"Man, come on. I got like damn near twenty gees on my books. I get out in June. I won't even be able to spend all that. Plus the money you, Scatter, and Tariq gave my mother for me. What's up with Scatter, man? He aight in the Feds?" Marco asked.

"I'm hot at him, Tariq, and Eddie," Sin said then looked in his cell at Slo Moe. He stepped closer to Marco. "Them niggas hit a lick for 100 mil. They straight robbed Scatter's Colombian connect. Them niggas did it three days before I got home. I guess the Colombian told Scatter the only way he was getting out the game was paying them five mil or dying. Dude must have thought Scatter was a peanut or something," Sin whispered.

"God damn! Them niggas caked up," Marco said.

"Shit, Scatter was caked up before that. He already had his real estate company and car lot. Then Tariq works for Taiochi Limited. He's the CEO. He makes like 2.5 million a year. He married my lawyer," Sin said.

"What's up with little Sha?" Marco asked.

"That nigga ain't little no more. Sha getting his money. He *had* this down-ass white broad named Erica. They got a four-year-old son. His new broad, Tenesha just had a little girl. I ain't feeling that bitch though. She seem like she shady. I fucks with Sha, but that nigga got a gambling problem or he spending too much. He don't stack his money. Other than that, everything's everything," he said.

"What's up with Lay?" Marco asked.

"Fuck Lay! I ain't seen her and don't want to."

"You still mad because she had that abortion?"

"Nigga, Lay was on some other shit."

"Sha ever find out you was fucking her?"

"Nah, because I wasn't fucking her no more. She came to me and told me she was pregnant after she started fucking Sha. Shit, Malika was gone. I was ready to wife her up. She says she got the abortion because she didn't know who she was pregnant by, and she was really digging Sha and didn't want to break his heart. Last I heard that bitch was in Miami married some corporate nigga."

"So you seen little Marco?" he asked.

"I bought that nigga a motorcycle for his birthday," Sin said.

"Yeah, Tara told me. She was mad about that too. So what's up with her?"

Sin didn't want to tell Marco his baby mama was dancing at a club. "She aight," he said instead.

"She told me she was dancing. I don't know why she doing that shit. Ya'll be looking out, plus I send her money. She be saying that all that money me and my niggas be sending her she uses for Lil' Marco," he said as he looked at his watch.

"I gotta get to my unit. Your counselor is this chick that used to go to Fremont with you. Her name is Jada Kerry. She's like a year younger than you. Tell her you want to stay in Quentin. Here, take this shit before I forget," Marco said as he handed Sin a Black & Mild box with five blunts in it, and the trash bag he brought with him. "I love you, blood. If you have any problems *I'll* handle it," Marco said as he looked in the cell, then yelled, "Nigga, let my brother have that bottom bunk!" Slo Moe didn't even try to argue, he just moved his stuff.

"I'll be by here tomorrow," Marco said and walked off.

Sin stepped back in his cell.

"Slo, you could keep your bunk. I ain't on it like that," Sin said. Slo Moe put his stuff back down on the bottom bunk.

The guards did count at 4:00, and as soon as they cleared the tier Sin pulled out a blunt.

"I always knew you was a smooth muthafucka, Sin," Slo said. Sin tossed him the blunt.

"Fire that up, cousin," he said as he posted up by the bars keeping point (watching out). Sin and Slo switched spots, and Sin hit the weed. About five minutes after they finished, the doors popped for dinner. Slo and Sin were over-high as they went to chow. After that first meal, Sin vowed right then to never eat in the chow hall again.

The next six months went by fast. Sin and Shaunté had conjugal visits every thirty days due to Sin having

Shaunté send the family visiting clerk a hundred bucks a month.

On February 10, 2000 Shaunté gave birth to a baby girl, whom they named Unique Simi Michaels.

Sin got visits from his mom, Malika, the kids, Maria, Anita, and one day when he talked to Mario, Sonia was over there. She came and saw him too. What really made Sin smile was Malika's commitment. She shot him mail every day, was home when he called, and shot him some pictures of her in lingerie. Well, all his chicks did it, especially Yanna, and surprisingly, Keena did it to. Keena was coming to visit every chance she got. Tracy came and saw him a couple of times. She let him know that the basketball player she was seeing had proposed, and she was thinking about marrying him.

Chapter Sixteen

Looking At Things Clearly

May 6, 2000, Sin stepped out of San Quentin. He heard a horn blow and looked in that direction and saw Shaunté's Benz. He walked towards the car as Shaunté got out holding the baby. Sin walked up and kissed her then the baby. They got in the car and Shaunté pulled off.

"Take me to your house to get my truck. What's the word on that sucka, Bo?" he asked.

"That nigga name poppin' like a muthafucka. He been getting money for real. I heard he be in North Carolina too. I can't believe muthafuckas still fuck with that nigga even though we put the word out he hot (snitching). I didn't want to tell you this, but him and Max done joined up together," she informed him.

"That's aight, because they about to die together.," Sin said.

When they got to Shaunté's house in Alameda by the beach, she pulled into the driveway. She hit the garage door opener and the door raised. Inside was her Range Rover and Sin's Navigator.

"Your SS and Chevelle are at your house on Sequoia," she said. They got out of the car and went in the house.

While laying on her bed with Sin and their daughter, Shaunté told him what had been happening.

"Them 61st Street niggas been at us. Them niggas shot at me one night when me and Déja were leaving the club. Sha went and lit a couple of them niggas up behind that shit."

"Don't even worry about it. I'm going to go on and have Carlos get them niggas. I let it go when them niggas shot me because Sha say he got the nigga that did it, and them other niggas didn't know about it. I ain't about to give them suckas no more passes. So how Davy been doing in school?" Sin asked.

"Since he came and visited you and you told him he had to go stay with Lisa, his grades went back up. June just gave his car back, but Terell still don't let him get money on the block."

"'Tay, what's up with you, baby?" Sin asked.

"Nothing really. I'm just glad you home so I can get out of the streets."

"I'm talking about with us."

"I'm seeing somebody, Sin. I haven't had sex with him yet because I've been fucking you. Those conjugal visits were for you. I'm never going to forgive you for fucking Lisa."

"I know I was wrong for that, baby, and I've constantly thought about it. I'm sorry, 'Tay. Baby, you had a nigga off his square. I love you though, baby."

"Sin, why do you want to be with me? The only time we really get along is when we're not together or when we're fucking. Man, you a dog. I can't take you doggin' me out like you do. You just don't know how serious I was about killing you and that smart mouth bitch, Sheree when you bought her on the block that day," she said.

"What if I bought you a ring and set a date? Would you marry a nigga?" he asked.

Shaunté shook her head no. Even though that's what she wanted more than anything in the world, she knew that Sin would never do right. "No, because it ain't in your blood to be a one woman man. I deserve to be treated like I mean something. When we first got together you loved me like your next breath," she said sadly.

"Tay, what fucked that up, huh?" he asked.

"You cheating on me with Jaunda and Shaunda."

"Oh, you mean the night that you were in Reno with that ancient ass nigga. You know what? You're right," Sin said as he put on his shoes.

"Where you going?" she asked.

"Where I should have went in the first place," he said as he put his coat on.

Sin kissed his daughter then kissed Shaunté. He went to the bedroom door and stopped and looked at

'Tay. "I don't give a *fuck* who you with. You know you mine forever," he said.

"I know."

"Can I have that pussy whenever I want it?" he asked

"No question. Can I have that dick whenever I want it?" she asked.

"No doubt, baby," he said and left.

Sin went in Shaunté's garage and pulled the cover off of his Navigator. He got in it and pulled out and left. Just as he was coming over the Alameda Bridge he saw a florist. He had a thought and pulled over. He went in and bought two dozen red roses and a bag of rose petals. When he got outside to the truck he called The Lucky Dragon and ordered food. He then got on Interstate 880 East. He pulled his phone out and called Anita.

"Hello?" she answered.

"Anita, what's up, baby?" he asked.

Anita sucked her teeth when she heard Sin's voice. "I can't talk right now," she said and hung up. Sin knew she was still salty. Anita had shown up to visit on a Friday when their regular day was Sunday. Sin had already had Sonia in there so he refused the visit. That was the last time Anita had tried to come see him, and she wouldn't except his calls. Sin laughed and dialed *67 to block his number, and then called Malika's cell number.

"Hello?" she answered.

"Pooh, I need you to be at home, by 12," he said.

"Who called me for you?" she asked.

"Terell's girl, Cynthia called you on the three way," he lied.

"Why do I need to be home at 12, baby?" she asked.

"Because something's being delivered for you, and before you ask what it is, I ain't telling you. It's a surprise."

"If it ain't you coming home, I don't want it," she said stubbornly.

"I bet you want this!"

"Okay, baby, I'll be there. You gon' call me later on and talk nasty to me again?" she asked.

"You like that freaky shit, huh?"

"Shit, I ain't had no dick in like three months. I may as well play with myself and get a good nut."

"What happened to that cat you was seeing?"

"You really want to know the truth?"

"For sure."

"He wasn't you, and he was a poor imitation of you," she declared.

That made Sin smile. Malika was his baby. He carried her like she was number one. He had even considered proposing. "You love me, Pooh?" he asked.

"You just don't know how much I love you."

"I love you too, baby. I'll be glad when May 24th comes so I can eat that pussy," he said.

"Sin, not right now, baby. You're going to make me touch myself before I go to my meeting."

Sin looked at his watch and saw it was 11. "Baby, you ain't got time to go to a meeting. I don't want what I'm sending you to be out on the porch. You gotta be there when the Over Night Express delivery person gets there."

"Sin, I only have to let my staff know that we'll be working this weekend, then I'm leaving."

"Aight, baby. Oh yeah, Terell dropped my Navigator off. The keys are in the mail slot," he said.

"Oh yeah, I almost forgot. Thank you for buying me the Benz! I'm dropping it off at Hashi's shop Monday to get the rims put on it."

"It's all good. You deserve more than that. You been holding me down as far as collecting my money and running the club."

"Well, don't forget to call me later. I love you, Sin."

"I love you too, Pooh," he said and hung up.

When Sin got off the freeway, he stopped at The Lucky Dragon and picked the food up, then went to Malika's house. He pulled up in the driveway and filled the card out. Sin opened the front door and put the roses on the doorstep. He then went in and went to the garage, and left the keys in the mail slot. He took the food to the kitchen, and went to the family room and looked in Malika's stash spot and found some weed. He stripped the Optimo, and rolled a blunt and smoked.

At 11:30 Sin took a bottle of Moët out of the fridge and put it on ice. At 11:40 he started filling the sunken tub. He went downstairs and got the 112 CD and skipped to *Cupid,* and paused it. At 12:05 he heard Malika pull up. He got undressed and got in the tub.

Malika parked next to Sin's Navigator and walked up the walkway to the front door. She smiled when she saw the roses. She picked them up and pulled the card out and read it. It said: *You're worth a million roses, a billion diamonds, and a lot more. If these flowers don't make you smile, you will soon get a surprise that will.*

Damn, I forgot the rose petals! Sin thought. He got out, grabbed a towel and wiped the suds off of his feet, went into the bedroom and grabbed the bag of rose petals, threw half on the sheets, and the other half in the tub. He got back in and sat back.

When Malika stepped into the house the first thing that hit her was the weed scent. *I'm going to beat this little bitch's ass! She thinks she's going to cut school and be up in here getting high,* Malika thought, assuming it was Simina. She dropped her purse and keys on the table by the front door, went into the kitchen and got a vase, and put her roses in it, then went upstairs. Malika went to Simina's room and looked in and saw she wasn't there. Just then she heard 112's *Cupid* coming from her bedroom.

"No this girl ain't!" Malika said as she stomped to her room. She walked in and saw the rose petals on the bed. Malika heard something in the bathroom. She looked back at the bed then the bathroom doorway. "Ahh *hell* nah!" she said and went to the closet and got the Glock .45 Sin had left there. She stomped into bathroom expecting to see Simina and some boy. When she saw Sin she started jumping up and down screaming, "You're home!"

Sin looked at Malika standing there in the blue Marc Jacobs skirt suit and blue sling back Cavallo heels. Her skirt was tailored fashionably short and fit her sexy wide hips and small waist perfectly. The white silk blouse was sheer enough to slightly see her white silk bra. She had her usually natural curly hair bone straight, looking silky and coming down to her shoulders. Malika was looking sexy as hell.

"Come get in with me and greet me like I been gone six and half months," Sin said.

Malika knew how Sin liked watching her undress. She felt her pussy getting wet at the thought of what was about to happen. She took her diamond necklace and bracelet off and sat them on the counter. She then lit the candles around the bathroom. She looked at Sin and slowly took the suit coat off. Next came the blouse. Malika's titties looked as if they were trying to escape the confines of the bra she was wearing. She reached behind her and unzipped her skirt. It fell to the floor leaving her in her heels, silk stockings with lace at the top, and the white silk g-string.

Malika slightly shuddered as she watched Sin lick his lips. She turned around so he could see her butt. The little string was literally missing in action in the crack of her big sexy butt cheeks. To entice him even more she bent over from the waist and took her shoes off. She rolled the stockings down her legs then unclasped her bra and released the twins. Sin looked at the fifteen-year-old tattoo of his name on her left tittie. Malika's nipples were standing at attention.

"Baby, fuck this slow shit!" she said as she hurried out of her panties and into the water into Sin's arms. They kissed each other passionately and then just stopped and looked at one another.

"Damn, Sin I missed you so much!" she said with tears in her eyes.

"You saw me every week, baby," he said.

Malika touched Sin's face then hugged him tight. "It's not the same."

"I missed you too," he said as he made her sit back. Sin took her feet and washed each one of her toes.

"Are you staying here?" she asked.

"Can I?"

"You know you can. What kinda arrangement will me and you have?"

"Malika, I love you with all my heart. You got my back on whatever, and I couldn't ask for more than that. I want to ask you to marry me, but I want to be strapped with a ring when I do it."

Malika's hand flew to her mouth. The old feelings that she had for Sin were once back again. This was what she wanted. "Sin, you already know what my answer's going to be," she said as the tears returned.

Sin bathed Malika then she bathed him. He carried her out of the tub and into the bedroom and laid her on the bed. He kissed every one of Malika's toes and licked the bottom of her foot, her ankle, and up her leg. He licked behind her knees, between her firm thighs, and across her hip. Sin licked under Malika's three-carat diamond navel piercing, across her toned abs, the side of her left breast and finally the nipple. Sin sucked Malika's nipple like he was a starving infant. He gave her right side, from her hip to her nipple, the same attention.

Malika's nude body squirmed from the sensations she was feeling. She pushed Sin's head downward. When Sin got to her shaved lips, he teased them with feather like strokes. With his thumbs he spread them open and there sat her clit. He wasted no time. He attacked the little man in the boat with his tongue.

Malika's legs, which were over his shoulders, started shaking. She grabbed the sheets and twisted them in her hands. "Oh, Sin, baby! Shit, got-damn! I love you, I love you, baby!" she moaned.

Sin stuck one of his fingers in her, never taking his mouth off of her clit. He reached up and found her lips. Malika took his finger in her mouth and hungrily sucked her wetness off of it.

"Oh, baby I'm about to cum! Sin, got-damn you!" she screamed out as she rotated her hips.

"Who's pussy is this?" he asked.

"It's your pussy, daddy! Ahhhhhhhh!" she screamed. Sin felt Malika's sweet juices when they hit his tongue.

Sin got up and backed away from the bed and just watched her as she laid there shaking.

Malika sat up on shaky arms and looked at him.

"Come here, daddy," she said.

Sin came over to the bed and Malika struggled to get on her knees. She licked Sin's mouth, his chin, and his neck. Only when she got to his chest did she notice how ripped he had gotten. She licked down to Sin's abs which weren't LL ripped, but were damn close.

When she got to his dick, Malika took just the head into her mouth while her tongue went down the underside of his shaft. She then relaxed and took all 9 inches down her throat.

"Oh, fuck!" Sin said as she deep-throated him. Malika started bobbing her head and sucking harder. Sin could only take so much of Malika's throat, tongue, and full lips. "Malika, baby stop. I'm about to bust, baby," he said as he held her head. Malika shook his hands off and kept doing her thing. She was about to get off too, and there was no way she going to stop.

Sin busted off in Malika's mouth and collapsed on the bed, but Malika was far from done. She locked her lips back on his dick again, and sucked it back to life. When Sin's dick was standing straight up again, Malika was on the verge of getting off again. She stopped and straddled him. As soon as Sin was in her she was getting off.

"Damn, I don't know what it is about you, but no one has ever gotten me off like that," she said. Sin frowned at her. "I already know what you're thinking. I've only been with two other people. Joe and ol' boy," she said.

Sin sat up and held Malika's cheeks and kissed her. They went at it, and when Malika started biting her bottom lip, Sin knew she was close to cumming. He laid back and let her do her. Malika grabbed the headboard as she moaned louder. Nothing but her hips moved, in an up-down, side to side motion. As soon as she came

Sin held her as he sat up and just stared into her tight half-closed eyes.

"Are we going to make this shit happen or what? Because for real for real, I'm tired of hoeing around fucking all these different bitches. I can stay at home and get some bomb-ass pussy and head. I ain't gotta be out there chancing that a bitch I stick my dick in might be an undercover cop, might be trying to set me up to get robbed, or worse, killed. I need you, Pooh. I trust you more than I trust anyone," he said all the while stroking Malika.

"Sin, that's all I ever wanted. I'm sorry that I was gone out of your life for as long as I was, and even more sorry for the pain it caused you. I'm more than ready to do this, baby," she said.

"Til death due us part?" he asked.

"Til death due us part." she agreed.

Sin laid Malika back and went as deep as he could, and he made love to her for next hour.

When they were both spent they laid there, and Malika told Sin how she had been meeting Kesha places and letting her spend time with Quesha. Sin had mixed feelings about that, but kept them to himself. He felt that as long as Kesha was with his enemy, then she wasn't above suspicion.

Sin and Malika took another bath together and had another session in the tub. When Malika was walking out the room Sin looked at the way her naked butt moved as if it had a mind of it's on. He reached over and grabbed his phone and called Mario's cell phone.

"Hello?" Mario answered.

"What's up, man?"

"What up, baby boy? You touched down?"

"Yeah, I'm at home."

"Which home? You lay your head everywhere," Mario joked.

"Nah, that shit's over. I'm at home with Malika," Sin said seriously.

"I'm in Fremont at the house. Me and Charmaine will be there in like forty-five minutes."

"Aight," Sin said and hung up.

Malika came back into the room with the Chinese food. They sat naked and ate.

"Sin, I want another baby. I want a son," she said.

"Shit, you gotta quit drinking them," he said and laughed.

"Fuck you, nigga!" Malika said laughing too. "You need to stop sucking my eggs out. You'll end up giving a bitch a hysterectomy," Malika said. They both busted up laughing.

They finished eating and then got dressed. Malika threw on a red Vickie bra and thong, a short, blue denim Baby Phat skirt, a white wife beater with boy beater across the front, and white and red beaded Jimmy Choo's.

Sin put on some blue denim Ecko shorts, a red Marc Ecko T-shirt, Nike ankle socks, and some white and red Nike Shox. He went in the closet and grabbed Malika's jewelry chest, sat it on the dresser, and opened it. He grabbed the platinum and diamond link with the diamond weed leaf, the matching bracelet, his Presidential Rolex with the diamond bezel, and the three-carat diamond earrings.

Malika put her diamond jewels back on except the necklace. She exchanged that with a very small platinum chain with a one-carat pear-shaped diamond pendant. She put the small face Cartier watch on to top it off. She then combed her hair back to perfection.

Sin grabbed a bag out of Malika's closet that had three guns in it. He took one out, checked the clip and put it in his pocket and covered it with his T-shirt.

After Malika cleaned the bathroom and they cleaned the room, they went downstairs. Sin pulled the Tahoe out and washed it up. Malika came out and brought him a bottled water.

"It's hot as fuck out here," he said, and pulled Malika to him and gave her a passion mark on her neck and another one on her cleavage.

Mario and Charmaine pulled up in their Range Rover. Sin walked over and helped nine month pregnant Charmaine out of the truck and hugged her. "What's up, big sis?" he asked.

"Damn, Sin look at you! You super swoll," she said and grabbed his arm.

"Shit, look at you! I didn't think it was possible for you to get more beautiful than you were," he said.

"Yeah right. My fat ass ain't beautiful."

Even pregnant Charmaine was a dime. She was brown-skinned, green eyes, and had a short Toni

Braxton cut, and a nice bubble butt. It wasn't as big as Malika's, but it wasn't far behind either.

Sin then hugged Mario. Malika then greeted them.

"What's all this, little sis?" Mario asked as he touched her neck and nodded at her cleavage. Malika started blushing.

"Well since you here, why don't you ride with me to pick the kids up," Charmaine said.

"Aight, let me get my purse," Malika said and went in the house.

"Sin, you better marry that girl. That girl loves you. When you first caught the case, and even after you got sentenced, she used to call me late at night crying behind you. She's a real rider. She held you down the whole time you were gone. Even though you weren't gone for that long, she didn't have to. You two weren't even together," Charmaine said.

"I kinda asked her today," he said.

"That's what I'm talking about, nigga!" Mario said and dapped him.

"Baby, I'll be back," Malika said as she came out. Sin kissed her. Malika and Charmaine started walking away.

"Baby, you got something on your chin," Sin said.

"What?" she asked as she looked in the passenger side mirror of the Range Rover.

"Theeeese nuuuuts!" Sin said.

"Yeah aight, nigga. Don't forget to floss. You gotta couple of hairs in your teeth!" Malika said. Her and Charmaine high-fived.

"How? You ain't got no hair," he replied.

"That's a little too much info, Sin," Charmaine said as she handed Malika the keys.

The girls left, and Mario told Sin what he had planned.

"Take a ride with me to the Benz dealership. My mama's birthday's tomorrow," Sin said.

"Damn, Charmaine took off with my weed," Mario said.

"Don't trip." Sin said. He went in the house and got an Optimo and a bud out of Malika's stash. He and Mario got in the Tahoe and left.

When they got to the dealership, Sin saw a tight CL600. The car was dark blue with white leather interior. Sin looked at the sticker and saw it went for 120,000. *Yeah, I'll be back for you on my birthday,* he thought. He saw a smoked gray SL500. The sticker said 80,000. There were like five white salesmen just staring at Sin and Mario. A black female approached them.

"Hello, gentlemen. I'm Geneva. May I be of assistance?" she asked.

"Yeah, Geneva. First tell me why them crackers looking at us like we trying to steal something," Mario asked.

"Those racist bastards probably think you are. Don't feel bad, they look at me the same way," she said as she stared at Mario.

Mario looked at her hand and saw that she was married. "Let me ask you a question, sweetheart. How is it that you work in this joint when you can't be more than 18?" he asked.

"That was very flattering, but I'm 30," she said as she grinned at Mario.

"Please say you're not happily married," Mario begged.

"I'm not happily married. What about you?" she asked as she saw the ring that Mario was wearing.

"I am, but for *you*, baby, I'll stray."

"Why don't you take my card," she said and handed Mario a gray business card.

"We having a party for my brother tonight at Club Sin. Why don't you come in and let me pop a bottle of Mo' with you? You do know where Club Sin is, don't you?" Mario asked.

"Shit, who don't know about Sin. That's the hottest spot in the Bay Area," she said.

"Well allow me to introduce you to the proprietor, Sin," Mario said and nodded towards Sin.

"It's nice to meet you, Sin."

"The pleasure's all mine," Sin said and took her hand and held it.

"Whoa, pimpin', unhand her!" Mario playfully said.

"If I must," Sin said.

Geneva started laughing. Both of the guys in front of her were fine, but Mario made her coochie wet. She wasn't getting hit right at home, and he was saying all the right things. She could tell they were having money, and she saw a nice chunky commission coming to her.

"I'm going to fuck the crackers over," Mario said and walked away. "I want one of those S600s, one of those SL600s and a ML," Mario said, pulling out his American Express platinum and the platinum Visa. The white salesmen rushed him.

"Geneva, I want to use this Tahoe as a trade in on this SL500," Sin said.

Geneva looked at the odometer and saw that there were 25,000 miles on the '98 Tahoe.

When it was all said and done, Sin got 20,000 on the trade in. He called Malika and told her to come there to the dealership.

Mario came over to Geneva's cubicle, grinning from ear to ear. "I had to teach the good ol' boys that you can't judge a book by it's cover. When they ran my info, they saw that I'm legally worth 2.8. So when it was time to sign the papers, I didn't."

"Malika's on her way up here with the business account stuff," Sin said.

"Geneva, my wifey on her way up here. I won't be able to say anymore to you. Why don't you take my number and call me when you get to the club and I'll come out and get you so you ain't gotta stand in the line," Mario said as he wrote his number down.

Chapter Seventeen

Daddy's Girls

When Malika pulled up at Sin's mother's house to pick the girls up, she saw that Tracy was there. She and Tracy had gotten cool ever since Sin had gotten shot. She honked the horn and Simina, and Mario and Charmaine's daughter, Ebony came out.

"Ask Tracy if I can take Malik and Quesha with me. Tell her I'll bring them home Sunday night," Malika said. Simina went back in the house and delivered the message. When she came back out, she was followed by Tracy, Ebony's little brother, Brandon, Malik, and Quesha. The kids all piled into the truck.

"Girl, what's up with this passion mark shit? Somebody got some, hmmm?" Tracy asked.

"What, ya didn't know?" Malik asked.

"Anyway, you can keep their little bad asses as long as you want to," Tracy said.

Simina leaned forward to get some gum out of Malika's purse and saw what Malika was wearing. As bad as she wanted to say something, she bit her tongue.

They pulled off and went to Sin. Malika pulled up in front and walked into the club. A new security guy stopped her. "I'm sorry, sweetheart, but we're not open until 9:00," he said.

"I know," Malika said and kept walking.

The dude headed her off. "Well if you know, why are you still trying to gain entry?" he asked getting irritated.

"Look, Fred, call Kira, because you about to piss me off," Malika said now starting to get irritated herself.

"And who should I say wants her?" he asked, not caring one way or another.

"The lady that signs the pay checks," she said.

Fred's eyes ballooned. "I... I..."

Malika raised her hand to stop him from saying whatever it was he was about to say. "It's okay. You're doing a good job," she said and walked away throwing her ass, because she knew he was looking.

She went to Sin's office, which she had taken over, and got the check book and authorization card. When she was leaving, she took in the decorations. The only thing Malika didn't like about the club was the size. It was huge. There were four bars, a kitchen that they hadn't opened up, pool tables, and card and craps tables downstairs. The only people that could go down there were VIP's, and not all VIP's. You had to possess a VIP card that had the Mad Circle hologram, and what High Council Mad Circle member was sponsoring you. At anytime there could be up to three or four hundred thousand dollars circulating down there.

The VIP area on the third level was huge. It could comfortably sit up to 35 people, max. There were high-backed leather sofas all around the perimeter of the area, and it was there that they only dealt with the high-end alcohol, wines and champagnes.

Something else Malika didn't like was the elevator that Sin had installed. You had to get on it to get to the fourth floor where his office, the manager's office, and the electronics room, which controlled the screens that showed videos, as well as the security cameras and monitors were. The lead security guy, Keith was assigned to that room. If anything went down in the club, from an employee stealing to people being let in without being electronically scanned, he was going to be held responsible. Keith had a twenty-man security team that covered the door, the hand-held body scanner, the VIP, the outside of the club, and the club's floor.

Sin was the hottest place to be in Northern California Thursday through Sunday. Malika was the one that started opening on Thursday for the ladies to see male exotic dancers. She knew Sin was going to cut that short when he found out.

Overall, the club made over $300,000, from Thursday through Sunday. The clubs payroll was 7500 for a staff of 30 that only worked 32 hours or less a week. The loans were paid off and it was all profit, and that's not even counting the gambling, which brought in another 100,000 a week, easily.

Malika loved that Sin put the liquor license in her name, and made her a 50/50 partner. She knew it was only on paper, but she still received $10,000. a month legal, and another 25 in cash from the gambling. She didn't have to use any of her paychecks, from her job, or the club. She lived off of that 25 gees a month, which lasted a lot longer than a month. All legal money she received she invested.

As Malika walked out of the club she saw Simina cut her eyes at her. She opened the door to the Range Rover and Simina looked at her in surprise, then turned her lip up.

"What the hell is that?" Simina asked as she pointed to the passion marks on Malika's neck and cleavage.

"I'm grown, child! You must have didn't get enough the other night. This is the last goddamn time I'm going to tell you, stay in your place. If you think I'm playing, we can get out this muthafuckin' truck right now and handle it like we did the other night when you called yourself pushing me!"

"She pushed you?" Charmaine asked.

"Yeah, girl, and I made this little bitch touch everything in that fuckin' room," Malika said.

"This sounds like some shit that got Ebony written all over it. She tried to play me like that, and I beat her ass like she stole something," Charmaine said.

"Well if Ms. Ebony *did* talk her into the ass kicking she got, she'll know better than to listen to that shit again," Malika said.

"Yeah, that's okay, Mama, because I *swear* when I see my daddy Saturday, I'm telling him about them hickeys on your neck and you beating me up," Simina said.

"Handle your business, sister," Malika said as they pulled off.

Simina knew not to say another word. She did not want to get the beat-down she suffered that night. As she thought of it she winced.

Three Days Ago

Malika went into Simina's room and told her to go clean her mess in the kitchen, and Simina sucked her teeth.

"You know what, smart ass? You on punishment," Malika said and unplugged Simina's phone and snatched her cell phone. "Little girl, you gon' make me slap the shit outta you!" she said.

"Mama, I'm not about to keep going for that slapping me shit!" Simina said as she stood up like she was trying to get down.

"You ain't *going* for it?" Malika asked in surprise. Her already tight eyes went to slits as she frowned. "Bitch, then what the fuck you gonna do?" she asked as she threw the phones down.

"Hit me and see, and I ain't no *bitch!* You a bitch!" Simina yelled.

"I'm the bitch that sold you the ass kicking you just bought!" Malika said as she walked up on Simina. Simina pushed Malika, to her surprise. That was all they wrote.

Malika balled up her fist and hit her daughter right in the jaw. Simina flew across the bed and onto the floor on the other side. She got up crying, and rushed

Malika. Malika stopped her in mid-motion, grabbed her shirt and slammed her against the wall by the door, then the wall on the other side of the room, across her vanity table, into the closet doors, through the bathroom door, into the wall in there, back out to the bedroom, and into the original wall again. When she jerked the neck of Simina's shirt, she purposely hit her in the cheek.

Simina started screaming and crying, and throwing wild punches, and hit Malika. When that happened, Simina eyes and mouth opened wide. She knew Malika was going to kill her.

"Mama, I'm sorry! I'm sorry, Mama! I swear to God I didn't mean to!" she screamed.

Malika touched her lip to see if she was bleeding, then her eyes blazed. The look Malika had on her face scared the shit out of Simina. She tried to push Malika and break for the door.

"Nah, bitch don't run now!" Malika yelled as she grabbed Simina's hair before she could get out of the door.

Malika held back a lot. All she wanted to do was show Simina that she was a kid. That's why her punches we're only being delivered with 65% of her power, and they were all head and body shots. She didn't want to mess up her daughter's pretty face for a few reasons. First being, that wasn't what this about. She wasn't the child abusing type of parent. Second, and probably just as important, she would have to take her to see Sin the following Saturday, and he would probably try to strangle her if he saw his daughter swollen up. And third, she wasn't trying to go to jail for chastising her child.

"You trying to kill me!" Simina screamed as she crawled into a corner. Malika slapped the hell out of her three times then stormed out the room. She went to the closet and got one of Sin's guns and took the clip out and made sure that nothing was in the chamber by pulling the slide back three times. *I'm going to put the fear of God in her young ass!* Malika thought. She stomped back into Simina's room with the gun in her hand.

Simina's cries stopped in her throat as she saw the gun. Not a word would come out of her mouth.

"I'm going to tell you like my mama told me. I brought your little spoiled ass into this world, and I'll take your little spoiled ass out of it. Now, who the fuck am I?" Malika yelled.

"M-m-m-my m-m-m-mama," Simina whimpered.

"And who the fuck are you?" Malika yelled again.

"A child."

"Now apologize to me, bitch!" Malika screamed as she started crying.

"I'm sorry, Mommy," Simina cried.

"You take the phones, PlayStation, N64, stereo, and that money you been saving into Malik's room, and leave it in there," Malika said as she wiped her eyes. Simina was still sitting in the corner crying. "Now, goddamn it!" Malika screamed.

"You promise you ain't going to hit me?" Simina asked.

"Girl, if you don't move your ass, me hitting you is going to be the least of your problems," she threatened.

Simina unplugged her games and the TV, and started to push the TV stand. She got as close to the wall as she could while passing Malika. After another ten minutes, everything Simina held dear was stored in her brother's room.

Malika went to her room and cried. She never thought in a million years that she would have to do her baby like that. Simina was Malika's best friend. They were all each other had since Simina was born.

Present

When Malika pulled into the Benz dealership, Sin walked out.

"Is that Uncle Sin?" Ebony asked. Simina and Quesha's heads snapped up.

"Sister, let me out! There goes Daddy!" Quesha screamed, trying to hurry up and get out.

Simina opened the door and flew out. "Daddy!" she screamed and ran to Sin. He hugged his oldest. Then Quesha, who was now 11 and in the sixth grade, came running, and jumped in his arms like she was still a little girl.

"Whoa, Princess. You ain't a little girl no more," he said as he held his girls.

Malik, who was now 10, came walking up looking dead on Sin, from his walk to his smile. The only thing different was Malik's braids, which were in a design and touching the center of his back. Sin pulled him in and hugged him. When Sin saw Ebony walking up, he knew Mario was going to have big problems. Ebony, was Charmaine's twin. Sin opened his arms, and she came to him.

"Welcome, home, Uncle Sin!" she said and kissed him on the cheek.

When Simina walked over to Mario to hug him, he saw how much more she had filled out. She was thicker than her mama.

Malika and Sin went inside and completed the paperwork.

"So now we got another Benz?" Malika asked.

"Not yet. I bought this for my mother's birthday," he said.

"Oh, she is going to love this. Look, I don't want no shit outta you, so I'm going to tell you what your daughter did, and what I did to her," Malika said and told Sin the story. Just telling him made her eyes water.

Sin was pissed off. They walked out, and Sin walked up to Simina gritting his teeth and snatched her arm. "If you *ever* put your hands on your mama again, I will beat your ass! Do you hear me?" he asked.

"Daddy, you're hurting my arm!" Simina cried out.

"Man, let my sister go!" Malik said as he got in between Sin and Simina. Malik was already 5-8, three inches taller than his 14-year-old sister was.

Sin snatched him by his shirt and held him away. "Boy, I will…"

"Let him go!" Simina screamed, pulling Malik back to her.

The way it was going down would be cute if the situation wasn't so serious.

"Ya'll down for each other, huh? Well if you don't answer me, you and this little nigga gon' get your asses beat," Sin said.

"I won't do it no more. She already beat me up. Am I going to get in trouble again?" Simina asked.

"Come on, bro," Sin said to Mario, and they went back to the house.

Sin sat at home with his family catching up on what's been going on with them. Simina went to her room, and didn't come back down. Sin went up and knocked on her door. When she opened it and saw Sin she went and sat back at her desk. He walked in and closed the door. He leaned against the wall and just looked at his daughter.

"Daddy, whatever you have to say, please say it. I know I was outta line, and I deserve whatever punishment you and Mama gave me," Simina said.

"Look, baby girl. I'm going to give it to you raw and uncut. If I would have been here when you put your hands on your mama, I would have put my foot in your ass. You don't do that! We are a family and we gotta be tighter than that. You been acting grown since you got here. I should have checked you a long time ago, but I didn't. So we'll blame that on me. Early tomorrow morning me and you going somewhere. I'm going to give you some responsibility. Since you wanna act like you running shit, that's what you gon' do." He looked at his daughter and laughed.

"What's so funny?" she asked.

"She gots a mean fight game, huh?" he asked.

"I ain't messing with her no more. She kicked my ass, Dad. I thought she was going to kill me!"

"You know she feels bad for that. After she did it, she cried all night. Baby, your mama loves you more than anything, but sometimes you gotta give your kids tough love. I on the other hand will more than likely have to do your brother like that, but I'm going to really fuck him up. So be on point. You ain't gotta worry about me putting my hands on you...unless you do some way outta pocket shit. Now go on in your mama's room, and apologize for that shit you said to her earlier. I ain't mad about that, because you thought she was creeping with some sucka. After you spend a little time with her, go get your stuff and bring it back in here. You got your ass kicked. So why be on punishment too, right?" he asked.

Simina walked over to Sin and hugged him. "I love you, Daddy," she said.

"You better, because your mama's mad at me for letting you off punishment six months early."

"Damn, she was going to leave me on punishment for six months?" she asked.

"Fa sho."

Chapter Eighteen

The King Is Back

At 9:00 Simina had just finished putting the last touches on Malika's hair with the comb. She put Malika's hair back into it's natural curly state and put it into braids at the front and sides for a few inches, and left the rest curly.

"Malika, hurry up, man!" Sin said as he walked in the room wearing light-blue Girbaud jeans, a white T-shirt and butter Tims, and serious bling. He grabbed the beige fitted hat and put it on backwards, and the beige leather coat.

Simina left, and Malika took her robe off. As she stood naked in front of Sin he thought seriously about giving Simina the keys to his Navigator and telling her to take the rest of kids and go stay at Mario's. He was ready for round two.

Malika put on a black g-string, a matching black bra, and skin-tight brown Marc Jacob jeans, which she couldn't zip so Sin had to help her. She put on a brown silk tank and black over the knee Manolo boots. Malika was really going to hurt them. She put on the four-carat emerald cut diamond ring, her diamond tennis bracelet, the three-carat diamond earrings, and her ladies presidential with the diamond bezel. Malika slipped on Sin's three-quarter length black leather coat. Sin grabbed their phones and his gun, and they walked out.

Simina and Ebony were downstairs watching the wide plasma screen. "Mama, ya'll look like ya'll some celebrities," Simina said.

"Pumpkin, ya'll know the drill," Malika said, and they walked out.

They got in Malika's S500 with Sin driving, and they left. When they got to their club, the line was around the block. Sin pulled up and the valet, Rafee came over. "Boss, welcome back!" he said and hugged Sin.

"Rafee, you aight? My wife gave you the raise, right?" Sin asked.

"No doubt. Ms. Malika done looked out, and she holding it down."

"Come up to the VIP and pop a bottle with me later," Sin said as he and Malika walked hand-in-hand to the door.

Sin saw Geneva and some super bad Spanish chick, and waited for them. When they got into the club, Sin sent Geneva and the girl that kept staring at him to get their photos taken for their VIP passes.

"Ol' girl looking at you like I won't beat her muthafuckin' ass," Malika said to Sin.

"Pooh, don't start that insecure bullshit. It ain't na bitch in here that can hold a candle to you. Plus, what I want with one of these sack chasers? You've been tried, tested and proven. I know I ain't got to worry about you doing some outta pocket shit. I should be the one getting mad. Look how this nigga just openly gawking at you like I ain't standing here," Sin said as he grabbed her ass while mean mugging the dude. Ol' boy must have gotten the picture because he quickly turned his head.

Fred, the bouncer, and Kira, the manager stepped up. Kira looked like a Megan Good copy with butt. What really appealed to Sin was her big pretty pouty lips.

Malika made the introductions. While Fred was escorting them to the elevator that would take them to the VIP, a gang of people were welcoming Sin home. The bouncer at the elevator slid a card through the swiper and the doors opened. They got on and Kira waived her pass in front of the card scanner, and the elevator went up. When the doors opened, Sin saw that his pride and joy, the VIP was looking even classier than before.

The first person he saw was Carlos. They hugged, and Sin held Malika's hand and walked to the back table.

"Big cuzzo, what's up nigga?" Shaqui yelled and got up and hugged Sin.

"What's crackin'?" Sin yelled. He hugged Hashi and his girl, Angel, Hasahn and his girl, Brianna, Tayshaun and his girl, Tyisha, and Tariq and his wife, Ayanna.

"Ya-ya, we need to chop it up," Sin said.

"You can take me to lunch Monday. Let's say, 12:30," she said.

Sin walked up and hugged his brother. "Good lookin' out, June" he said. Sin had Mario feed June with a long handle spoon while he was gone. He let June get the work for 10 a key. June moved the work and split the profit with Sin.

Malika was picking up money from June, Sha, and Shaunté, whom she couldn't stand because of how she bragged about how she was taking the baby up to see Sin on conjugals. She was picking up money from Lisa and Yanna too.

Mario looked up and saw Geneva come in. He immediately looked at Malika to see if she was paying attention. He slid away from their table and headed Geneva and her friend Elaina off, and directed them to another table where they all got familiar.

Unfortunately, Malika did peep them. She moved away from Sin while he was talking to Hasahn. She stepped up to the table where Mario and the females were and sat next to him.

"Big bro, what's really going on?" she asked as she looked at Geneva. "Geneva, right?" she asked.

"Yes," Geneva answered.

"I wanted to talk to you about something else anyway. You remember that blue CL600 *my husband* was looking at?" Malika asked for Elaina's benefit.

"Yeah, I remember. He said he was going to come back and get it for his birthday," Geneva said.

"I would like to order it with every option on it. His birthday's next month on the 15th. So that means we have a month."

"Come in tomorrow and we'll do the paperwork."

"I get off at 2." Malika said.

"That's fine. Will you be needing financing? That's my girl, Elaina's department," Geneva said.

Malika looked Elaina up and down. "I don't think so. I'm paying cash."

"That car fully loaded is going to cost you 125,000," Geneva said.

"So, you better be ready to count," Malika said. She gave Mario the 'I'm watching you' look then left.

The DJ played DMX & Eve's *Why Do Good Girls Like Bad Guys*. Malika took Sin's hand and led him down to the dance floor. As they were grooving, Sin saw something that he knew he had to be imagining. He focused again, and sure enough, it was Bo, Marv, Max, and some cat Sin didn't know coming in.

"Go up to the VIP and get Sha, Hash, Tayshaun, and Hasahn! Then go to the office and stay there. Some shit about to jump off," Sin told Malika.

"Sin, be careful," she said and kissed him and hurried to the elevator.

Sin kept his eye on the enemy. He discreetly pulled out the Glock 45 and racked the slide.

Sha, Mario, Hash, Hashan, June and Tayshaun all got off the elevator and came face to face with Max and Bo and company. Sin walked up behind them.

"You niggas must be high to come up in here!" Sha said.

"Nigga, this shit ain't ya'll shit! We can come up in here if we muthafuckin' want to," Max said.

"Nah, bitch ass nigga, that's where you wrong," Sin said. Bo and Max turned and saw Sin and got spooked. "You didn't see the name on the sign? It says *Sin*, muthafucka. You and this hot (snitching) ass nigga already living on borrowed time. I suggest you take this pass I'm giving ya'll and go spend it with your families, because I'm killing you niggas."

Max nodded at somebody, and Sin heard guns cocking. Tayshaun, Hasahn, June and Sha all pointed their guns at Max and Bo. Sin and Mario pointed theirs at them also. Sin was going to fuck the dude doing the electronic scanning up. There was no way that many people should have gotten in with guns.

"Check, nigga!" Shaunté said as she moved in and stood in front of Sin with her gun pointed at Max.

"Is it going to be a mate?" Sin asked.

Max motioned for his boys to put their weapons away. The crowd sighed with relief. Sin had just noticed that the music went off, and everyone was looking at them.

As soon as the bouncer in front of the elevator saw what was going on, he contacted Kirk in the electronics room.

Kirk zoomed in with a camera. He picked up his walkie-talkie. "Code two, VIP elevator!" he yelled. His men knew a code two meant there were guns in the club and a potential threat. When they got there, they saw that there were at least twelve guns out.

Sin and his folks tucked their guns. Kira rushed over to Sin and he leaned down and whispered something in her ear.

"Escort these gentlemen out," she said to the bouncers.

Max gave Sin a look of hate. Bo didn't even make eye contact.

"Max, you fucking with that weak-ass nigga. He get pressed by the police, he telling," Sin said.

After the enemy was escorted out, Sin whispered some other stuff in Kira's ear before he and his clique got on the elevator.

"Drinks on me!" she yelled to the bartenders.

Kira tapped her earpiece and looked at the DJ. Juvenile's song, *G-Code* came on pounding. Kira looked at Big Fred. "Have someone go relieve Greg of the scanner and bring his ass to my office," she said as she called for the elevator. She got on and went to the fourth floor. She got off and went to Sin's office where everyone was.

When Fred knocked on the door, Kira opened it and stepped to the side. Fred pushed Greg in. Sin pushed 'play' on the remote, and the wide screen showed a picture of Marv sliding Greg some money, and he and the others passing by Greg without getting scanned.

Sha walked up to Greg and put the Sig Sauer to his head. "Empty your pockets, bitch," he said. Greg took about a gee out his pocket.

Sin stood up and opened the office door. "Kira, you might not want to see what I'm about to do this nigga," he said.

"Boss, I'm a big girl," she said and licked her lips. The look she gave Sin made him want to take her down right then. He shrugged his shoulders and shut the door.

Sin grabbed a lead crystal paperweight and wrapped it in a cloth napkin. He walked up to Greg and swung it, and cracked his kneecap. Greg screamed out and fell to the floor.

"Nah, Cuzzo that ain't the one," Sha said as he looked around the office. His eyes stopped on a steak knife on the counter where the sink was. He walked over and grabbed it, some salt, and a bottle of Bombay from the bar.

"We ain't fixing to get all that blood in my office," Sin said. Everybody looked at Sha like he was crazy. Sin went to work on Greg's body. When he got tired Sha started in. When it was over, Greg was barely hanging on to his life. Most of his bones, from his feet to his shoulders, to his hands, were broken or shattered.

"Get him out of here," Sin said.

Later on while enroute to the house, Sin thought about what he did and felt bad. He was only going to fire Greg at first, but he got to thinking about if some gunplay had jumped off and innocent people got hurt or worse if Malika got hurt. He looked at her and squeezed her hand.

Malika looked at him, and read what was in his eyes. "I love you too, baby," she said.

When they got home, they had a slow deep session then went to sleep.

The next morning the alarm went off at 6:00 waking Malika up. She slipped out of the bed and went and got in the shower. When she got out, she put on a red thong and bra, a pair of tight fitting blue DKNY jeans, a DKNY T-shirt, and some DKNY sneakers. She brushed her teeth and took the scarf off of her head. She kissed Sin then left to work.

Sin got up at 8:30 and planned his whole day out as he took his shower. When he got out of the shower, he put on loose fitting blue Polo shorts, a crisp white T-shirt, a blue sweater vest over that, and some white and blue Air Max. As he brushed his teeth his phone rang. "Yo?" he answered.

"Sin, you could have at least called a nigga and told me you were out," Davy said.

"Nigga, you lucky I ain't seen you. You outta pocket for them bullshit-ass grades. Meet me at my mama's house at 3:00," Sin said and hung up.

He put on his ice and grabbed his gun, phone, two-way and white Cal hoodie and went downstairs. Quesha was in the family room on the computer. Sin came up behind her and saw that she was on a music preview website.

"Daddy, can I go to my mama's house this weekend?" she asked. In light of what happened last night he wanted to say "Shit no", but he didn't want to deprive Quesha of spending time with Kesha.

"I'll let you know later. Why don't you go upstairs and get dressed. I'm going to get the other kids something to eat. Be ready to leave when I get back."

Sin picked the phone up and called Denny's and ordered everyone their favorite meals. He walked out of the house and went and got in his mom's SL500 and went and picked the food up. When he got back 30 minutes later and took the food in, Quesha was dressed and ready.

"Go wake your sister up and tell her you going with me" he said as he went to the kitchen.

Sin took Quesha out to breakfast then they went to Princess Cuts in San Francisco. They walked in the store and Sin pulled Malika's three-carat yellow diamond ring out and went straight to the ring section.

Quesha looked around at the other stuff. "Excuse me, ma'am. May I see these earrings?" she asked an Asian saleslady. The girl came over and pulled the half-carat diamond studs out.

Sin got a white saleslady's attention. She walked over, looking unenthused. She evidently didn't know who Sin was or that he spent so much money in the store, or that he and the store manager, Joseph were on a first name basis.

"May I please see this ring?" he asked. The lady pulled out the ring. It had a huge yellow diamond in the center surrounded by four regular diamonds. "How many carats are the diamonds?"

"The yellow diamond is five-carats. It has a princess cut. The other diamonds are all 1½-carat baguettes. The yellow diamond is raised a sixteenth of an inch higher than the other diamonds, and they are all set in platinum. The band is also platinum," she said.

"Now the big question. How much is this beautiful ring?" he asked.

"One hundred thousand dollars."

"Damn! If I propose to someone with this ring do you think she'd say yes?" he asked.

"Hell, if she doesn't, you come back, because I sure as hell would!" she said.

Sin smiled and the woman almost melted. "Tell Joseph an old friend of his is out here," Sin said as he gave her the platinum American Express.

Quesha came walking over with the look that Sin knew meant she wanted something. "Daddy, I saw these banging earrings over there. May I please have them?" she asked.

"Yes, princess. Tell them you want four other pair for your sisters and Ebony too," he said. Quesha hurried back over to the saleslady.

Joseph Giraud came out of the office area. The pale 4-11 blue eyed white man looked like a racist, but that was the furthest thing from the truth. The only color Joseph took preference to, was green.

"Sin, welcome home. A few days after that unfortunate incident, Shaunté came in and told me about it firsthand." he said as he clasped Sin's hand.

"Joseph, I came in here to get an engagement ring. Hook me up, 'cause I ain't trying to spend 100 racks," Sin said.

"I'll tell you what. Give me 90,000," Joseph said.

"Well you need to catch the chick with my credit card. Oh, and that's my daughter over there, put her stuff on the bill too. I want that ring sized the same as this one," Sin said as he gave Joseph Malika's ring.

Once Sin got his card and Malika's ring, Joseph told him to come back and pick the new ring up at 12. Sin looked at his watch and saw it was 10. He and Quesha left. Sin thought about Tia. He knew she worked Saturdays so he called her.

"This is Tiara Evans," she answered.

"What's up, Ms. Evans?" he asked.

"Sin?"

"No other."

"Oh, are you home?" she asked.

"No, not for a couple more weeks. I'm calling to tell you that my little brother, BG that you met is about to drop a gift off for you."

"What's his real name again? I'll have security to let him come up."

"It's David. Look, Tia, I'll call you later. They calling lock down," he said.

"Sin, take care of yourself. I'm going to try to come see you this coming Friday."

"Aight, baby," he said and hung up.

Sin pulled up to Bank of America's Western Regional offices and parked right in front. "I'll be right back, baby," he said to Quesha. "And don't drive off!"

"Wrong daughter, Daddy," she said.

Sin walked up to the door and pushed the call button. A middle-aged white guard stepped up. "I'm here to see Tiara Evans," Sin said. The guard let him in.

Sin entered the elevator and went to the 21st floor. When the doors opened, Tia was standing there. She saw Sin and dropped her purse and jumped into his arms. Sin wasn't expecting this type of reaction. He sat Tia down.

"Oh, I didn't know you were out!" she said and hugged him again, pressing her body tightly against him.

Sin's dick started getting hard. "Damn, you miss me or what?" he asked.

"It feels like you missed me too," she said as she backed away and looked down.

"I can't stay long. My daughter's in the car. Damn, you look good!"

"So do you. Look how big your arms got," she said as she backed away a little further. Tia felt her juices flowing. She wanted Sin in a bad way. He could have already had her in her hot tub if he would have been persistent against her playing hard to get, because for real that's all it was, playing.

"So how's the wife and kids?" she asked.

"They're good. The kids are growing too fast. Look Tia, fuck the beating around the bush. What I gotta do, to taste you?" he asked.

"I'm tempted to take you in my office and let you have your way. If you're serious, be at my house tomorrow night at 7:30," she said.

Sin looked at her in surprise. He couldn't believe she conceded. "You really going to give me some?" he asked.

"Eat you a pound of oysters, pop a Red Bull, or take some ecstasy, because you're going to have your work cut out," she said while pointing down to her crotch. "Nothing that wasn't battery powered has been in here in two months."

"What happened to the little white boy?"

"You just said it, little!" she said and spread her thumb and forefinger three inches apart.

"Oh, you ready for some of this Mandingo, huh?"

"Shut up!" she said and playfully pushed him.

Sin pulled her to him and they kissed. Tia slipped her tongue in his mouth. He slipped his hands in her sweatpants and squeezed her butt.

"Come downstairs and meet my little girl. Well her ass ain't little no more," he said. They got on the elevator and Sin and Tia kissed all the way down 21 floors.

Chapter Nineteen

Play The Hand Dealt

Sin went back home and got Malik and Simina, and let Simina drive them around in the Navigator. The first place Sin went was to look at an apartment. It was not too far from where he and Malika stayed when they were younger. It was a two-bedroom apartment in a secure building. It fit what he needed it for. The rent was a thousand dollars a month.

Sin went and got five postal money orders, which totaled five-thousand dollars. He went back to the apartment and told the manager if he let him move in right away he would pay the two-thousand dollar security deposit and the rent up for ten months right then. He agreed, and Sin gave him the money orders and seven-thousand cash.

Their next stop was to Reed Brothers Security where Sin purchased a safe that was so big they would have to remove the apartment's front door and closet door to fit it into the closet in the spare bedroom.

Their last stop was to the mall. They went into the furniture store and Sin bought furniture for the whole apartment. They went to Circuit City and got all the electronics. They then hit Super K-Mart and got everything else the spot would need.

"What I'm going to be doing is giving you money to go in that apartment and count, and lock in the safe. The only two people that know about that apartment are me and you. I don't want anyone else knowing about it. You and me are the only ones that know the combination, and have keys to the spot. Under *no* circumstances do you fuck with that money. I'm going to give you 500 every week, and if you be cool I'll take you and buy you a car on your next birthday," he said.

"Okay, dad. Don't even sweat that. I got you," Simina said.

"I'm serious. *No one* goes in that muthafucka but us."

After Sin dropped the kids off at home he went to the club to go over the books. Time slipped away and before he knew it, it was 3:00. His cell rang and he saw the house number on the caller ID.

"Hello?"

"Sin, you know that we have to hurry up and get to your mama's house," Malika said.

"Baby, I'm at the club. Just bring me something to wear."

"I'm going to drop the kids off then come there."

"Aight," he said and hung up.

When Malika got there, it was 3:45. She was in a yellow Tracy Reese original. The dress was a halter that was sexy and classy. On her feet were yellow beaded Jimmy Choo's. She was absolutely beautiful.

She handed Sin a bag and he went in his private bathroom and showered. When he finished, he put on the beige silk boxers and came out. Malika helped him lotion down. He took the outfit out of the garment bag and nodded. He slipped on the beige button up, then the tan Hugo Boss suit, the tan tie, and his tan gator boots. He kept on the same jewelry minus the chain. That he put on Malika.

Malika had on her left ring finger the half-carat diamond solitaire that Sin bought her for her fifteenth birthday. On the right ring finger was the three-carat yellow diamond. On her wrists were the diamond tennis bracelet and her Cartier watch. She had another tennis bracelet on her ankle.

"You look beautiful, *mami*," he told her.

"You looking pretty dapper yourself, *papi*."

Malika slipped on her tinted lensed Cartier frames, and Sin slipped on his Hugo Boss clear lenses. He handed Malika his gun and they left.

When Sin pulled up at his mother's, there were two extra-long Hummer Limos parked out front, and the kids were all outside. Sin tied the red bow around the Benz and went in.

"Boy, when you get out?" Sin's Aunt Barbara asked.

Sin's mother, Jackie turned quickly and saw her baby boy standing there and screamed, "My baby! My baby's home!" Sin hurried to his mother and hugged and kissed her on the cheek.

"Granny, come look at what my daddy bought you," Quesha said as she took her grandmother's hand and led her to the door.

"Oh, baby, thank you!" she said and kissed Sin on the cheek.

He dropped the keys in her hand, and as they went down the stairs, Tracy and her fiancé were pulling up. *This bitch's outta pocket,* Sin thought.

Shaunté and her male friend came next. Sin stood there stunned. He couldn't believe either one of them had the nerve to do some shit like that. Shaunté walked up and handed Simina her baby sister. Tracy and her dude walked up next. Sin was going to check them both.

Just then Yvette pulled up in her new BMW X5 truck.

Simara jumped out of the truck before it came to a complete stop. "Daddy!" she screamed and ran to Sin.

"Hey, 'Mara," Sin said and kissed her.

"Happy birthday, Grandma!" she said and hugged Jackie.

When Tracy walked up she knew Sin was mad. They all went back in the house and Sin pulled her to the side. "You outta pocket for bringing ol' boy over here! Since you wanna play foul, we gon' play foul. Quesha's going to come live with me," he said.

"Nigga, you crazy! My baby ain't fixing to be raised by one of your bitches," Tracy said.

"She's going to live with me and Malika. The next nigga ain't going to raise my daughter."

"But he can raise your son?"

"Malik's *our* son. Quesha's *my* daughter. This ain't up for debate. I told you what's up and that's that," he said and walked away.

Sin caught Shaunté in the kitchen. "Bitch, I ought to slap the shit outta you! How the fuck you just gon' bring the next nigga to my mama's house?" he asked.

"Sin, I already told you if you put your hands on me again I was going to *kill* you. Now if you think I'm playing, try me!" Shaunté calmly said.

Sin snatched Shaunté by her shirt and slammed her against the refrigerator. "Hoe, don't you ever threaten me again!"

"Let me go! You just mad because I ain't chasing behind you no more," she said.

Sin let her go and said, "Girl, if I didn't love you I'd fuck your pretty face, up." He then walked out the kitchen and went and sat next to Malika.

"Baby, you know I've loved you for fifteen years. You are smart as hell, you're beautiful, you got a banging body, the sex is straight fire, and the way we do our thing is unbelievable. What I'm trying to say is, baby you gonna marry a nigga or what?" he whispered in her ear as he pulled the box out of his pocket and opened it.

Malika gasped and screamed. Everybody in the house came to see what was wrong. All the females gasped at the sight of the ring. Tracy unconsciously looked at the ring her fiancé, Steve bought her. It was no where as lovely as Malika's. Tracy's ring was a clear five-carat emerald cut solitaire.

Malika had tears in her eyes. She pulled Sin's face to her and kissed him. When she pulled away, she was smiling. "Nigga, that was a ghetto-ass proposal. What the hell is, *Baby, you gonna marry a nigga or what*, Sin?" she asked.

"Tell him girl!" Sha's mother, Sin's Aunt Barbara said.

"I love that ghetto shit though. Yeah, nigga, I'll marry your ass!" she said.

Sin took the little half-carat off her finger and put the new ring on it. He then kissed her.

Mario and Charmaine, June and LaToya, Sha and Tenesha, and his brother, Brian and his baby mama, Sanaa came in. Everybody went outside, got in the Limos, and went to Spenger's in Berkeley.

Sin really didn't want to go to Berkeley because of the war. Sha and June had their boys go there to make sure that the other side didn't catch them slipping. So far everyone has been respecting the code of leaving one's family out the beef, unless they were in it. Sin's mother actually lived three blocks from 61st Street, on, 63rd.

When Davy walked in, Ebony's eyes lit up. Sin caught them making eyes at each other. He pulled Davy out of the banquet room. "Look, nigga, you been running too wild. I want you to go get your shit from Lisa's. You moving to Dublin with me. I'm only going to tell you this once, and if you violate, I'm killing you. Don't be fucking around with my daughter."

Davy frowned at Sin and said, "Nigga, that's like my sister! Man, if you thinking like that, fuck you! I don't want to mess with you no more. On no level, business or otherwise."

"Man, who the fuck you talking to? I'll beat your muthafuckin' ass, fool!" Sin said as his temper rose.

Malika couldn't hear what was going on across the room, but she saw Sin looking like he was going to do something to Davy. She got up, and went over to them. She didn't want Davy to have any drama with Sin. Davy was like a son to her, and he worshipped Sin.

"Man, I ain't scared of you! You outta pocket for even saying some shit like that to me!" Davy said like he wanted to get down.

"What's up with ya'll?" Malika asked as she got between them.

"This nigga gon' tell me he want me to come live with ya'll, then say I bet' not be fucking around with 'Mina or he gon' kill me. I ain't never looked at 'Mina no other way than being my sister!" Davy said looking at Sin crazy.

"First off, you better watch your mouth! You ain't grown! Second, Sin, you wrong! Davy keeps them little niggas away from our baby. Ya'll need to squash that shit," Malika said.

"Yeah, whateva'. Nigga, you think you hard, huh? We gon' see how hard you are next time you get in trouble at school or get outta line," Sin said as he walked away.

Malika gave Davy her house keys and told him, "Go get you a set of keys made, then go get your stuff."

Davy looked into the banquet room and mean mugged Sin again then left. Malika came back in and sat next to Sin. She took his hand. "The girls wanna have a ladies night. Is that all right with you?" she asked.

"Where ya'll going?" he asked.

"More than likely we'll just get a suite somewhere and get drunk and talk shit all night."

"Bro, let her go. We can go have a guys night," Mario said.

"Aight, it's cool," Sin said.

Sin found out that Malika, Simone, Cynthia, Charmaine, Tracy, and Sonia were going. When they got back to Sin's mom's house, everybody made plans on where they were going to meet. Sin took the kids home.

"Shamika, Ebony, and Jasmine are staying the night," Malika told him as they changed clothes.

Sin just looked at her.

"Sin, if you don't want me to go, I won't," she said as she walked up to him in her underwear.

"Nah, go on and do your thang, baby," he said as he put his arms around her and grabbed her cheeks. "Can I see if the pussy's any different since we're engaged now?" he asked.

"Baby, it's too many kids up in here right now."

When Mario and Charmaine came back, Sin had just finished packing his overnight bag.

"Mario, don't be giving my money to none of them bum-ass stripper bitches!" Charmaine warned him.

Sin and Malika kissed, then he got in the Range Rover and Mario pulled off. Sin fired up the weed as Mario told him the plan. "I'm fuckin' Geneva tonight. Her potna, Elaina wants to see you about something," he said.

"Hook it up," Sin said half-heartedly.

"Call the fellas and see if they all wanna go to Reno. We can leave by 7 and get there by 10:30."

Sin called Sha, who was with it, Hash was with it, June Bug was with it, and Hasahn was with it.

At 7, Sin and Elaina were in the car with Mario. Hash and some chick named Debra were in the car with Hasahn and his kids mother, Marie. June and Jae, who came down for the weekend, were in his Suburban, along with Sha and Teesa.

"So, I finally get to spend some time with you," Elaina said.

Sin had to admit that she was fine as hell and had a cold body. "Yeah for sure, baby. So what you trying to do?" he asked her.

"I'm trying to get a room with a hot tub, take my clothes off, and what happens after that, just happens," she said.

"I'm feeling that. So you gotta man?" he asked.

"Yes, but tonight *you're* my man," she said as she got closer to Sin.

"Is that right?" he asked.

"For sure, boo," she said as she rubbed his chest. "I know you have a woman. So let's leave what happens in Reno, in Reno!"

"I ain't got no problem with that. So what you cut (mixed) with?" he asked.

Elaina started laughing. "Why can't I be Mexican?"

"Too much ass."

"I'm Dominican," she said as she got even closer. "Look up front," she whispered.

Sin saw that Geneva's head was in Mario's lap, bobbing up and down. Sin smiled and looked at Elaina.

"Don't even think about it!" she said as she licked Sin's neck as she grabbed his dick.

When they finally got to Reno, Elaina put the suite in her name and she rushed Sin upstairs. They walked into the plush suite and she went and filled the hot tub. Sin rolled them a couple blunts.

Once the hot tub was filled, Elaina stood in front of Sin, pulled the sash on her dress, and took it off. She stood there naked in nothing but her Cavallo heels. She looked like Mariah Carey, but had an ass like Jennifer Lopez. Sin nodded his head in approval. Elaina took her heels off and came over to Sin and started undressing him. She took the .40 caliber Sig out his waistband and put it on the table, then pulled his Sean John shirt over his head and admired his tattoos. Sin stood there as she rubbed her finger over the bullet grazing on his neck. She stepped closer to him and kissed it. She then unbuckled his belt and unbuttoned his Sean John jeans.

"You are so fucking sexy, Sin! You going to be my gangster?" she asked as she pushed him onto the sofa. When Elaina said that, Sin thought of the movie, *Dutch*.

"Baby, I can be whatever you want me to be as long as you play your position. I got a wife, and nothing and no one is going to come between what we have. If you cool with that then we can see where we're going to take this," Sin said as she pulled his Tims off.

"Like I told you, Sin, I have a man. All I'm looking for is some side dick without having a bunch of one-night stands," she said.

"Cool," Sin said as he raised up and let her pull his pants and boxers off.

"Damn!" Elaina said when Sin's dick popped out pointing at her.

Sin smiled at the compliment. She pulled him up and led him to the hot tub. They both stepped in and settled back and talked for a minute. Sin looked at the clock and saw that it was 10:30. He wondered what Malika was doing.

Elaina straddled him and started kissing on his neck. Sin grabbed her butt and kissed her shoulder. Elaina reached over to her purse and pulled out a ribbed Rough Rider condom.

"Sin, I haven't cum since the last time I had an affair on my husband. That's been like four months," she said as she slid down on his dick. "Make me cum, *papi!*" she demanded.

Sin started fucking her softly, going as deep as he could then pulling out. He repeated the process over and over until he put Elaina in a dick frenzy. He started going fast and hard, and Elaina came extra hard.

Sin got behind Elaina and lifted one of her legs to the rim of the tub and slid in her. As he hit her from the back, her ass jiggled and that made him think about Malika and how her ass jiggled and bounced. Not that Elaina's ass was the size of Malika's, but it was big and juicy. Sin wanted to see how far she would let him go. While he had her moaning he rubbed his finger across her butt hole.

Elaina felt it, and smiled a little, and backed up prodding him to go further. Sin stuck his finger in her butt and she came so hard it was scary.

"Sin, baby, please don't cum inside me! If I got pregnant I would lose everything," she said.

He made Elaina cum two more times before he felt his nut coming. He pulled out, and spun her around and pushed her head down. Elaina put her lips on Sin's dick and started sucking. *Damn, this bitch's head's on 1,000!* he thought. "I'm about to cum, E! *Goddamn*, girl suck that muthafucka!" he said.

"Call me a dick sucking bitch!" she demanded.

"Man, do your thang, you dick sucking bitch!" he yelled out. "Oh yeah, bitch, make me cum! Swallow this nut, you cum drinking bitch!" he said as he busted off in her mouth.

"Oh, I'm about to cum again!" she mumbled with her mouth full.

Sin looked in the mirror behind her and saw that she had two fingers in her pussy and her thumb in her ass. Elaina came again even harder. She and Sin washed up then went to the bedroom. Elaina was out as soon as she hit the pillow. Sin looked at his phone and saw it was now 11:30. He dialed Malika's number.

• • • • • •

Malika and the girls had a suite at the St. Francis Hotel in San Francisco. Four male strippers were entertaining them. As Malika was putting a $20.00 bill in one of the stipper's g-string she felt her phone vibrate. The stripper that was dancing for her was a 6-4, 250-pound God. The boy's name was De'Angelo. He danced at Sin on Thursdays. The rest of the group also danced at the club. De'Angelo had been flirting with Malika since she hired them. The most they ever did was have a drink together. She was in love with her baby's daddy, and judging by the size of the ring she was wearing, he was in love with her too.

Malika looked at her phone and saw Sin's number. *Shit!* she thought. She got up and went to the bedroom. "Hey, baby," she said.

"What's up, Pooh? Where are you, baby?" he asked.

Malika thought about lying. "At the St. Francis," she said.

"Damn, that music loud. Ya'll must be having a party."

"We got strippers in here dancing," she said truthfully.

"What? Man, I know you didn't just say that," he said angrily.

Malika knew he was going to react like that. "Baby, I'm not trying to start this off lying."

"Hold on," Sin said and picked up the hotel's phone and called Tariq.

"Hello?" Tariq answered sleepily.

"Cuzzo, is your company's jet in the town?" Sin asked.

"Yeah, it's out here."

"Man, I need Malika in Reno as soon as possible."

"Cuzzo, by the time we file a flight plan, get the pilot, and the jet ready, she could have driven out there," Tariq said.

"I didn't think about that," Sin said. "Aight, go back to enjoying your new bride," Sin said and hung up.

"Pooh," he said into his cell.

"Yes, baby?" she answered.

"I want you to come get me. We getting married tonight!"

"Nigga, that's what the fuck I'm talking about! I'm leaving right now!" He told her where he was.

"And come by yourself," he instructed her.

"Okay, baby. I love you!" she said and hung up.

Malika came out the room, and De'Angelo was standing there. "Look, Malika why won't you give me the time a day?" he asked her.

"I told you what my situation was, De'Angelo," she said as she noticed he was butt-ass naked. She looked down at his dick and shivered. "And anyway, there's no way that I was going to let you put all this up in me," she said as she grabbed De'Angelo's 11 inches.

"I only wanted to put half of it in you, and all of this," he said as he stuck out his long, thick tongue

Malika felt her panties getting wet. *I better hurry up and get away from this muthafucka before he gets me and him killed!* she thought. She released the python, and hurried into the living room and went over to Simone and Charmaine. "I'm out. I'm going to Reno to marry my nigga. I should be back tomorrow, but if I ain't, one of ya'll go check on the kids and make sure they still alive," she said and picked up her purse and left.

When Malika got to Reno, she called and found out Sin was at Circus Circus. When she pulled up, he was standing outside with his duffel bag. Malika slid over and he got in on the driver's side. She put her arms around him and kissed him.

"You nervous?" he asked.

"No, I've been waiting for this forever, baby. What about you?"

"Shit, I'm straight. I'm marrying the baddest bitch that ever walked the earth."

"You better know it, and that better be the last time you call me a bitch," she said and mushed his head.

They pulled up at a twenty-four-hour wedding chapel, got out, and went hand in hand inside.

Right before the ceremony took place, Malika pulled Sin to the side and said, "Sin, be a hundred-percent sure you want to do this, because after we do it I won't have any understanding about you falling weak. I'm going to literally kill you if you break my heart."

"Baby, I want this more than anything."

"Well let's do this!"

Within five minutes, Malika became Malika Michaels.

Sin rented them a suite in the Hilton and sexed his wife up all night. There was no holding back on anything. Sin licked Malika everywhere. He even did something he said he would never do. Right after Malika got out of the shower, he licked her butt.

Malika did something she didn't think she would ever do. She licked his, and let him hit her in the butt. It hurt her in the beginning, but after a while she started enjoying it.

While Sin was hitting her from the back and squeezing her luscious butt cheeks, he looked at the platinum band on his ring finger and smiled. *I made the right choice*, he thought as he stroked his wife.

Chapter Twenty

Loyalty & Betrayal

The next six months had been hectic. Sin and Sha and their crew were bringing the heat to Max and his crew, and to Bo and his. Sin found out that the dude Bo was getting his work from was the Colombian he and the girls had put work in on when he first started dealing with Maria. This dude was the one that got away, Pedro Garza.

Mario and Sin had been flying back and forth to the southeast putting together a network. They had finally gotten things the way they wanted it. Sin and June were doing their thing on the next level. Money was coming in from everywhere. Everything was so cool that Sin got scared. He had Simina counting so much money that they devised a way to do it faster. All Simina had to do was separate the denominations. Each bill weighed one gram. So a hundred pounds of hundreds was close to 4.5 mil. 4,480,000 to be exact. Ones and fives they just threw into pillowcases without counting.

Every Saturday that Sin was home, he, Jamila and Simina put the money in ten-gee stacks at Jamila's house. Nobody knew about the apartment other than Sin and Simina. They didn't even tell Malika.

Sin settled with the city for 2.5 million for his civil case. Then on top of that, the lady Malika was close to had kept her word and sent Sin a check for 2.5 million. He gave that to Malika. Sin's illegal worth was a staggering 5 million dollars. He and his family's (Malika and the kids) legal worth was about 6.4 million.

Malika and Sin were having a house built in Castro Valley, complete with a man made lake. They were still going strong, although Sin still tipped with Elaina, but she knew what time it was with Malika.

Sin bought a house in Atlanta in the Stone Mountain area, and he and Mario went half on another in Charlotte, North Carolina. Since Sin was out that way in each city at least once a month, they thought it to be a good investment.

Malika quit her job at J.A. Drake because it was evident that they were not going to allow her to make partner. The "good ol' boy" network would never make room for a mixed blood female, and her being half black was all the more reason.

Malika took her impressive list of clients from all over the world and started working from home. She represented famous ethnic athletes, politicians, authors, actors, and other celebrities. Most of the time, when Sin went out of town she went with him, especially since she was now five months pregnant.

Marco came home and jumped into the game headfirst. Even after all the talking that Sin had done, Marco still went wild. He was smashing on every dude that claimed The Circle that didn't pay the six-month dues. He and his crew of misfits started kidnapping cats and burning their Mad Circle tattoos off of their bodies. Dudes that were up under The Circle that didn't ride during the war with Bo and Max were killed. There wasn't a middle ground with Marco. It was like the mob with him. Either you were with it 100%, or you weren't. This attitude is what caused Marco's name to be ringing negatively.

Sin was pulling up at Terell and Cynthia's house on 98th, when he saw that Terell had his burnt orange convertible Corvette parked in the driveway. Sin got mad as hell. He had told Terell not to have that car parked there because it was too noticeable, and while they were at war with Bo and Max, he didn't need to be noticed, especially since Cynthia was pregnant.

Terell had just beat Cynthia up a week prior, and Mario wanted to kill him. He didn't, on the strength of Sin, but let it be known that if it continued to happen, God wouldn't be able to save Terell.

Sin got out of his new green CL600 and went to the door and knocked. Terell opened the door. The way he was acting made Sin's antenna go up. He looked behind him then came in and closed the door. "Man, I told you about parking your car over here. You want muthafuckas to run through here and whack you, Cynt, and the baby?" he asked.

"Bro, muthafuckas ain't trying to see us. Them niggas will end up like that nigga, J.B.!" Terell said as he opened the closet and grabbed a duffel bag and tossed it to Sin.

This nigga on something, Sin thought as he saw how Terell was acting.

"I need 10 more keys of that cream, Sin," he said.

Sin unzipped the bag, looked at the money, then turned and went to the door. He was mad enough to do harm to Terell so he just left. He pulled his Glock 40 out, eased the door open, and looked both ways before stepping out. Something wasn't right and Sin felt it. He pulled his phone out and called Malika.

"Yes, baby?" she answered.

"Meet me at Simone's. I need you to do something," he told her and hung up.

As Sin pulled off, he stayed checking the mirrors. When he got to the top of the 98th Avenue hill and was about to hit Golf Links, he saw a blue Task Force car get on him. He changed direction, and instead of going to Simone's, which was on Golf Links, he turned into Knowland Park.

The cop car hit its lights. Sin pulled over and took his gun out, put it in the console, reached over to the glove compartment and grabbed the registration. He looked through his side view mirror as the cop was getting out and saw that it was Anita.

She walked up to the car looking pissed off. *What's wrong with this bitch?* Sin wondered.

"Sin, you need to be at my house at 5:00 today," she ordered.

"I don't *need* to be no goddamn where," Sin replied.

"Sin, don't make me come to Dublin and fuck up your happy home. Be at my house at 5. I need to talk to you about some serious shit. Now let me see your license and registration so nobody thinks you working for the police," she said.

Sin handed her his paperwork. She went back to her car and acted like she was running his information.

Some girls drove by admiring Sin's Benz. He had it painted dark green with white leather interior, and it now sat on 20" chrome Ashanti's.

Anita came back and gave him his stuff back.

"Can I come over there and stand up in something?" he asked.

"You can *never* stand up in me again," she said as she walked off shaking her ass.

Sin pulled out of the park and saw Malika on her way to Simone's in the Navigator. He blew his horn and she pulled over. He pulled the bag out of the car and took it to her. "I'll be home about 9," he said and kissed her.

He got back in his car and went to the freeway. He then went to Shaunté's and kicked it with his daughter until 4:30, then left to Anita's.

Sin pulled up just as Anita did. He followed her into the house and pushed up on her butt.

"Sin, take your hands off my ass!" she said and stepped away from him. "You know a nigga named Terell Hodges?" she asked.

"Yeah, that's my young potna. We like brothers," he replied.

"Well your *brother's* a hot ass rat! He got pulled over on a routine stop, and the officers found he was high off something. When they searched his car, they found 180,000 and two kilos of cocaine. As soon as he got to the station he was trying to make a deal. He said he worked for you and you bought your shit from a guy named Mario Perez. Then that little punk muthafucka said that you were fuckin' with some bitch that worked for the police department. He didn't know if it was the Oakland or Berkeley police department, but that's how you didn't have any dope on you when you got busted."

This little hoe-caked muthafucka! I brought that nigga up from nothing. Muthafucka was homeless when I started fuckin' with him, and this is how he's going to repay me? I'm killing this nigga! Sin thought.

Anita saw how Sin was looking and knew he was shocked. A person that he claimed as family went out like that.

"Nita, don't worry about it, baby. I'll handle it," he said.

"Sin, you better. This is *my* life this nigga playing with, as well as yours," she said with tears in her eyes.

"I got it, *mami*. Don't trip. Baby, you ain't been nothing but good to me. You're a loyal muthafucka and I want to do something for you. I'm going to give you 100,000, baby," he said.

"Yeah, *right!* Sin, just tell me why you did me like you did."

"Look, baby. I gave you a day to come visit for a reason. Sundays were somebody else's day," he said.

"Did that someone bring her ass up to the jail house and give you some pussy and some weed? Did this someone risk her *career* by keeping you from possibly having drugs on you when you were being set up by a snitch?" she asked.

"Look, Anita. If you didn't just cut me off, I would have been able to tell you that she was a friend of mine that drove all the way from Arizona to see me."

"Sin, keep it 100 with me. Are you selling dope again?" she asked.

Sin really didn't want to answer her. She was *those* people after all, but she had a soft spot for him. "Anita, I'm in this shit for six months, then I'm done. I got the opportunity to make a gang of loot and I can't pass that up," he said as he stepped into her comfort zone and kissed her cheek. "Change clothes and follow me somewhere."

When Anita came out of her room, she was dressed in blue jeans, a white blouse, black leather boots, and a black leather coat. She put her Glock in her purse, grabbed her phone and umbrella, and they went out.

"Meet me at 7-Eleven on 27th and Harrison," Sin said as he helped her into her car. He went to his car, got in, and pulled his two-way out and sent messages to Tayshaun, Hasahn, Amir, Shaqui, Marco, June Bug, Mario, Boss Mann, and Tariq. The message read:

"There's a crack in the circle.
Let's link up at my job.
Sin 4 Life!"

When Sin got to his apartment, he looked around before pulling into the underground parking area. When he got out of the car he cautiously walked to the elevator then decided on the stairs. He ran up the four flights to the fourth floor then went down the hall to number 405. He heard music coming from inside the apartment. He stuck his key in and turned the lock and tried to open the door. The chain was on so he knocked.

"Who's there?" Simina asked.

"Your dad," Sin said.

Simina opened the door and Sin went in. On the dining room table were stacks of money.

"Give me a hundred racks," Sin said.

Simina went to the safe and took ten $10,000 stacks out, and put them in one of the back packs that were on the floor.

"How much more you have to do?" he asked.

"I only have to put rubber bands on the money, then I'm done."

"Let's do it. Then we can leave together."

They bound the money then Sin locked it in the safe.

"Dad, what's wrong?" Simina asked.

"Nothing, baby," Sin said as they locked the apartment up. When they got to the garage Sin handed Simina the keys, and she knew something was wrong because he never let her drive his Benz, in the rain at that.

"Go down the hill to 7-Eleven," he said. Simina hit the button on the key ring and they got in. Simina skillfully navigated the car to 7-Eleven. Sin had taught her how to drive without Malika's knowledge before he went to jail.

Sin saw Anita parked at the curb in front of 7-Eleven when Simina stopped at the stop sign. He had her pull into the parking lot.

"Go in and get me a soda," he said to his daughter. They got out and Sin went and got into Anita's Denali. He leaned over and kissed her. Anita saw how stressed Sin was.

"Baby, if you want me to, I'll do that hot muthafucka," she said.

This made Sin smile. "Nah, don't worry about it," he said and gave her the backpack. "This is because you're by far one the realest people I ever met, but don't look in it until I pull off."

Anita saw Simina come out the store. Some dude was trying to get at her. "Your girl's popular," she said and nodded towards Simina.

"*Girl?* That's my daughter!"

"Damn, she looks grown!" Anita said.

"Anita, can I get some more of that good stuff?" Sin asked as he rubbed between her legs.

"Ain't you married?" she asked.

"Yeah, and? Man, a muthafucka can't knock me for trying to get some more of the best pussy I've ever had," he said as he rubbed her crotch.

"I'm not going to do your wife like that," she said and removed his hand.

"I need to run, baby," he said and leaned over to kiss her. To his surprise Anita turned her head towards him and their lips met, and she slipped her tongue into his mouth.

"You might be able to come eat the best pussy you ever had, and I might think about letting you beat it up again," she said.

"Aight, I'll be at you," he said and got out.

Sin stepped to the dude that was trying to talk to his daughter.

"Daddy, before you get mad at me, I told him how old I am," Simina said.

"Homie you got three seconds to be out of my sight," Sin said and lifted the front of his shirt revealing the Glock .40. The dude took off.

"Go to the club, baby," he said.

●●●●●●

As Sin and Simina pulled out the parking lot, Anita unzipped the backpack and saw all the money, and quickly zipped it back up while looking to make sure no one was spying on her. She went home and dumped the money out and counted it. When she got to the total she screamed and jumped up and down. She picked up her phone and called Sin as she stripped so she could roll around naked on the money.

● ● ● ● ● ●

At the club Sin was listening to what his folks was saying when his phone rang. He looked at the caller ID and saw Anita's number. He put his finger up, silencing Sha who was now talking.

"What up?" he asked.

"Sin, I love you, baby! You can come get this pussy right now! Hell you can come get this ass and head too!" she said excitedly.

"I'm glad you're in a better mental than you were earlier. I'm taking care of something right now. I'll holla at you later," he said and hung up.

"Look, cuzzo. That nigga gotta dee-zy (die). He done even put Mario's name in it. Mario ain't even in the Circle," Sha said.

"Straight up, Sin. I know dude was your lil' mans at one time, but he gotta catch it, Sun," Hasahn said. Everybody looked at him like he was crazy.

"*Sun*? Nigga, you be around them East Coast niggas so much, you starting to talk like 'em," Tayshaun said. He then looked at Sin. "Sin, if you can't kill that nigga, I'll do it, but one way or another, dude gots to go."

The High Council voted and that was that. Terell would be killed.

"I'll do it," Sin said as he stood. Everyone else stood too and they all filed out the office.

Kira was coming out of her office as they waited for the elevator. She walked right up to Shaqui and kissed him. "I'll see you tonight, big daddy," she said and switched over to the video room.

They got on the elevator, and as soon as the doors closed Sin was on Sha. "Nigga, is the pussy cool?" he asked.

"It was bomb, but her head is *super* bomb. You see them big pretty lips? She knows how to use them," he said.

Sin and Simina went home. Sin called everyone in his crew and told them Terell wasn't allowed to get any dope. At 9:00 Sin and Malika got in bed. Sin told Malika the story.

"Well, you know what you gotta do. That punk is putting us and our family at risk. If you don't kill him, I will. I am not having you going to jail and being away from me again. Fuck that nigga!" Malika said.

Three months ended up going by and Sin put off serving Terell as long as he could. The rest of the Circle was getting impatient.

●●●●●●

Tariq, his wife, Ayanna, and Tayshaun and his girl, Tyisha were all in Lake Tahoe at Black Ski Week when the opportunity presented itself. Tayshaun and Tyisha had an argument and he left the cabin they were staying in to cool off. While walking through the snow to the store, which was across the road, he saw Terell pull into the parking lot.

Tayshaun approached the Expedition that Terell was in as he was getting out. "What's up, cuzzo?" he asked greeting Terell.

"'Tay, what's up, my nigga?" Terell said and hugged him.

"Man, my bitch trippin'. I had to bounce for a minute. Where the hoes at?" Tayshaun asked.

"Nigga, I got four bitches at the motel room freaking, and all them hoes off E (ecstasy). You with me or what?" Terell asked.

"For sure, nigga," Tayshaun replied.

"Aight, let me slide in here and get some drank and rubbers," Terell said and tossed Tayshaun the keys.

As Terell walked in the store, he wondered what happened to Tayshaun. Tayshaun was a fly ass dude back in the late '80s, early '90s, getting some real money with Sin and them. Then something happened and he just stopped. He and his girl, Ty lived in some Housing Authority apartments, and he was broke. If it weren't for his hustling ass woman who was boosting clothes out the stores, he would be a bum ass nigga.

Sin and Sha used to talk about how Tayshaun puts work in when he's needed. Terell thought that was highly unlikely. This assessment came from Tayshaun's pretty boy looks. That's where everyone got it twisted. Tayshaun might have had more bodies than anyone in the Circle, except for Scatter and Sha.

Terell came back out and saw Tayshaun sitting in the passenger seat. He slid into the truck and started it.

"Tee, you know you violated the code," Tayshaun said. By the time Terell's mind registered what was going on, and he was reaching for his gun, Tayshaun had a grip on his head, exposing his neck. Tayshaun put his knife on Terell's jugular and sliced quickly.

Tayshaun slid out of the truck when Terell stopped moving. He went back to the cabin and told Tyisha to pack because they were leaving.

He then called Tariq. "Nigga, I just saw Terell's hot ass," he said.

"I'm at that fool. Where he at?" Tariq asked.

"It's too late. I'm on my way to the house. Come by my house and pick your Range up when you get back to The Town," Tayshaun said and hung up.

'Tay pulled his two-way out and sent a message to the Circle's High Council. It read:

"The crack in the Circle has been repaired.

Breathe easy."

The messenger's screen name was, "*Taysheezy*".

● ● ● ● ● ●

When Sin got the message, he was at home, with Malika on top of him riding. He looked up at her and smiled. She took the two-way and read the message and looked at him confused.

"Terell's no more," he said as he sat up and grabbed Malika's butt and moved her faster.

"He should have *been* no more, baby!" she kissed him.

When Sin got up the next morning, he looked outside and saw that it was raining hard. He showered and threw on boxers, blue Pelle Pelle jeans, a red Pelle Pelle T-shirt, some tan Tims, and a tan and blue leather Pelle Pelle jacket. He went downstairs, got his keys, went outside and got in his 600 and left.

When Sin pulled up at the apartment, he did his normal recon of the area, then pulled in. Once inside the apartment he went and cracked his safe. He looked at all the money and smiled. His phone rang, and he answered. "Hello?"

"Let's take a trip to N.C.," Mario said.

"When?"

"Our plane leaves when we get to the airport. We flying private so be suited and booted."

"Aight, pimp shoe. I'll call you when I'm ready," Sin said and hung up.

He snatched two million dollars out. It was time for him to move his money around. If he got knocked in his apartment they would get it all. He put the money in a duffel bag and left. When he got home, he saw that Malika was back. When he got in the house she was upstairs packing a bag for him.

"You ain't going?" he asked

"No. Somebody has to be here to pick Quesha up later," she said.

"I ain't staying out there long. I don't know why, but I can't stay away from your ass," Sin said as he walked up behind her and put his arms around her. Malika gave him a knowing smile. Sin looked at her. "Don't let me find out you put some voodoo on me," he said.

"Just don't go in the back yard. You might find a few pairs of your drawers I buried," she said.

"Yeah, whatever. You been feeling better in the mornings?" Sin asked.

"Yeah, I've been a little better. I still get a little queasy. What about you?" she asked as she pulled out the blue Ralph Lauren suit.

"I only feel fucked up when I first get up. Shit, it's better than when I was waking up being sick for the first five months of your pregnancy. I think I had more of your morning sickness than you did," Sin said as he sat on the bed and pulled Malika between his legs. He lifted her shirt and laid his head against her eight-month pregnant stomach. Just like always, the baby kicked.

"We only have four weeks left and you'll have your junior," she said.

"You going to let me put another one in there?"

"Yeah, but I want to wait until SJ (Simian Jr.) is at least two."

Sin unbuttoned Malika's shirt and looked at her bra-bound titties. "Damn, they got hella bigger!" he said as he rubbed them.

"They went up to double D's. After S.J. is born, they'll be back to normal," she said.

"We will have to get you some implants then. I like them like this," he said.

"I ain't about to go get no *implants!*" she said as she stepped away from him. She grabbed the white button-up, the black belt, the black Feragamo shoes and Sin's blue Ralph Lauren overcoat.

"Go ahead and get dressed," she said as she opened the duffel bag he brought in. She saw the money, took it out and packed it in his suitcase.

Sin took off his jewels and Malika packed them. She grabbed his Movado, the platinum wedding ring with the three one carat stones that she had bought him, the Ralph Lauren clear lenses, and the platinum link bracelet.

Sin got dressed then looked at himself in the mirror and nodded. Malika packed his laptop in his black gator briefcase and he was set. She buttoned up her shirt and grabbed her keys and went downstairs

Sin pulled his phone out and called Shaunté.

"Hello?" she answered.

"Lil' mama, throw on one of those business suits and pack a bag. We going to Carolina."

"When?"

"It's 10:30 now. Be at North Field at twelve."

"North Field? We flying on a private jet?" she asked.

"Yeah, now hurry up," he said and hung up.

Sin went downstairs and got in the 600 with Malika, and they left. When they got to North Field at the Oakland Airport, Sin saw Mario outside in his Range Rover.

"Be careful, baby, and come home when you finish whatever ya'll going out there to do," Malika said and leaned over and kissed him.

"I love you, baby," he said.

"I know, and you know I love you too," she said and kissed him again.

Sin got out of the car, got his stuff, and went and got in the Range Rover. There were two women in the back that Sin recognized as Gayle and Carla. They were both dressed in business suits and both of them were fine as hell. Mario was fucking Carla and Sin tried to fuck Gayle, but she wasn't having it. She told him guys had dogged her out all her life, and she was trying lesbianism.

Carla was like 5'3". She was dark-skinned, had slanted pretty brown eyes, and medium length black hair, and a sexy body.

Gayle was cocoa-brown, had pretty brown doe-like eyes, and short brown texturized curly hair. She had lips like the girl that played Ronnie in *Player's Club*. Her body was unbelievably stacked. Girl was playing with something sweet. Her titties were average, tiny waist, wide inviting hips, big legs, small feet, and a big ass. She was in a gray business skirt suit and black heels. Carla was wearing a black suit.

"Shaunté's going with us. She should be here in about thirty minutes," Sin said to Mario.

"Who's Shaunté?" Gayle asked.

"My baby's mama," Sin said.

Carla and Gayle both started laughing, then Gayle got serious. "You got some bad timing, playa. I was going to go ahead and break down and give you some," she said.

"Baby, I ain't got no time for games. If you wanted to fuck me you should have been done it," Sin said angrily.

They pulled into the hanger where the G5 jet was sitting. They all got out of the truck. The pilot came down the stairs and helped them take their bags up. Sin liked the jet. There was a nice sized room and a bathroom complete with shower at the rear of the plane. There was also another main bathroom. There were beige leather sofas and six reclining Lay-Z-Boys that all become one bed when let down. There was a bar, a flat screen TV, and a lot of other audio visual stuff.

Shaunté called at 11:50 and said she was at the gate. Sin took the Range Rover and went out to meet her. He had her follow him to the parking area.

When Shaunté got out of her Range Rover Sin's mouth dropped. She was wearing a blue Chanel skirt suit that was short and sexy, white monogrammed Chanel stockings, and blue Chanel heels.

"God damn, baby!" he said as he got out of Mario's truck.

She walked up to him and kissed him on the lips. "You look handsome, baby," she said. They got a ride back to the jet.

The call came from the pilot notifying them of takeoff. Sin sat across from Shaunté and Gayle. Mario sat across the isle with Carla. Once they were airborne, Mario and Carla retreated to the stateroom.

● ● ● ● ● ●

Malika had just put the last of the dinner dishes in the dishwasher when she heard something, a noise in the front room. She walked out of the kitchen, and sure enough she heard somebody messing with the locks. She ran into the family room where Davy was. "Somebody's trying to get in the house!" she whispered.

"Come on," he said and led her to the living room and up the stairs. Malika went into Simina and Quesha's room and made them get in the closet. She then went and got her registered Glock .40 out of her nightstand, put the clip in it, and cocked it. She grabbed her extra clip and met Davy in the hallway.

"Malika, go back in there with the girls. I got this," Davy said as he cocked his 9. They heard the door as it squeaked open. Malika heard footsteps, then they saw two guys. She took a deep breath and said a quick prayer.

When they heard the bottom stair squeak, they knew it was now or never. Malika stepped around the wall surprising the dude on the stairs. He never got to say a word. Malika held her Glock .40 with two hands the way Sin taught her, and pulled the trigger twice, hitting the guy in the chest and knocking him down the stairs. The other guy came running out of the kitchen shooting up the stairs. Malika ducked back behind the wall just before the slugs hit where she had been standing.

Davy stepped out and started getting off at the other guy as he tried to help his friend who was now on his feet. The guy Malika shot raised his Desert Eagle and started shooting. The slugs knocked huge chunks out of the wall.

Malika pointed her gun around the corner and let five slugs off down the stairs. Davy stood and let five off at the dudes as they tried to get to the door. He ended up hitting the dude Malika shot, in the back and leg. "Aaahhh, I'm hit!" he screamed out. His man raised his gun and popped off a few more shots as he pulled his friend out. "Light it up!" he screamed.

Malika and Davy heard the fully automatic machine guns going off. They both fell to the floor as bullets whizzed passed their heads. The two dudes standing outside with the AK-47s chewed the walls and windows up, upstairs and downstairs.

Malika wasn't scared at all. Her kids were in the house, and whoever did this was going to die! *This shit just got real!* she thought as she met Davy's eye and smiled.

Davy frowned at her. *This shit ain't funny! Malika must be in shock,* he thought as the shooting stopped. They heard sirens coming near, and heard two car doors slam and somebody hit the gas, leaving rubber.

Malika went straight into effect mode. She ran in the girls' room and saw that it was wrecked. There were bullet holes in the windows, walls, and... closet door.

She yanked open the door and didn't see anyone. "Pumpkin!" she screamed out.

Quesha and Simina came running out of the bathroom and right to Malika.

"You two okay?" Malika asked with tears in her eyes.

"Yes, Mama," Simina said.

Malika put a pair of Simina's shoes on, ran into her bedroom, got the other two guns, then grabbed Davy's gun from him. "You got anything in here?" she asked.

Davy ran in his room and got ten gees. Malika ran to the garage and put the stuff in her 500.

Just as she was coming up the stairs the police came screeching up. When they ran in with their guns drawn, they ordered Malika to drop her gun. She complied and told them that she was coming out of the kitchen and heard someone messing with the door. She went and got her gun because the first thing on her mind was protecting her children. When she confronted the two dudes from the top of the stairs, they started shooting. She said she shot back and that's when the dudes ran out and the machine gun fire started. She explained that she owned a very profitable club in Oakland and they may have been trying to rob her. She also showed them her gun permit.

"Call your father," she told Simina, who was standing at the top of the stairs.

Simina went and got her cell phone and called Sin.

Sin's phone rang just as he and the girls were coming in from a strip club. He looked at the caller ID and saw Simina's cell phone number. He looked at the time and saw it was 2:15 a.m. East Coast time, so that made it 11:15 p.m. in Cali. If she was calling this late, Sin knew something was wrong.

"Baby girl, what's up?" he answered.

"Daddy, somebody broke in the house! Mama and Davy was shooting at them and they was shooting back! Then they shot the house up, Daddy! They messed the *whole* front of the house up!" Simina said.

The first thing Sin thought was that something happened to one of them since the girls' rooms windows were upstairs at the front of the house. "Ya'll aight?" he asked.

"Yeah. Daddy, come home. I'm scared!" she cried.

"Stop crying, baby. Where's your mama?"

"She's talking to the police."

"I'm about to get a flight out. Tell Malika to call me as soon as she's done," he said and hung up.

"What's up?" Shaunté asked.

Sin had a tear in his eye. *These niggas changed the game. It's on now for real!* he thought.

"Some niggas ran up in my house. Malika and Davy got at them and then niggas lit my house up. I can't figure out how they know where I live. Only a handful of my closest friends know where I live." He looked at Shaunté and she shivered. "Somebody's whole fam is about to come up short. From their mamas to their kids. Book me a flight home. We moved all the work we brought out here, so there's no reason to stay," he said as he ran upstairs to Mario's room and walked in without knocking.

Carla was on her hands and knees and Mario was behind her pumping. When Carla saw Sin standing in the door she made no move to cover herself up.

Mario saw the look on Sin's face. "Some shady shit jump off when you went and met them niggas?" he asked.

"I gotta get home. Niggas ran up in my house while my family was there," Sin said.

"What? Is everybody okay?" Mario asked as he pulled out of Carla and pushed her away.

Sin turned his back while Mario put his draws on. "Everybody's straight. Simina said that Davy and Malika got into a shootout with them then they shot the front of the house up. I got Shaunté making flight arrangements for me," Sin said.

"Fool, we on the jet!" Mario said as he pulled his phone out of his pocket and called the Holiday Inn. He was connected to his pilot's room. "Change of plan. We're leaving right away. There's an emergency back home. Call and do whatever you need to do. We need to be in the air in an hour. Call me back when it's done," he said and hung up.

Carla went to her bag and got some underwear and jeans and stood at the door waiting for Mario to come get in the shower with her. Sin noticed that her pussy was bald. When she saw him looking she stroked herself once.

Sin walked out, went to his room and got rid of any evidence that another woman had been there. He even went and washed his sheets, pillowcases, blankets, and comforter. He had Gayle go clean his bathroom while Shaunté cleaned the dishes.

As he thought about what he was going to do to Max and Bo and their families, his phone rang. When he saw Malika's number he felt better. "What happened, baby?" he asked.

Malika explained everything, not leaving one thing out. She told him she thinks the dude had a vest on when she shot him because he got up shooting.

"So tell me what happened after I left."

"I went and checked the books at the club, went and got groceries, and went home. Kesha called me and told me she was bringing Marquesha home. Then I cooked din..."

"Whoa, whoa, *whoa!* What you mean Kesha called and said she was bringing Quesha home?" he asked cutting her off.

"I mean exactly that. She said she was going to drop her off," Malika said.

"Baby, I never told Kesha where we live," he said.

"I told her. I thought it..."

"Malika, I'm at war with her man! Why in the fuck would you tell my baby's mama where I live if I didn't tell her?" he yelled.

"Sin, stop fuckin' yelling at me! I'm sorry, baby! I didn't know you was at war with her boyfriend!" Malika cried.

"I'm sorry, Pooh. I'm just going crazy. That bitch told them niggas where I lay my head. Look, pack and go to Simone's. I'll be there as soon as I can," he said.

"Okay, baby. I love you, Sin," she said.

"I love you too," he said and hung up.

Chapter Twenty-One

Lie In The Bed You Made

June, Sha and Sin sat in a gray nondescript GM Van Conversion looking out of the tinted windows.

"Heads up!" Sha said. They watched as Max pulled out in the red convertible Corvette ZRl. He pulled away fast.

"Man, I should have just killed that nigga right then," Sin said.

"Nah, nigga, we need to get at this nigga's loot too," Sha said.

As they watched the house, they saw Carlos run to the side of it. About three minutes later, Sin's phone rang. "Yeah?" he answered.

"I'm in. She's in her room with the baby, and there's a nigga out back by the pool," Carlos said.

"Aight, open the front door," Sin said and hung up.

As they were getting out of the van, Marco, Shaunté, and Déja pulled up in Marco's brown 99 Buick

Skylark. "You know I wasn't going to miss this!" Shaunté said as she put her black skully on her head.

Sin looked sad as he walked across the street. He was going to see what Kesha had to say. He already knew that if the shit didn't add up he was going to kill his daughter's mom.

"Sin, nigga, fuck that shit! That bitch could have gotten one of your kids killed. She didn't give a fuck enough about her own kid that she did some scandalous shit like that. If you don't kill this hoe, if we find out she guilty, then I will!" June said as he looked around to make sure that they were undetected.

Carlos opened the door and they slid in. Sin nodded for Marco to go to the back with Carlos. Déja went with them. Sin, Shaunté, June and Sha went up the stairs. They walked down the hall with their silenced weapons ready.

Shaunté and Sha stepped into the room first. Kesha saw them and grabbed her baby. "What the fuck ya'll doing?" she screamed. "Shaqui, you guys got rules! You ain't suppose to harm the family!" she screamed.

"Ain't no rules. Kesha, just tell me why?" Sin asked as he and June stepped in.

"Sin, what's going on? What are you talking about?" she asked.

"Kesha, my muthafuckin' house got shot up two days ago," he said.

"What? Is my little girl okay?" she asked un-convinceingly.

Sin, at *tha*t exact moment, knew that Kesha had something to do with it. "Them niggas shot about a hundred rounds through her window! Why did you tell that nigga where I live?" he asked.

"Nigga, I ain't told Max where you live! Do you think I would put my daughter in danger just to get to you? Sin, I told you that I wasn't going to be in the mid..." Kesha stopped talking when a thought hit her. "That bitch! Sin, I know what happened. I had this bitch named Josie in the car with me when I dropped Quesha off. She fucks with Curtis who is Max's cousin. That bitch told them. It had to had been her," she said.

"Well since them niggas don't care about my family, I don't care about theirs, and since your hoe ass wanna lie, I'm at you too, bitch!" Sin said and turned to leave.

There was a sudden movement then the distinct sound of a silenced weapon letting off three rounds. When Sin turned around, he saw Kesha laying there bleeding from her chest, and in her hand was a 9mm. Smoke was coming from Shaunté's silenced Beretta. Sin didn't have an ounce of regret for Kesha. Everyone looked at him, wondering what was going through his mind.

"Fuck her! Lets find the cash, and someone go tell Carlos to bring that nigga upstairs," Sin said.

Sha, as if reading Sin's mind, lifted Kesha's body into a sitting position and grabbed her hand that had the gun in it.

"'Tay, move that baby," Sin said.

Shaunté picked the baby up and put her in her crib.

June, Carlos, Déja, and Marco all escorted the dude in and quickly moved away from him. Sha pressed Kesha's trigger finger and two loud pops could be heard. All the while this was happening, Marco was looking for the money.

"Come here, baby," he said. Déja walked her big butt over to where he was in the closet. Marco pointed up at a trap door that went to an attic. "You see how the paint is kinda chipped away around the frame?" he asked.

"Yeah," she said.

"It means that somebody's been going in there. Then this," he said as he pointed to a ladder print in the carpet. "I'm going to boost you up there. Tell me what you see," he said. As soon as Déja opened the door she saw bags of money and started handing them down to him. Once they had all the money and were leaving, Sin looked back at Kesha's body.

As they were heading towards the freeway, Sin told Sha to pull over at a phone booth. Sin went and dialed a number.

"911, what is your emergency?" the operator asked.

Sin stuffed his mouth full of paper and dropped the tone in his voice a couple of notches. "I just heard shooting coming from a house I was walking past."

"Sir, can you give me that address?" the operator asked. Sin did, and when she asked who he was, he hung up.

●●●●●●

Later on that day, not having been home yet, Max had Bo in the car with him on their way to 61st. As they were passing Alcatraz and Shattuck they saw Sin and June turning off from 63rd onto Shattuck.

"Man, that's them niggas!" Max said as he followed them. He and Bo both cocked their guns and continued to follow.

Chapter Twenty-Two

It's a Wrap

Sin pulled his SS Chevelle over at the Everett & Jones on Telegraph and he and June got out and went in. After Sin ordered Malika's food and paid for it, he got an eerie feeling in his stomach. He just chalked it up as it being about what happened earlier. He bought a soda and a link sandwich for himself.

Sin and June stepped out of the restaurant and he looked around. As he was walking to his car, the red Corvette pulled up on them from out of nowhere. When Sin turned around he already had his Glock in his hand, but it was too late. The Mack 11 that Bo was shooting, lit him up. Bo then turned the gun on June and stroked the trigger. Sin saw his brother fall. He raised the Glock and shot through the door, hitting Bo in the stomach. Max hit the gas, taking off fast.

Sin touched his jacket to see if he was bleeding. The Kevlar vest saved Sin's life. He hurried around the car and went to check on June. Sin saw that June wasn't wearing his vest and that he was hit bad. In the distance he could hear sirens.

Sin grabbed his brother and put him in the car and got in and pulled off. "Sin, I ain't gon' make it. Man, take care of my family. My money's at my house under the doghouse. I love you, blood!" June grunted.

"Man, you trippin'! You gon' be aight! We'll be at Kaiser in a minute!" Sin yelled.

When they pulled up in Kaiser's Emergency's entrance, June had exhaled his last breath.

Sin started crying and he swore he was going to personally kill Bo, Max, and everything they loved. He stopped and thought about it. If he hadn't had J.B. whacked, none of this stuff would have happened. *Fuck that! Them niggas struck first. I was going to let this shit ride, but these muthafuckas kept it going!* he thought.

As the weeks went by, Sin killed Bo's brother, Max's father and his sister. Anyone affiliated with them wasn't safe.

Bo and Max moved the rest of their families out of Northern California. They went down south to North Carolina of all places and set up shop.

Sin ended up expanding his enterprise. If you weren't buying a hundred keys or better, you couldn't see Sin. In turn, this brought Hasahn and Sha up. Hasahn was in it to win it. Sha was on some spend it as soon as he got it shit.

Sin left all his strays alone and put a hundred-percent into Malika. Not a day went by that he didn't think of his brother. Marco weeded out all of the fakers in the Circle. They were now back where muthafuckas feared them. The Circle was known nationwide and that was something Sin didn't want. Because for real, he knew the big boys (the Feds) were going to be knocking at his door soon. He would be ready though. He and Marco had important people in their pockets. They had so many go-betweens that the trail would never come back to them. The only people ever to see Sin with dope were Sha, Mario, Shaunté, Marco, Hasahn, and Davy, his Circle in the Circle.

Street Knowledge!
"So Real You Think You've Lived It!

Street Knowledge Publishing LLC
P.O. Box 345
Wilmington, DE 19899
TOLL FREE: 1.888.401.1114
www.skbookstore.com

Date: _____

Purchaser _____

Mailing Address _____

City_____**State**_____**Zip Code**_____

Qty.	Title of Book		Price Each	Total
	978-0-9822515-6-0	Bloody Money	$15.00	
	978-0-9822515-9-1	Bloody Money 2	$15.00	
	978-0-9799556-4-8	Bloody Money 3	$15.00	
	978-0-9799556-0-0	Tommy Good Story	$15.00	
	978-0-9822515-0-8	Tommy Good Story II	$15.00	
	978-0-9746199-1-0	Me & My Girls	$15.00	
	978-0-9746199-0-3	Cash Ave	$15.00	
	978-0-9822515-1-5	Merry F$$kin' Xmas	$15.00	
	978-0-9799556-1-7	A Day After Forever	$15.00	
	978-0-9822515-3-9	A Day After Forever 2	$15.00	
	978-0-9799556-2-4	Court & the Streets	$15.00	
	978-0-9822515-5-3	Court In The Street 2	$15.00	
	978-0-9746199-6-5	Don't Mix the Bitter with the Sweet	$15.00	
	978-0-9799556-9-3	Playing For Keeps	$15.00	
	978-0-9799556-3-1	Pain Freak	$15.00	
	978-0-9799556-5-5	Dipped Up	$15.00	
	978-0-9799556-6-2	No Love No Pain	$15.00	
	978-0-9746199-4-1	Dopesick	$15.00	
	978-0-9799556-7-9	Lust, Love & Lies	$15.00	
	978-0-9799556-8-6	Money and Murder	$15.00	
	978-0-9746199-7-2	The Queen Of New York	$15.00	
	978-0-9799556-5-5	Dipped Up	$15.00	
	978-0-9746199-8-9	Sin 4 Life	$15.00	
	978-0-9822515-4-6	A Little More Sin	$15.00	
	978-0-9746199-5-8	The Hunger	$15.00	
	978-09746199-3-4	Money Grip	$15.00	
	978-0-9822515-7-7	Young Rich & Dangerous	$15.00	
		Total Books Ordered	Quantity	
			Subtotal	
SHIPPING/HANDLING (Via U.S. Priority Mail) $5.25 for 1st book, $2.00 for each additional book			Shipping Total	
Institutional Check & Money Order (No Personal Check Accepted)		**Total** $		

www.ingramcontent.com/pod-product-compliance
Lightning Source LLC
Chambersburg PA
CBHW070303260626
47160CB00003B/698